GIVE NO QUARTER

Barbara Korsness

PublishAmerica
Baltimore

PublishAmerica has allowed this work to remain exactly as the author intended, verbatim, without editorial input.

Hardcover 978-1-4512-8020-3
Softcover 978-1-4512-8021-0
PUBLISHED BY PUBLISHAMERICA, LLLP
www.publishamerica.com
Baltimore

Printed in the United States of America

For all my grandchildren
Theresa, Loren, Brenna, Abby, Jessica and Charlie

CHAPTER ONE

The thunder of cannon fire sent Catana and Louis, along with a flood of civilians from the small village, darting through the fort's wooden doors. Splintering walls shattered behind them in clouds of dust and flying debris.

Coughing, she held her hand over her mouth and darted through the soldier's dining room where cracked beams supported the ceiling. Bits of wood rained down. Motioning for Louis to hurry, she called out, "Follow me to the drill field before the ceiling caves in."

Louis hesitated. "We'll be targets for cannon fire out there."

Catana tugged on his arm. "The walls will stop any artillery fire before it goes that far."

They dashed toward the drill field in the middle of the fort and joined the small group of women and children huddled in the center.

Catana's Aunt Jacinta grasped her by the shoulder. The wisps of hair that had escaped the bun stuck out like chicken feathers. Her gaunt frame stood on tiptoe to look her seventeen-year-old niece in the eye. "Where is Inez?"

Brushing a lock of sable hair from her cheek, Catana looked around but saw no sign of her younger cousin. "I thought she was with you."

"She told me she was spending the night at your house," her aunt replied. Jacinta turned her attention to Louis, who was hovering behind her niece. "What is that *Frenchman* doing here? Do you realize it is the French who are attacking?"

"*Sí*, Tia Jacinta. But Louis has nothing to do with the assault."

Her aunt returned her gaze to Catana. "No matter. Inez is missing, and I hold you responsible. You do not look after her properly when she is with you."

Catana clamped her teeth together to keep from saying something she might regret. Her aunt blamed her every time Inez went astray. Since Jacinta was unable to control the daughter's actions, she needed someone to accuse, and Catana was her target. Now French ships were pounding the fort, Inez was missing, and Jacinta was looking at Catana as if she was the cause.

"I will look for her," Catana said and turned to leave.

Louis caught her sleeve. "Let me go with you. It is the least I can do to help."

Nodding, she darted for the wall. With Louis close behind, she climbed the steps to the upper level where Spanish soldiers returned cannon fire. She approached two men reloading their cannon for another shot.

"Have you seen Inez?"

The two soldiers shook their heads and continued with their work. Approaching each group of men, she asked the same question and received the same answer. The two friends left the fort, and, dodging stray fire, ran toward the village of Santa Maria de Galve. Catana slowed her pace, knowing it was no use to rush and possibly miss seeing Inez, and her eyes darted from building to building in search of a blue dress. They found no sign of Inez.

A few streets from the water the sound of cannon fire rolling from the bay grew louder. Reaching the beach that ran along the length of the village, Catana paused and studied the silver sand dunes fringed by oat grass, but to no avail. She slid down into a valley between two high dunes and sat in silence. Louis followed and sank down next to her.

"Don't blame yourself because Inez is missing," he said, trying to comfort her. "She is wise and is probably hiding in a safe place. You know her better than her mother. Think. Where would she have gone?"

Catana shrugged. "I have no clue."

Another cannon ball arched over their heads toward the village. Crawling to the crest of the dune to her back, Catana scanned the settlement. A column of fire rose above the rooftops, and smoke drifted to the sky. Suddenly a blast of sand erupted near them with a deafening roar. The concussion knocked them to the foot of the dune. Flying grains of sand stung the back of Catana's neck and her arms. When she looked around, she saw Louis flat on his back moaning softly. Catana staggered to her feet on weak legs, grabbed his hand, and pulled him to a sitting position.

"Are you all right?" she asked looking into his wide blue eyes. His face and dark brown hair were caked with a chalk white covering.

"*Oui*, just frightened out of my wits. We were lucky the blast came from behind. Otherwise, the flying sand would have blinded us." Louis stood and brushed loose sand from his shirtsleeves "Do you notice anything different?"

Catana shook her head, thought for a moment, then smiled. "The sound of cannon fire has stopped."

The two friends crawled to the top of the dune nearest the beach and looked over the edge. On the wide expanse of the bay were thirteen French ships spaced out of range on the wide expanse of the bay. One stood engulfed in flames from stem to stern.

Look there is a small boat leaving the fort under a flag of truce," Catana said "We are surrendering to the French."

She turned and slid down the dune. When Louis reached the bottom she heaved a deep sigh. "I do not understand. Why has France come here to attack us? I know neither of our nations has been friendly toward one another, but it has never come to this. If it had not been for French merchants, like your father, the people of Santa Maria Galve would have starved in years past."

"When my father allowed me to remain here until his return, it was because there was no sign of trouble. Whatever happened, it was sudden."

Catana crawled up the dune again to observe what was happening. The small boat had come alongside the French flagship. Scanning the bay, her eyes rested on the burning vessel in the distance. It had listed to one side and was slowly slipping beneath the waves.

"Four of those ships are large man-of-wars. The others are smaller *feluccas*," Louis remarked.

"The French must realize we only have one ship for protection and that it is a small *pirogue* at Saint Joseph's harbor." She stood atop the dune and brushed powered grit from her skirt. "Now that there is a lull in the fighting, I am anxious to find Inez. I pray she is safe."

Catana and Louis headed back to the settlement. When they entered, they trudged up and down streets and ducked into buildings calling for Inez with no success. Taking in the scene before her, Catana shook her head. She realized the damage could have been worse. The main target of the French had been the fort. Catana decided to go to the church to pray that her cousin was safe and well.

In the dark interior, she heard hushed voices. When her eyes grew accustomed to the dimness, she saw two figures sitting on a bench near the altar. Approaching them, Catana recognized that one was Father Ortega and with him was Inez. She rushed to her cousin, embraced the younger girl, and thanked the Lord. Catana stood back, her hands on Inez's shoulders, and looked into her sepia eyes.

"We all have been worried. Where did you disappear to last night, and why did you tell your mother you were with me?"

"If I tell you, do you promise not to tell Mother? She would be furious."

Catana looked at Inez, then the priest. "Do you want me to lie to your mother?"

"No, just keep the truth to yourself."

Father Ortega stood, looked at Catana, and then Louis. "If you will excuse me, I better see if I am needed at the fort. Thank the Lord the French are gone."

"But, Father," Catana said, "the French are sitting in the bay. We have sent a boat with a surrender flag."

"What! That cannot be. I am not going to have those atheistic Huguenots invading my church. I must see the governor right away and learn what is happening." The priest, mumbling some unholy words about the French, stormed out of the church.

Catana cleared her throat. "Now, Inez, explain yourself."

Her cousin eyed Louis. "What is he doing here?"

"Louis is not the blame for what has happened. He knows no more than we do." Catana took Louis by the hand. "It's better that you make yourself scarce until we learn what is going on. Some Spanish soldiers may not feel too friendly toward you right now."

"But where shall I go? Although Governor Matamoros and my father are close friends, I doubt that I will no longer be welcome in his home."

"Go to my house. It will be safe there. When I learn more, I will come to you."

After Louis stepped out the door, Catana turned back to her cousin. "Well?"

"Do you remember when I told you about Juan?"

"One of the soldiers at the fort?"

"Sí, that one. We love each other and want to marry. Mother does not approve of him. I was with him last night. At daybreak, we heard the first cannon fire. Juan ran to the fort while I came here to hide."

"What does Father Ortega think of all of this?"

"The good father does not realize I spent the night with Juan. He was here to say daily mass. When I refused to leave and join the others at the fort, he stayed with me."

"Why remain here? Wouldn't you prefer to be near Juan during all the chaos?"

"No. If he was in danger, I was afraid I would give my feelings away, and then Mother would know. Please don't tell her. She has a lot of influence with the governor. She would have Juan sent away."

"Spending the night with a man is something I cannot condone. If I promise to keep your secret, you must promise it will not happen again."

"But nothing happened. We only talked and enjoyed one another's company."

"Maybe this time, but next time you may not be able to use self-control."

Anger flashed in Inez's eyes. "You should practice what you say. There has been more than one time when you and Louis were together all night."

"That's different. We're only friends. He is like a brother to me and has been since we were children. In your case, you and Juan are in love, and sooner or later, you both will want to consummate that love, be it with or without marriage."

"Then Juan and I will run away and marry in secret."

"Please don't do anything foolish. Give me time to reason with your mother. Maybe she will accept that you love Juan and sanction your marriage."

Inez let out a deep sigh. "Since father's death she has been overprotective and smothering me."

"Do as I ask for now. We have greater worries. If the governor does surrender to the French, we will find many changes in our lives."

* * * *

Late that day Catana received a message from the governor to come to his office. Because she was apt at reading and writing in both Spanish and French, she had been requested to record the events of the council meeting held by Governor Matamoros to discuss their next line of action. The governor often asked Catana to his office to record meetings he conducted. Politics normally bored her, but she was curious about what would take place at this gathering. As she headed toward the governor's office, she wondered what would happen to the civilians in the settlement if the Spanish surrendered. Would the French allow them to remain, or send them away to fend for themselves?

Once the council was seated around the table the governor spoke. "When we sent our soldiers out to learn the reason for the attack, the French leader Bienville informed them that France has declared war on Spain."

"But why?" a council member asked.

"Our king has revoked the pledge he made twenty years ago that he would relinquish claim to the throne of Louis XIV. This is why the French have orders to make an immediate attack on our fort."

The governor turned his attention to Captain Martinez, the commanding officer of the fort. "What took so long to receive word of the French's arrival this morning?"

The commanding officer called for the sentry that had been on duty. The frightened man entered the room and shifted from foot to foot until he was ordered to sit. The sentry took a deep breath before he answered. "I saw the first small French boat as it appeared off Point Seguenza after daybreak. I thought it was our *pirogue* returning from Saint Joseph's Bay. When the other boats appeared, I and the other guards became suspicious. That is when Corporal Armagosa fired a warning shot."

"Then what happened?" the governor asked.

"The French circled our position"

The governor slammed his fist on the wooden table. "I asked Governor Salinas to leave at least one ship here for protection. He declined because it violated his orders. Instead, he set sail with his ships to map out a new settlement at Saint Joseph's Bay. The only defense we have is our *pirogue*, and even that is not here."

Catana looked over to Captain Martinez. Would his information spell doom for Santa Maria de Galve and her people? She continued to write as he spoke.

"I received word that the French have captured our fort at Point Seguenza after swarming ashore on Santa Rosa Island. They overpowered our small unit and pounded spikes into the fire holes, rendering the cannons useless. We will have no help from Point Seguenza."

Governor Matamoros shook his head. "I managed to dispatch a messenger to Governor Salinas in Saint Joseph's Bay, but I do not know if he and his men will arrive here in time. The French leader has sent a demand for surrender and will allow us until ten o'clock tomorrow morning to respond. We have only one hundred sixty defenders. The French outnumber us five to one."

Everyone started to talk at once, and Catana gave up trying to write. Finally, the governor held up his hand requesting silence. "As you know, an engineer from Spain was sent here to examine this fort. He recommended that we abandon it and move the whole company to Point Seguenza on the island. He said that Fort San Carlos could not be defended for long. Its construction is weak. If the French send troops ashore here, they could attack from the higher ground to the rear. I was unable to comply with his suggestions because it would exceed my authority. Although we have made improvements to this fort, it is no enough. Now Point Seguenza has been taken."

The council discussed and argued the situation through the night. When put to vote, the Spanish council chose to surrender to the French. Once the decision was made, they prepared the terms of surrender. It included the safe conduct for all personnel to an appropriate settlement and amnesty for the Indian allies who remained loyal to the Spanish.

A tight knot gripped Catana's heart with the thought of losing the only home she had ever known. There must be a way for the Spanish to regain Santa Maria. What would happen to her beloved Church if the Huguenots took over?

"Please include protection for our Church and priest," Catana added.

"Your job is to write and keep your opinions to yourself," a heavyset counsel member grumbled.

Catana glared at the stern-looking man with resentment.

"She is right," a counsel member, who reminded Catana of a nervous cat, said in her defense. "Many French are Huguenots and do not respect our Catholic Church."

A warm flush of satisfaction filled Catana when the governor agreed and added it to the list.

The heavy-set counsel man spoke again. "She should know. She is always seen with that Frenchman, Louis whatever his name is."

"His name is Louis LeClaire, and he is a Catholic," Catana replied in a cool voice. "There is a number of Catholics among the French, but we do not know if those to whom we are surrendering are of our faith or Huguenots."

The governor raised his hand to silence Catana. "That is enough. Let us continue with our business. We will also ask for an inventory of supplies captured."

* * * *

The governor met with the French leader later that morning, and both sides agreed to the twelve terms. After the surrender of the Spanish was signed, Catana watched with pain in her heart as the Spanish soldiers laid down their arms and marched from the fort. From a distance, she gazed at the Spanish garrison being herded aboard the French frigates *Conde de Tolosa* and *Mariscol de Vilalars*, which would take them to Havana. The few women and children of the settlement were to be relocated in Saint Joseph's Bay, only a few leagues from Santa Maria de Galve. Catana wondered why Governor Salinas at Saint Joseph's Bay had never responded to Governor Matamoros' plea for help.

She knew she must get Louis out of Santa Maria before the French discovered he was here. If they found him, he would be arrested for treason.

CHAPTER TWO

Catana had brought Louis to a small Indian village not far from the captured Spanish settlement. The houses in the hamlet were small with one room and constructed of wood poles covered by thatch. The fire provided the only light in the round room with no windows and one doorframe covered by an animal skin.

Louis sat watching Catana pace around the fire pit in the center of the room. He shifted to a more comfortable position on a wood bench that sat against the wall. Catana's pacing was growing on his nerves. "Come sit down, there is nothing we can do."

She slumped down next to him. "All my people are gone."

"I know," he said and gave her hand a squeeze. He and Catana had known one another since his father started bringing him, as a child, from Mobile to the Spanish settlement on his trading voyages. They became close friends and shared many adventures. His father allowed Catana to sail on his merchant ship numerous times and she had learned the ways of a sailor. He looked into her soft brown eyes where golden flecks of light danced from the fire.

What he admired most about her was her ability to never give up no matter how desperate a situation seemed. When her mother died of Yellow Fever three years ago, her father returned to the sea as captain of his own ship. Catana was put under the care of her Aunt Jacinta, who disliked her niece. Rather than live with the intolerable woman, she found work as a scribe for the governor and was able to persuade him to give her a house of her own.

The houses in the Spanish settlement were but poor wooden shacks compared to what he was accustomed. His parents owned a large home on Mobile Bay. His father's generous income as a coastal trader provided his family with a pleasant lifestyle. Since Louis enjoyed adventure and Catana's company, his father allowed him to remain with Governor Matamoros, his father's friend, in Santa Maria de Galva between visits several times a year. This visit proved to be at a bad time. He wondered how long it would be before his father would come to pick him up or send someone.

Several years ago, Catana had introduced Louis to the people of this village. Escaping the British, they joined the Indians in Spanish La Florida. The people were a mixture of Apalachee and several other tribes that came from farther north. "You know they will return," Catana said in a soft voice.

"What?" Louis replied coming back to the present.

"My people. They will return and drive the French out."

Louis shook his head. "I do not see how. The people of your colony have been scattered to the east and the south."

"Poor Inez is probably despondent over her separation with Juan. They wanted to marry, but now he is in Havana and she is at Saint Joseph's Bay. I wish there was something I could do to restore our settlement to the way it was."

"This is out of your hands. Try to relax and enjoy the company and hospitality of the natives while we have the chance."

"If I pray, maybe the Lord will send me an idea," Catana said.

They stood and stepped out the door into the bright sunlight where they were greeted by excited shouts. Tokala, a young warrior, grabbed Louis by the arm and pulled him to their playing field. "Join us in a game."

"They have come to challenge us," Tokala confided, "and they want their honor returned, for we won the last two games against them."

Tokala and his warrior brothers treated Louis and Catana as part of their extended family. Louis had participated in their games several times and enjoyed playing. Catana and the village natives stood on one side of a small clearing while the people of a neighboring tribe lined the opposite side.

15

Since the Apalachee wore little clothing, Louis stripped off his shirt and handed it to Catana. About fifty players poured onto the field. Louis felt a mixture of apprehension along with eagerness to play. The game could become dangerous. Sometimes players were badly injured; a few killed.

In the center of the clearing, a tall post shaped like a pyramid with a nest on top reached toward the sky. The players could only use their feet to move the hard clay ball to the goal. Each time a team hit the goal with the ball, they scored one point. If they kicked the ball into the nest, they scored two points. The first team to score eleven points won.

Louis managed to play well and scored three points in a row. The players on the opposing team singled him out to stop him, and then things got tough. One man tripped Louis as he lunged toward the ball. Louis hit the ground, and a number of the opposing team piled on top, knocking the wind out of him. When they got off to chase the ball, he pushed himself into a sitting position and tried to clear his head. Focusing his eyes, he froze. The last thing he remembered was the ball flying straight toward his head.

* * * *

Later, when Louis opened his eyes, his head throbbed with pain. Catana stood over him, holding a wet cloth to his forehead.

"Welcome back to the land of the living," she whispered with concern on her face. It took Louis a minute before he realized that he was lying on a bench against the wall inside of one of the houses.

Tokala stood next to her with his arms crossed over his bare chest and a big grin on his face. "That was a nice block, but I do not recommend you use it often."

Louis managed to give him a weak smile. The name Tokala meant fox in the Indian's language, and although he had black piercing eyes and a hooked nose that reminded Louis of a hawk, his name fit for he was clever.

Louis noticed someone hovering in the shadows. Tokala motioned for the man to come forward and introduced him. "This is my friend

Jabulani." A large bull-like man emerged from the darkness of the far wall. The light from the flames of a fire danced on large muscular arms and barrel chest. His skin was black as coal.

"Are you able to sit up?" Tokala grabbed Louis by the hand and pulled him into a sitting position. Louis winced with pain.

The Indian gave him a nod. "I will get some willow and make a drink for you. It will help the pain and swelling. Catana, you sit to his left, and, Jabulani, on his right to steady him."

Catana touched the wound on Louis's head lightly. "You have a nasty bruise and cut, but at least the bleeding has stopped."

To get his mind off his pain, Louis started a conversation with Jabulani. "You are new in the village. Do you live here now?"

The black man nodded. "Tokala and his people have welcomed me into their village. I can teach them to farm the white man's way. I learned this as a slave."

Catana leaned in front of Louis and whispered, "Are you a runaway slave?"

"I escaped from the whites in the north and hope that here in Spanish La Florida, I can live as a free man."

Catana rubbed her temple. "I pray our French invaders don't endanger your chance of freedom"

Louis gave a grunt when she straightened up and bumped him. "Why would the French turn him over to the British?" he asked. "There is no love between our countries."

Catana shrugged. "The people of this village are allies to Spain. If the French capture Tokala and his people, along with Jabulani, they would sell them all into slavery." She sighed deeply. "If only there was something I could do to return our colony back to Spanish rule, I…" She sat up straight and a wide smile crossed her mouth. "I have an idea, and, Louis, you are going to help me."

"Oh, no. Every time you get an idea, we end up in trouble. Remember the time we—"

Catana placed a finger over his lips. "Let's forget about that. Look, Tokala has returned with your drink."

* * * *

Louis felt better that evening and sat at a campfire eating roasted duck with Catana and Jabulani. Tokala and his warriors were at a council meeting with the chief and wise men of the tribe. Set at the center of the village, the counsel lodge was a replica of the houses, but much larger.

"The natives are concerned about the French," Catana confided to the two men.

"Oui," Louis added. "The French also have Indian allies. They could make war on this village at anytime."

Jabulani's eyes took on a fierce glow in the firelight. "If this is true, I will fight with my new brothers. I will no longer be a slave to any man. I would rather die free."

"It's sad," Catana replied. "My religion teaches us that all men are created in the likeness of God, yet we do not treat everyone as equals but make slaves of one another. Even the Spanish are guilty."

After a few moments of silence, Louis spoke. "In what way can I help you return Santa Maria de Galva to the Spanish, Catana?"

"Your injury gave me an idea. Here is what I want you to do. It is simple. Go to the fort and spy on Bienville. Learn what you can of his plans, and then we will relay the information to Governor Salinas in Saint Joseph's Bay. He, in turn, can send a message to the Governor of Havana and ask for help."

"It does not sound that simple to me. Why would Bienville or any French soldier allow me into the fort? I am a stranger to them."

"You are also a Frenchman. Tell them you are one of the civilian volunteers who joined in the siege of the fort, but you were wounded and rendered unconscious. When you awoke, you were dazed and lost, but you finally found your way to Santa Maria. You have the wound on your head to prove it. There were over five hundred volunteers involved in the attack. They will believe your story."

"I don't feel comfortable spying on my countrymen, and I don't understand why what transpired in Europe should leave such a devastating effect on us here."

"This will give you the opportunity to find out, and we can find a way to settle this peacefully."

* * * *

Louis departed the Indian village the following morning. When he saw the Santa Maria in the distance, he noticed there were already a number of changes. The *Philippe*, one of the French warships, was tied to the dock along with two merchant ships. Supplies were piled along the waterfront and a great number of people were milling about.

It was easier than he imagined mingling with the soldiers and colonists. He approached four soldiers sitting around a campfire. "May I join you?" he asked. A sergeant moved over on a log to made room for him.

"Are you one of the settlers who just arrived?" asked a young corporal who sat across from him.

Louis thought he would stick to Catana's story for he had rehearsed it in his head often on his way from the Indian village. "No. I was with a group of colonists who joined in the siege, but I was wounded in the process."

"The volunteers were a great help," the sergeant said

Louis looked around at the four men and felt a twinge of guilt; then it died. If Catana was right, what he learned might settle this dispute peacefully.

"It was an easy battle from what I understand," said a round-faced, heavyset soldier. His uniform was straining at the buttons.

"You were not involved with the attack?" Louis asked.

"No. We are a part of a group that arrived earlier today," the heavyset soldier replied.

Louis knew he had asked the wrong question when the tall lanky soldier at the left end of the log eyed him with suspicion. "I would think you would be aware of what is going on here."

"See this wound on my head?" Louis replied with anger in his voice. "Because of my injury, I was in and out of consciousness until several days ago. Some natives in the forest cared for me, and it is only now that I have made my way back here."

The round-faced man nodded. "I have heard that some of the civilian volunteers, who attacked by land, were aided by Indian allies."

"Exactly," Louis replied. "Several of the natives remained behind until I was well enough to come here, then they returned to their people."

The soldiers seemed satisfied with his story, and the sergeant proceeded to tell Louis what was going on. "After the siege, Bienville received orders that Santa Maria de Galve is to become the new capital of French Louisiana. The three ships you see brought supplies and more soldiers to be permanently stationed here."

"Oui," the lanky man on the end replied. "And we have the misfortune of being sent to this backwater hole."

The heavyset man punched his fellow soldier in the arm. "You better not let our captain hear such a comment."

The lanky man rubbed his arm. "We all feel this way. I heard that many of the Spanish soldiers felt the same. This is definitely not New Orleans, nor Mobile."

"Maybe so, but it is better not to voice such opinions in public," the sergeant said.

"That explains the ships and soldiers, but who are all the civilians?" Louis asked.

"There were three hundred colonists aboard the ships as well as soldiers," the young corporal replied. "I do not know how this small colony will handle them all."

Louis excused himself and then wove his way through the confusion of humanity in the streets to Catana's small wooden house. No one was inside so he made himself at home. If anyone came, he would claim it as his own and would remain here several days to glean further information. What he had learned so far was not good news for the Spanish.

* * * *

Three days later, Louis left the colony and met Catana at a prearranged spot on the edge of a clearing in the forest. In the light of a waxing half-moon, he found her pacing between two pine trees. When he called to her, she spun around quickly to face him. He was unable to see the expression on her face hidden in the moon shadows, but fear mixed anger edged her voice.

"You were supposed to meet me here last night. I thought something had gone wrong. Thank God you are safe." She threw her arms around him, hugged him, and then stepped back. "What happened?"

He explained how Bienville had started colonizing the settlement. "This will make it difficult for the Spanish to reclaim Santa Maria, and there is more."

"Is it good or bad?"

"I think it will be good news for Governor Salinas. Remember the *Philippe,* one of the warships involved in the attack?"

Catana nodded.

"It is in port at Santa Maria. Bienville is faced with an overcrowded colony. He plans to send some of the settlers and supplies to Mississippi Landing and others to Mobile. His brother, Serigney, has been assigned to take settlers to the riverside settlement while Bienville sails a ketch to Mobile with the others. This will leave Santa Maria unprotected."

"*Buena,*" Catana said with a smile. The chance of returning home to a normal life looked promising. "I must get this news to Salinas."

"I will go with you. If the French at Santa Maria knew what I was doing, they would hang me as a traitor."

"Sí, you must come with me. We should leave right away."

Louis and Catana followed the shoreline east all night. By midmorning, they spotted the new colony nestled on the shore among the dunes. There were a few wooden houses, all about the same size, clustered around a larger building in the center, which was the Governor's headquarters. Off in the distance sat three Spanish ships bobbing on the water.

21

They entered the settlement. Louis knocked on the door of the large building, and a kind, old gentleman greeted them.

"Please tell the governor that Catana Molino and Louis LeClaire have an important message for him." Catana announced.

Standing at the open door, they waited patiently as the old man shuffled down the hallway to make the announcement. On his return, he invited them in and led them to the Governor's office.

Governor Salinas stood when they entered and moved out from behind his desk to approach them. The governor's grey beard and thick grey hair reminded Louis of his father. His warm brown eyes held a smile for his visitors.

"Welcome. I am happy you are safe from the attack on Santa Maria, Catana, and I am surprised to see you here, Louis."

"I was at the settlement when it was seized and unable to return to my parents in Mobile. Catana and I have been in the Apalachee village."

"Louis has some important information," Catana added.

After Louis relayed what he had learned at the French-held fort, Governor Salinas thought for a moment before speaking. "I will send the information on to the Governor of Havana, but I have heard rumors the Spanish plan to make an assault on Santa Maria. This information will help them with their plan of attack."

"Señor, Louis has nowhere to go at present," Catana said. "May he stay here in Saint Joseph's Bay until we find a way to return him to his family?"

A wide smile spread across the Governor's face. "But of course. You are most welcome. We are indebted to you for acquiring this information. I have extra room in the barracks attached to this building. We only have a few soldiers here at present and there is plenty of room."

The Louis gripped and shook governor's extended hand. "Thank you, señor," Louis said, "I am most grateful."

The Governor turned and called to the old gentleman. "Manuel, show this young man to one of our empty rooms in the barracks."

Returning his attention to Catana, he added, "Will you be staying with your aunt? She lives but a few houses to the north of this building."

"Sí, I am anxious to learn how Inez is dealing with all these changes."

After Louis and Catana left the governor's office, Louis stopped her in the corridor. "Since you don't get along well with your aunt, will you be all right?"

"It will only be until the French return what is ours. I want to give Inez some moral support. I know she misses Juan, and my aunt is not sympathetic to her feelings."

Louis stifled a yawn.

"I'll go now," Catana said. "We both need sleep."

Later, as Louis lay in bed thinking, he realized the French would not hand Santa Maria back to the Spanish without a battle, which would take many lives. He prayed it would not include those he knew and loved.

CHAPTER THREE

A month later, the Spanish fleet from Havana, led by Don Alfonso Carrascosa de la Torre, arrived in Saint Joseph's Bay to gain more information on the situation at Santa Maria de Galve. A dozen ships made up the Spanish fleet. When Inez learned that the man she loved was with the fleet, she asked Catana to help and arrange a meeting with Juan. Catana wanted to talk to Juan herself and learn if there was any word of her father in Havana. She had not heard from him in over two years and was worried he may have run into trouble.

On the second evening after the fleet's arrival, the governor arranged for Catana and Inez to meet Juan on a lonely section of the beach. Catana planned to stay long enough to learn what she wanted and then leave the two of them alone.

The early August evening breeze from the gulf was refreshing after the hot, humid day. Tired of watching her cousin wring her hands while they waited, Catana strolled to the edge of the water and stood, the surf barely tickling her bare toes as each wave washed ashore. Looking across the expanse of the bay, she saw the Spanish Fleet silhouetted against the moonlit sky. It gave her a sense of hope that soon she would be able to return home. She heard Inez squeal and turned to see the lovers embrace.

Approaching them, she greeted them with a smile. "Welcome, Juan. I would like to speak to you briefly, and then Inez can have you all to herself."

They made their way to a dune and sat in the soft sand at its crest.

"While in Havana, did you hear any word about Don Antonio Molino de Cataluna, my father?" Catana asked.

"The only thing I know is that Don Antonio and Captain Carvajal had a dispute about a year ago, then your father disappeared. The Captain has come with the fleet. You could ask him if he has further information."

Catana decided she would seek out this captain and question him about her father before the ships sailed for Santa Maria. She did not know how much time she had before the fleet departed. "Tell me about Don Alfonso's plans."

Juan shifted his muscular frame to a more comfortable position next to Inez. His black hair absorbed the moonlight and his eyes sparkled with its reflection. "Let me tell you first about our capture. It was quite an amazing experience. After our garrison boarded the French frigates in Santa Maria, and we were in route to Havana, adverse winds delayed us. When the French vessels neared the coast of Bahia Honda, they sited a Spanish Fleet."

"How many ships did the Spanish have?" Catana asked.

"Ten grandaleres and smaller ships, having four to ten cannons each."

Catana imagined the looks on the Frenchmen's faces when they saw the fleet, and she smiled.

Jose continued "The ships carried a large number of Spanish troops who were en route to Saint Augustine."

"Saint Augustine?" Catana asked. "Why were they heading there?"

"Saint Augustine is having their problems, too. The British have threatened to invade the settlement. But as I was saying, the troops of the Spanish Fleet had been alerted of our war with France. When they saw the French ships we were on, they forced them to halt for inspection. The Spanish discovered we were aboard as prisoners, arrested the French crews, and turned the ships over to Havana, where the French were imprisoned."

Inez clapped her hands in glee. "What good fortune."

Juan nodded in agreement. "Once we were in Havana, Don Gregorio prepared a counterattack against the French at Santa Maria. He met with Governor Matamoros and Cuban officials. Within a few days after capturing the French ships, they loaded them with supplies.

The *Conde de Tolosa* was selected to serve as the command ship. Our garrison from Santa Maria was rearmed along with one hundred fifty volunteers." Juan swept his arm across the horizon. "Don Alfonso was ordered to command these ships. Not only is our Spanish Fleet out there, so are the two captured French ships. In the next few days, we sail for Santa Maria"

Catana stood and brushed the sand from her skirts. "Thank you, Juan. This news lightens my heart."

Leaving Inez and Juan on the beach, Catana walked swiftly to the barracks and taped on Louis's window. When he opened it, she told him what she had learned. "I want to join the volunteers and find Captain Carvajal," she added. "He is the only link I have to my father. I would like you to join me, but I understand if you refuse. We will be attacking your countrymen."

"Let me think about it," Louis replied. "To run from them while under siege was an easy choice, but to face and fight them would be difficult."

Catana left the barracks and walked slowly back to her aunt's house deep in thought. If her people were unable to return to Santa Maria what would she do? She did not want to live with her aunt again. The two of them never got along and never would. When she entered Aunt Jacinta's house, the woman was sitting by the fire waiting. Shadows danced on her rigid, unsmiling face.

"What are you doing out so late, and where is Inez?"

Catana suspected that her aunt would question her. She and Inez had concocted a story in the event Jacinta noticed they were not in their beds.

"A group of us gathered at the governor's headquarters to wash and mend clothing for the soldiers. We also served a fine meal to the officers. It was the least we could do, for they will be leaving soon to liberate Santa Maria."

It was true that some of the village women were doing this, but Catana and Inez had only participated for an hour. Catana rubbed her temples. "I started getting a headache and returned here. Inez will be safe. Someone has promised to escort her home when they are finished."

Before her aunt could mutter a protest, Catana stepped toward Jacinta, took her hand, and squeezed it. "Just think, soon we will be able to return home."

As she started for the room she and Inez shared, Jacinta called after her. "Did you get the message?"

Catana turned to face her aunt. "What message?"

"The governor wants to see you in the morning."

"Oh…Sí." Catana had received no such message, but if she had just left headquarters, she would have known about it. She knew she had better leave her aunt's company before she was put into the position of telling more lies. "Good night, Aunt Jacinta."

* * * *

After breakfast the next morning, Catana excused herself to go to the governor's office. Inez was in a cheerful mood, and her aunt smiled several times during the meal. Inez must have returned home at a decent hour and had convinced her mother of the wonderful things the Spanish troops were doing.

Why did Governor Salinas want to see her? She hastened out the door and dashed toward the governor's building. She saw no one around as she raced up the steps and darted through the open door. Turning a corner in the hallway that led to his office, she collided with Louis.

"Salinas summoned me here this morning," she said when he gave her a questioning look.

"He has asked me here, too," Louis replied.

"Do you think we are in trouble?"

Louis shrugged. "It is difficult to know. The only way to find out is to go inside."

He knocked at the office door, and a voice summoned them to come in. Opening the door, Louis gave Catana a slight bow. "After you, my lady."

As they entered, a tall gentleman with shoulders almost as broad as he was tall stood to greet them. The man reminded Catana of the soldiers who entered wrestling matches to entertain the troops.

Governor Salinas moved from around his desk to introduce them. "Don Alfonso, this is Catana Molino and Louis LeClaire. They left Santa Maria after the French attack. Louis later returned to our captured settlement and gained information that will help you. Tell him what you told me, son."

Louis conveyed to the Spanish Don all that he knew.

"And the French have no fear of a prompt reprisal?" Don Alfonso asked.

"Not to my knowledge, sir."

"Buena, Don Gravois will commence an attack on Santa Maria then serge on to attack Massacra and Mobile."

"You will be to going Mobile?" Louis asked.

Catana shifted back and forth from one foot to the other. They planned to assault Louis's home? Now what will he do?

Louis cleared his throat. "Excuse me, sir, but I would like to volunteer and join you. It may be the only way I can find to return home."

Don Alfonso rubbed his chin and thought for a moment. "You realize that if you join us, you will be fighting against your own countrymen."

"If it is possible, I would like to stay out of the fighting, unless my or Catana's life depended on defending ourselves. I will do nothing to jeopardize your attack."

Don Alfonso's eyes shifted to Catana. "Do you plan to volunteer as well?"

"Sí. My father taught me to use a sword and bow. I will be more of a help than hindrance to our cause."

"Who is this father of yours that he would teach a girl the ways of fighting?"

"Don Antonio Molino de Cataluna."

"Ah. I know that name. He was once known along the Spanish Main as a great protector of our fleets. When any of our gold shipments were in danger of attack, he came out of nowhere with his small fleet of schooners and fought off the aggressors."

"That is my father," Catana said, standing straight with pride.

"But he has disappeared, and no one knows what has happened to him."

"That is one reason I would like to volunteer, Señor. I understand that a Captain Carvajal was last to have seen him and that he is with your group."

"Carvajal is captain of one of our ships. We will see what we can do to learn more information. The Caribbean has become increasingly dangerous for us. Both the British and French fight and overrun us in that area. I hope he has not been scuttled or captured. We are also having problems with the Dutch. It seems everyone is against Spain." Don Alfonso shook his head slowly and looked Catana in the eye. "It is too dangerous for a woman."

"I will look after her," Louis said.

Catana had to fend for herself since her mother's death and father's disappearance. She spun around to face Louis. "I do not need you to protect me. I can take care of myself."

Don Alfonso chuckled. "That is part of a true soldier's duty. Not only must he fight the enemy, but he must also do all he can to protect his comrades. It will be a joint effort to defeat our foe, not an individual vendetta."

Catana's face flushed with embarrassment at his admonishment. Now he would never allow her to join them.

When the Don spoke again, it was with a smile. "I will allow you to volunteer. Although what I said is true, the military will not have time to take responsibility for what might happen to you or the other volunteers."

With a gracious nod, Catana thanked him. Grabbing Louis by the hand, she pulled him out the door.

"We have much to do to get ready."

CHAPTER FOUR

On an early day in August, the Spanish fleet sailed out of Saint Joseph's Bay and anchored that night a half league from Santa Maria de Galva. Before dawn the next morning, Don Alfonso dispatched some men in small boats to fight against Point Seguenza.

"He is sending only a hundred troops," one of the volunteers said as Catana and Louis joined him at the rail. They peered into the darkness lit by a quarter moon.

"He will not need more," Louis replied. "The fort is lightly occupied."

When dawn broke, the Spanish flag flew over the fort on Point Seguenza indicating that her people had successfully taken it. Catana noticed a small boat sailing into the bay. "What are they doing now?" she asked the young man next to her.

"Don Alfonso has sent men out to survey the area. All I see are those two French frigates off shore."

Suddenly a loud explosion broke the silence of early morning. Catana made the sign of the cross as a cannon ball landed short of the small Spanish boat. Sustaining no damage, the survey boat retreated and returned to the flagship. Once the men were safely aboard, Don Alfonso signaled to all his ships, except his frigates, to pass over the sand bar. The volunteers were on a schooner with a shallow draft, and she easily glided over the shallow area.

Their captain called out orders. "Come around, men. Don Alfonso wants us to cut the French frigates off from the shore batteries."

Cannon fire belched from the French ships and from Fort San Carlos on the mainland. The captain of the schooner was a good seaman and was able to bring his ship close to the French frigates to return their fire. The crew was young and daring, and soon, along with other Spanish ships, they isolated the French ships from the shore batteries. One of the Spanish warships put several smaller boats into the water readying to board the French man-of-war.

When the schooner lowered a dinghy to join the others, Catana strapped on the sword her father had given her. She wore loose breeches and blouse to give her freedom of movement.

"I am going with them," she told Louis.

Louis grabbed a sword from a pile on deck. "So am I." As an afterthought, he stuck a dagger in his belt.

"No," Catana shouted. "If you are captured by the French, it would mean certain death. They would hang you." She caught up with him as he was climbing over the rail and grabbed his arm. "Please, this is not your fight."

He pulled away and stepped down the ladder to join the others in the small boat. She followed close behind and dropped into the dinghy in front of him. "Louis, this is not your fight."

"I have decided to make a stand and join you. I believe this is what my father would do in the same situation. I could never forgive myself if I let you go and I watched from the deck of the schooner while you were injured or killed."

"You are not responsible for my actions. I—"

A loud crack ripped through the air and a cannonball plunged into the water next to their craft, rocking the dingy and spraying water on them. Louis clutched Catana's arm to steady her. "Let's stop arguing and concentrate on staying alive." Both turned toward the bow and watched a French ship loom closer.

The volunteers' dinghy joined the fleet of small Spanish boats ready for an attack. Upon reaching a French man-of-war, the leader of their dinghy threw a rope with a grappling hook attached to the end that arched through the air and grabbed the gunwale of the French ship. A man quickly climbed the rope and threw down a rope ladder. Screaming and waving their swords, the volunteers pushed Louis and Catana aside and stormed aboard the French ship. By the time the two set foot on deck, the fighting was almost over. There were few Frenchmen aboard, and all but two were subdued.

A Spanish officer who had boarded from another craft called out to the two Frenchmen. "Throw down your arms and we will not harm you. As you can see, you are greatly outnumbered and to die now for France would be to no avail."

The two Frenchmen dropped their swords and joined the rest of the prisoners surrounded by the Spanish.

"Run up the Spanish flag," a lieutenant shouted.

Catana ran to the rail to see if the Spanish had captured the second French warship. At first, she observed a trail of black smoke rising from its deck. As it thickened, licks of flame traveled up the ropes and soon the canvas was ablaze. She turned to one of the Spanish soldiers. "Why is Don Alfonso destroying that ship? We could have added it to our fleet."

"I do not believe our leader ordered it set afire. See the Frenchmen swimming to shore? They set their second ship afire so we would not capture it."

"Look over there," the lieutenant pointed out. Spanish troops were pouring ashore and surrounding Fort San Carlos.

With the French ship secured, the volunteers returned to their dinghy to join the landing party. When its hull scraped the white sand, Louis and Catana jumped ashore and ran along the beach. Ahead of them, Don Alfonso and his men had a group of French at gunpoint. They shouted at their enemies standing on the wall of the fort. "Surrender or your men shall die."

A moment later, an officer appeared at the top of the fort wall with a white flag and called down. "I am Commander Chatubuei. Give us until ten o'clock tomorrow morning to make our decision."

Don Alfonso thought for a moment, and then replied, "I agree, but we will keep these men as our prisoners."

* * * *

At ten o'clock the next morning, Don Alfonso approached the gate of the fort. A French officer appeared and handed the Spanish leader the keys. Santa Maria was in Spanish hands.

Catana and Louis entered the fort once it was secured. In the center of the drill field stood three hundred Frenchmen without weapons. By late that evening, the captured troops were placed on the French frigate under sixty Spanish guards. Now that Santa Maria was under Spanish rule once more, Catana invited Louis to stay with her until he was able to return home. As the two strolled past the church, Catana heard Spanish officers singing *Deum Laudamus* in thanksgiving for their victory.

"Ah, it is good to be home," Catana said, stepping into her familiar living room. She started a fire in the fireplace and settled on the settee next to Louis.

"I heard that Governor Matamoros was on the flagship and will return to his duties as governor here. I will visit him tomorrow and have him help me locate Captain Carvajal. I am anxious to learn if he knows where my father is. I will go see him tomorrow and ask him if he will hire me back as his scribe after I return from Mobile. It will be interesting to record all that has gone on."

"You want to join the attack on Mobile? Why? You have what you want. Your colony was returned to you."

"We must ensure the French do not retaliate and try another siege. We will drive these French so far away, they will never return."

* * * *

When Catana arrived at the governor's office the next morning, she was about to enter when she heard angry voices.

"Don Alfonso, Governor Matamoros," a strange voice shouted. "The troops are disgruntled because of your order not to loot the village. They fought hard and want some reward for their efforts. They have no idea when, or if, they will be paid. Always when we capture an enemy holding or a town, we have been rewarded by taking what we find."

She recognized Don Alfonso's voice when he replied. "Perhaps if we permit thirty of your men to attack a nearby Indian village and capture some of the natives, the enlisted men will be satisfied having their own slaves. They can also divide the nonmilitary supplies found in the settlement."

"But, Don Alfonso, Captain," the governor replied. "The nearest Indian camp belongs to our allies. "I do not think—"

Don Alfonso interrupted. "Is it not better to have them inconvenienced than have dissatisfied soldiers? Everyone must cooperate if we want to continue our successful campaign against the French."

When Catana heard the governor give in, she had to place her hand over her mouth to stifle a sob. She knew that anything she had to say would fall of deaf ears. She had to warn Tokala and his people. If Jabulani knew he was to be taken as a slave again, he would fight and die to remain free.

Catana slipped out of the building and flew down the streets to her house. She quickly explained to Louis what she had heard. They sprinted through the village, dodging soldiers ransacking and looting houses. The captain had not wasted time giving the order.

"We must hurry," Catana said between gasps of air. "Men could be on their way to the Indian village at this moment."

When they arrived, the village was quiet. There was no sign of an impending disaster. They found Tokala and Jabulani on the opposite side, skinning a black bear.

The Indian stood to greet them. "You will eat with us later?"

"This bear is large and will provide food for the winter," Jabulani added. "We are getting ready to cut and dry strips of meat.

Tokala gave the two visitors a wide grin. "And we prepared some for a feast this evening."

Catana grabbed Tokala by the arm. "You do not have time for that, my friends. Spanish soldiers are on the way here to attack."

"But this cannot be," Tokala replied. "We have word that the French were defeated. The Spanish are our friends."

"Not any longer," Catana replied. She explained to Tokala and Jabulani what she had overheard.

Tokala shook his head in disbelief. "We are not prepared to fight. We do not have guns like the French and Spanish."

"This is why you and your people must leave, hide, or anything, to avoid capture." Catana said, helping Tokala to his feet. She and Louis followed the black man and Indian to the chief's house to warn him.

"I will call a council meeting," the chief announced when he heard the news.

"There is no time for that," Louis said.

"That is the way or our people," the chief said in dismissal. "Tokala, call together the leaders of the tribe and bring them to the council lodge."

Catana, shaking her head in frustration, followed Louis out of the chief's house. "What a waste of effort."

"No matter what happens, Catana, you did your best to help."

"It is not good enough. While they conduct their meeting, the Spanish move closer with each moment."

The door of a hut flew open. A woman stepped outside and scanned the village with a wild look in her eyes. When she saw Catana and Louis, she ran toward them.

"Help me. My children have gone into the forest and have not returned.

Catana glanced at her, then at Louis. *Could the soldiers have already taken them as slaves?* As the thought struck Catana, the woman voiced her fears. "Do you think white warriors have stolen my children?"

"I do not think so," Louis said and put a comforting hand on her shoulder. "We will help you look for them."

They entered the forest in the direction the mother said her children often went.

"I am Ktomi. My son and daughter enjoy playing in a small stream near here but have never been gone this long."

When they came to the stream, the children were nowhere in sight. The native woman found their tracks, and the three searchers followed them deeper into the forest. Looking closely at the signs, the mother gasped. "Tracks of a young panther are mingled with my children's."

"Do you think the panther is stalking them?" Catana asked in a whisper.

"This is possible, but I think they are the ones stalking the panther. The tracks of the children overlay that of the cat."

As they continued to follow the signs, a strange scream penetrated the air. Then there was silence.

"The cat," Ktomi uttered.

She broke into a run with Catana and Louis at her heels. The Indian woman came to a sudden stop, stood still as a rock, and stared ahead. Catana halted before she ran into the woman and followed her gaze. Two young children stood in a clearing facing a young panther that was crouched and ready to spring. The cat's tawny coat shined in a pool of sunlight as it prepared to attack the boy and girl that stood huddled together.

With slow, deliberate moves, Ktomi pulled a knife from the cinch tied around her waist. As the cat sprang toward the children, Ktomi's arm snaked out. The knife cut through the air, intercepted its target, and sank deep into the panther's chest. The cat dropped to the ground, like a sack of rocks, at the children's feet.

Before Catana could let out a sigh of relief, the two children were in their mother's embrace.

"The attack! We must return to the village." Catana called, reminding them of their other dilemma.

"You go on. The children and I will slow you down. I will follow as fast as I can."

Catana and Louis headed back the way they had come, but since they were not good at tracking, nor were they familiar with their surroundings, they got lost. It was dusk when they found their way back to the village. No one was around.

"Do you think the council is still in session?" Catana asked.

They stole toward the counsel house but heard no voices. Opening the door a crack, Catana peeked inside. There was nothing but darkness and silence.

CHAPTER FIVE

Catana did not know whether the Indians were hiding in the forest or captives of the Spanish. Either way, there was nothing more she or Louis could do, the natives were either safe or it was too late. They headed back to Santa Maria. There was little moonlight to see by, and it took most of the night before they entered the settlement.

When they stepped into Catana's house, her heart sank. The table was overturned and what was left of her belongings was strewn about the room. Shards from two clay pots were scattered on the dirt floor, and all their food was gone.

"Looters," she muttered in disgust. Tears welled in her eyes when she noticed they had taken a small chest containing the simple jewelry her mother had left her and letters her father had written before his disappearance. She sank down onto a pile of animal skins in the corner and sighed deeply. "It was my dream to return home, but I had no idea it would turn out like this."

Louis made a place for himself next to her. "I know it is not the same, but maybe in time—"

"Don't you understand? The Spanish soldiers care nothing of the only home I remember or of the people who once lived here. Will I ever be able to go back to the way things once were?"

"I don't know, Catana. Try and get some sleep. Things will be brighter with the morning sun."

* * * *

The first thing that entered Catana's mind when she awoke was the fate of the Indians. She decided to go to the office and see if Governor Matamoros wanted her to record any official business. Maybe he would have word. She told Louis to stay hidden until their departure for Mobile. She did not know or trust many of the soldiers who now occupied the settlement. Many of the original men assigned here were under the influence of the newer troops. What if they turned against Louis like they had the natives?

Arriving at the fort, she knocked lightly on the governor's office door and heard a muffled "Come in." She stepped inside and found Governor Matamoros sitting at his desk with a pile of papers stacked in front of him.

"I am glad you have come. As you can see, I am buried in administrative work and need your help."

"That is why I am here, sir."

"Buena. First, let me clear away some of these papers." He handed her a stack. "Put these in the cabinet while I fetch some ink and a pen from the supply room. All this sitting has tightened my back muscles," he muttered as he limped out of the room.

Once he was gone, Catana straightened the pile of papers and noted several forms were notices of freedom. The paper declared that if a slave possessed such a document, they had been set free. The other documents were Letters of Marquee, like the one her father had received before he sailed to Havana. His gave the right to attack enemy ships and divide the loot with the Spanish crown. With a Letter of Marquee, a privateer was protected by international law and could not be arrested or tried for piracy. Both types of documents were written with room to insert the name of the person who was to receive it, the date, and the governor's signature.

Tucking the forms into drawer, she slowly closed it while scanning a paper on top of the desk. Picking it up, she read it.

Our soldiers returned to the fort with 160 captives.
These captives have become the property of the enlisted
men. Among those captured are two black men. One

*was killed; the other imprisoned with one of the native
warriors. They prove too dangerous to remain with the
other prisoners. With their unchecked anger and ability
to incite a revolt, I deem it necessary to put them
in chains.*

Captain-General Miguel Carvajal, the last man who had seen her
father, signed it. Was Jabulani dead or in chains? "Please, Lord, let him
be the one who lives," she whispered.

As she shuffled through the papers to learn more, the governor
returned. "Here we are, my dear, enough ink to write a book," he
chuckled. "I have several letters I would like to dictate. One will go to
the governor of Havana, thanking him for his help, but first, I must
make a report to the viceroy on how things stand."

Catana's pen scratched away as the governor recited. He had
assigned a work party to Point Seguenza to resume improvements of
expanding the fort and adding guns. The place was given a new name:
Principe de Asturias. Don Alfonso would authorize dispatching three
sloops and a *pirogue* to scout the coast to the west, especially Massacra
and Mobile. Included in the party would be thirty French nationals,
including Monsieur Rogue, a French official from Mobile, who had
deserted to the Spanish side. She asked her employer when the scouting
party was due to leave for Mobile and learned it would be the next
morning.

Catana spent the remainder of the afternoon helping the governor
with his paperwork. As soon as he gave her leave, she sprinted out the
door and ran home. Charging inside, she found Louis sitting at the
table. He had repaired the damages, straightened up, and found some
food for them. She pulled a chair up across from him and took a deep
breath. "They are leaving tomorrow."

"Don Alfonso leaves for Mobile?"

"Sí, I mean no. The Don has put Don Antonio Mendieta in charge
of a small fleet to scout the west coast. The best part is that there will
be thirty Frenchmen who have come to our side with him. Do you know
what that means?"

"That I am not the only one confused by this?"

"Maybe so, but it also will make it easer for you to reach Mobile without being bothered by Spanish troops with a bad attitude."

"I also have bad news. A number of natives were taken prisoner. I think a few got away and hid, but our enlisted soldiers now have their own slaves."

"Do you know if Tokala and Jabulani were taken?"

"Jabulani is either dead or chained in a cell. There were two black men captured. One was killed. I do not know which one. As for Tokala, I do not know. There is an Indian imprisoned with the black. It may be our two friends."

"If it is, I cannot go to Mobile and leave them."

"But, Louis, it may be the only chance for you to return home safely. Besides, we do not know for sure."

Louis stood. "There is one way to find out. We will go and see for ourselves."

"The guards will not let us near the brig, unless…"

Catana searched in her desk until she found her writing materials.

* * * *

Several minutes later, Catana handed a note to the man guarding the two prisoners. It was from the governor's office and allowed them to see the captives. They approached the barred window of the brig, and Catana called out, "Tokala, Jabulani, are you in there?

No answer. She peered into the interior until her eyes became accustomed to the darkness. She managed to make out the form of two men bound in chains against the opposite wall and heard a strained whisper. "Catana?" It was Tokala's voice.

Turning to the guard, she gathered her courage and looked him in the eye. "Unlock the door. I want to speak with the prisoners."

The guard gripped his flintlock tighter. "I cannot do that, señorita."

Putting her hands on her hips, she glared at him. "Oh yes you can. If you fully read that letter I gave you, you will see that the governor has given me permission to enter the brig and speak to the prisoners if I deem it necessary. And I do!"

The guard slowly looked over the paper, grunted, and unlocked the door. Catana and Louis rushed in to see how badly the prisoners had been treated. A knot gripped her stomach when she saw the cut and bruised face of the Indian warrior. Her eyes traveled to the black man's face, and a mix of relief and pity overcame her. Severely beaten, Jabulani was alive, but barely.

She lightly touched Tokala's swollen and bruised eye. "Dear Lord, what have they done to you?"

Tokala smiled weakly. "We put up a fight and lost."

"So I see," Louis said hunkering down to get a closer look. He turned and peered at the black man. "Is Jabulani all right?"

"He spends much of his time in the dream world," Tokala answered."

Catana wiped away a tear trailing down her cheek. *"Dios,* such treatment. Who ordered this done?"

"The captain-general did it himself," Tokala replied through swollen lips.

"I did not realize what a cruel lot my own people are," Catana said through clenched teeth. "I am going to see the governor about this. I may not be able to free you right away, but once Matamoros realizes that his captain-general has treated his prisoners in this way, he will end it." She slammed her fist into the palm of her hand. "One way or another, I will free you. Guard! Get in here!"

CHAPTER SIX

Louis ran his fingers through his curls. He squinted against the sunlight that reflected off the water and watched Santa Rosa Island disappear as the ship headed for Mobile. He should not be leaving Catana to deal with the governor alone, but she had insisted she had the situation under control. As long as he had known the governor, Louis had thought him a fair man. If anyone could help Tokala and Jabulani, it would be Catana. The governor treated her like the daughter. Louis had seen her talk the Spanish leader into doing things when others failed. Still, he did feel guilty leaving at such a time.

Although he did want to see his family again, Catana seemed like part of his family too. After her mother's death and her father went to sea, he felt that he had become her only true friend whereas her Aunt Jacinta treated Catana as an inconvenience.

By evening, the small Spanish fleet approached Massacra, an island off the coast of Mobile that was occupied by the French. Louis peered into the distance and saw that a French man-of-war had run aground on the island. When the Spanish fleet drew closer, he noticed a group of soldiers, Indians, and sailors milling around the beached ship.

"Is that one of the ships that attacked Santa Maria de Galva?"

A Frenchmen who stood next to him answered. "Oui, it is the *Philippe*. It departed Santa Maria under the command of Serigney. It must have run aground because the bay here is shallow." As the Spanish scouting party proceeded on to Mobile the Frenchman continued his conversation with Louis. "You look familiar, are you the son of Monsieur LeClaire, a merchant from Mobile?"

"Oui."

"I talked to him several weeks ago. He is as upset about this war as we are. If it were not that it would endanger his family, he would be with us now."

A thought struck Louis. If the French in Mobile caught him with these French deserters, and on Spanish ship, it would put his family in danger. He certainly did not blame his father's position. He was protecting the ones he loved. If the French considered his family traitorous, they all could be hanged for treason. The more he thought, the more it weighed on his mind. The best thing he could do for his family was to remain where he was. He would get word to them that he was safe, but he would say nothing about siding with the Spanish.

Under the cover of darkness, the Spanish fleet silently crept into Mobile Bay. Louis felt uneasy when soldiers from one of the Spanish ships went ashore and captured two small boats laden with military gear. Everything was so unsettling. He hated going against his countrymen who had gone to war over something that happened in Europe.

His mind snapped back to the problems at hand when a Frenchman grabbed him by the arm. "The captain is sending men ashore to destroy the military defense. Are you coming?"

"Will civilians be hurt?" Louis asked.

"No, there are only a few soldiers defending Mobile, and if we can overpower them, Mobile will be under the control of the Spanish. There will be little bloodshed."

In the darkness, the Spanish and French who had joined them sailed ashore on smaller vessels. Once the Spanish and French were engaged in battle, Louis stole away. This was the opportunity he had needed to get a message to his family. He headed for one of his father's warehouses. He was familiar with the area and had no problem finding his way. Slipping through a side door of the building, he headed for the office. Once inside he lit a lantern and searched through the desk where he found pen, ink, and paper. He wrote a note to his parents saying he was safe and was returning to Santa Maria to help Catana. By the time he returned to the beach, the fighting was over, and the men from the

Spanish colony were pushing their boats into the water. Once they were back aboard the sloop, the captain announced they would be returning to Santa Maria to describe what they had found.

* * * *

The morning that Louis left for Mobile, Catana marched into governor's office to confront Matamoros.

"Señor, are you aware of how the captain-general has treated Tokala and Jabulani?"

The governor looked up from the papers on his desk and gave her a questioning look. "Who?"

"The Indian and black man imprisoned in the brig. He had them beaten."

"Captain-General Carvajal is one of the officers who joined us in Havana. Although he is strict, his men are well disciplined, and he gets things done. If prisoners are troublesome, it is his duty to see that they do not harm anyone. He told me that two slaves attacked and tried to kill two of his men."

"They were only defending themselves. Tokala and his people have saved your hide more than once in the past."

The governor stood. His face was red with anger, and the veins in his neck throbbed. She had never seen him look at her with such anger.

"You have gone too far, señorita. What I, or the Spanish soldiers do, is no concern of yours. Now leave. I do not want to hear another word on the subject."

Catana opened her mouth to speak but snapped it shut before she said something she would regret. If he learned she had presented a false letter to the guard in order to see the prisoners, he would have her head. She turned on her heel and walked out of his office, slamming the door behind her. There was no use reasoning with him. Don Alfonso would be of no help either. She would help Tokala and Jabulani some other way. Oh, how she wished Louis was here.

She strode directly to the brig to see if Tokala and Jabulani were all right, and to keep up their spirits.

"Guard, I have come from the governor's office and would like to see the prisoners." At least it was not entirely a lie.

"Sorry, señorita, Captain Carvajal left orders that no one goes in there without his permission."

"*Madre de Dios*," she muttered under her breath. Pulling herself up to her full height, she looked the guard in the eye. "Did your Captain say anything about speaking to them through the window?"

"Well no, but…"

"Buena." She hurried to the window before the guard could say another word. "Tokala. How is Jabulani?"

The Indian came to the window, and Catana leaned closer to him.

"Did they remove your shackles?"

"Yes," he replied in a low voice so the guard would not hear him. "Jabulani and I have agreed to cooperate with our captors, for we know you will find a way to free us. We want to make it as easy as possible for you. Do you have a plan?"

"I…I am still working on it."

"The Spanish plan to send us to Point Seguenza tomorrow to join the other slaves working on the fort."

Catana rubbed her temple lightly with her fingers. She felt a headache coming on. "I cannot help you before then, but I will get word to you when the time comes."

"That is enough talk, señorita," the guard called out. "Leave before you get us both into trouble."

Catana whispered, "*Adios*, my friend. Tell Jabulani I hope to have you both freed soon."

Stepping back from the window, she turned for home. When she entered her house, she felt frustrated. The pounding in her temples worsened. She would rest. Once her head felt better, maybe she would come up with a plan to rescue her friends.

* * * *

On the second evening after Louis had departed for Mobile, Catana was still trying to think of a way to free the two men. They were at Point

Seguenza now, which would make it more difficult. How would she free them, and take them far from here, when she had no help, no plan, and no idea where they would go? Deep in thought, she stared into the cooking fire, watching the flames slowly burn down to glowing embers. A noise outside her door made he jump. Grabbing her father's sword, she hid behind the door as it slowly inched open.

"Catana, are you in there?"

She had not realized she was holding her breath and exhaled. "Louis?"

"Oui. I have returned with the scouting party. Would you please put that sword down?"

She lowered the weapon. "But why? Are your parents all right?"

"It is better to stay away from them for a while. There are some French who might associate me with Monsieur Rogue and the French Nationals. If I return home, some exuberant colonist might accuse my parents of being traitors. It is better that I remain incognito." He settled into a chair near the fire.

Catana pulled her chair around to face him. "Things have not gone well here. Captain Carvajal eased up on his torment of Tokala and Jabulani, but now they have been put to work at Point Seguenza helping the soldiers reinforce the fort. The governor is of no help. He warned me, not so nicely, that what happened to those two slaves was none of my affair. If I attempt to go near them, I am afraid he will have me arrested."

"Then you must humble yourself and apologize."

"I will not. It is he who is wrong, not I."

Louis held up his hand, palm out. "Stop and think. If the governor believes you have conceded to his way of thinking, the matter will soon leave his mind. It will erase any suspicion he may have, and we can act on our plan."

"But we do not have a plan."

"Not at the moment, but we will soon. Return to your duties in the morning as though nothing has happened. I will volunteer to join the work party at Point Seguenza."

"The men who are working on the fort are staying on the island to save time."

Louis shrugged. "Then I will sail a boat over and join them. We will need to know where they are billeted, how heavily they are guarded, and alert them to be prepared. It may take several weeks to make the arrangements, but if they know we are planning a rescue, maybe they can help in some way."

Catana brushed a stray lock of hair out of her eyes. "Once we rescue them, where can we go? Not to the French and we will have the Spanish pursuing us."

Louis thought for a moment. "I do not know. I am sure we will find an answer."

* * * *

A beam of sunlight caressed Catana's cheek, its warmth waking her. She looked up at the thatched roof, where the light worked its way through small openings, and then she rolled over to gaze at the pile of animal skins where Louis had been sleeping. Sitting, she cleared her head and remembered that he was going to Point Seguenza this morning. She stood and shook out her bedding. It was time to get ready to humble herself. She walked briskly up to the office door and paused. She was not sure what she would say. It would be hard for her to admit she was wrong when she knew she was right.

Knocking lightly, she entered to his summons and was surprised to see a tall, good-looking gentleman with the governor. She guessed him to be in his mid-thirties, with handsome features, and piercing brown eyes. His air of authority intimidated Catana.

"Let me introduce you." Governor Matamoros said. "Captain Carvajal, this is my secretary, Catana Molino. Catana does not approve of some of the army's treatment of prisoners."

Catana shifted from one foot to the other as the captain's cold stare fixed on her.

The governor chuckled. "Women know nothing of what must be done to win a war. They are too softhearted."

Catana choked down her anger. He seemed to think the whole thing was humorous. At least he did not seem upset with her. Crossing her fingers behind her back, Catana spoke in a meek voice. "You are right, Señor. When I saw those two men, it touched my heart. I thought over what you said, and I must not let my sympathy go to the enemy under any circumstances."

"Most appropriate thinking," the captain said. "Let up your guard for one moment and they will kill you."

"Sí," Catana agreed. "That is why I have come to apologize. May I continue to work for you, Governor?"

"Of course," he replied. "I, too, apologize. I was under stress at the time of your visit and lost my temper. Let us pretend the disagreement never happened."

Catana nodded and smiled. That is exactly what she wanted. "Leave us now, my dear. You can return to your duties after the midday meal. The captain and I have urgent military business to talk over."

The captain's smile did not reach his eyes when he turned to her and spoke. "We would not want to tempt you to pity our enemies any further."

Catana clenched her teeth so she would not speak. With a nod, she turned and left the room. As the door closed behind her, she heard the two men laughing. Had they made a joke at her expense? At least she was back in the good graces of the governor and privy to information that might help her and Louis.

With Louis gone and with no work at the present, Catana strolled toward the beach. It was a cloudless September day. The mornings were pleasantly cooler, and a walk along the shore would help melt her anger before she had to return to work that afternoon. Sinking down atop a sand dune, she gazed across the water at Santa Rosa Island. What was Louis doing now? Had he been able to contact Tokala and Jabulani? Out of the corner of her eye, she noticed sunlight reflect off a piece of metal sticking out of the sand at the bottom of the dune. Sliding down to it, she brushed the sand away and saw her mother's jewelry box. She set it in her lap and opened it. Her mother's jewelry was missing, but her father's letters remained inside. Whoever took it had thought only the jewelry worth taking. Her mother's shiny bobbles were not worth much, and to Catana mere keepsakes. The only piece of value was the ring her father had given her mother when they were married. It was the ring Catana wore.

Closing the box, Catana stood. She would take this home and put it in a safe place. It was the only link to her father she had. Captain Carvajal did not seem to be an easy person to approach, but if she had to humble herself before him to learn what he knew about her father, she would.

She crossed the dunes to her house. After hiding her retrieved box in the corner of a cupboard, she sat alone at the wooden the table, slowly chewed on a piece of bread, and tried to think of a plan to rescue the two prisoners. Noticing at the length of the shadows on the floor, she realized she had been away from the office too long. The governor must have work for her by now. She grabbed a piece of cheese and an apple to eat along the way and hurried back to the office. As she settled into a chair at her small writing table in one corner of the room, a messenger burst through the door without knocking. The governor was behind his desk leaning over some papers and his head snapped up as the man stood at attention in front of him. The messenger took several gulps of air before speaking.

"Sir, our scout ships report three man-of-war ships under the command of Admiral M. Demos de Champmeslin, have arrived in Massacra. The ships include the *Hercule, Mars,* and *Triton.* With them are two lesser ships."

The governor sighed deeply. "Did the French indicate what their plans are?"

"I am not sure, sir. I did learn that the fleet has over five hundred soldiers, colonists, and prisoners. There is also a large shipment of food and supplies aboard."

"No indication that they plan an attack on us?"

"I was dispatched to give you the information before I learned more."

Catana pretended to be absorbed in her writing but listened carefully. If the French attacked the fort, what would happen to her and Louis's rescue plans?"

CHAPTER SEVEN

Catana slept poorly that night. She had nightmares of the French overrunning Point Seguenza and killing Louis, Tokala, and Jabulani. She awoke feeling depressed. At work, she had a hard time concentrating on the mundane words and numbers of the supply report she was to copy. The governor was out of the office, and she sat staring into out of the window. Maybe she should take a boat to Santa Rosa Island and speak with Louis. Hearing the governor's voice outside the door, she bent over her work and started writing.

"This message from Don Antonio Mendieta has me worried," the governor said as he came through the door with Captain-General Carvajal and Captain Martinez. He stepped behind his desk and indicated that the two men to have a seat. "Don Antonio's sloop has remained near Massacra to keep an eye on the French. They are preparing an attack on Santa Maria."

Martinez cleared his throat. "I suggest we abandon this fort and move all the men and equipment to Point Seguenza. It is well fortified, and, as I told you before, this fort is vulnerable to attack because it is an easy target from the rear."

The governor nodded. "You are probably right. I will—"

"It is a bad idea," the Captain Carvajal cut in. "If we abandon this fort and the village, the French would over run them and have a foothold in Santa Maria."

The captains argued back and forth, until finally, the governor agreed to call a meeting so the colony's leaders could vote on the subject. At the meeting, everyone spoke at once, and Catana was unable to record any of the conversations that filled the room. The disagreements became heated and the governor was unable to resolve the issue. When the conference was over, an exhausted Catana returned home.

The next morning Governor Matamoros doubled the perimeter guard around Santa Maria to prevent Indian attacks and gave orders to improve both defensive positions. Catana was kept busy recording his instructions. She was unable to find a way to join Louis.

Several days passed, and the governor began to doubt the report. "Maybe what the scouting party saw were not warships," he confided to Catana. "They might be merchant ships. We have found no sign of them and there have been no Indian attacks."

Catana was more than ready to agree with him. The Spanish grew confident that it was a false threat. This gave Catana time to get away to visit Louis. After she received permission from the governor to go to Santa Rosa Island, Catana boarded a sloop laden with food and supplies for the soldiers at the fort. As they approached Point Seguenza, a crewmember noticed sails in the distance.

The captain squinted at the horizon. "It must be the Windward Squadron. The governor of Havana promised to send five of their ships for support."

As soon as Catana jumped ashore, she asked a worker if he knew where she could find Louis. Nodding, the man pointed to the top of a wall overlooking the sea. She waved and called out to him. "Do you have time to talk?"

"Come on up," he called back.

She joined him and they sat facing the gulf while Louis shared his lunch with her. Catana popped a piece of bread into her mouth and chewed slowly as Louis explained that Tokala and Jabulani were billeted in separate areas of the fort.

"I will have to find a way to first free one and then the other," he explained. "Will you be able to sail a small sloop alone to the eastern point of the island and beach it on the north side? Once I free both men, we will need you to be waiting for us."

"And where will we sail?"

"South is all I know for now."

"I should have no problem. The sloop I sailed here is small, and the distance from mainland to the island is not far."

"If you bring it over as the tide is going out, you greatest worry would be beaching it. When I arrive with Jabulani and Tokala, we should be able to get it back into the water easily."

Catana swallowed her last piece of cheese and licked her fingers. "You are skilled at sailing, and I know enough to get by, but Tokala and Jabulani have no experience."

"Jabulani has. He was a slave aboard a three-masted merchant ship for a while. A sloop will be much easer for him to handle."

"Look, those ships are growing closer," Catana said, scanning the water. "From their shape, and their flags, are they French?"

Louis peered at the incoming fleet. "Oui, they are French, and the lead ship is flying the flag of a full admiral."

At that moment a sentry called out a warning. By the time Catana and Louis had scrambled to their feet, the fort was in chaos. Louis gripped Catana by the arm. "We will do it tonight."

"What?"

"We will rescue Tokala and Jabulani tonight while the Spanish soldiers prepare for battle."

"Are you crazy? If I try to sail a sloop from the mainland mid-battle, I will be shot out of the water."

"The French will have their guns trained on the forts. If you sail to the east of the village, they may not notice you."

Catana was not happy with the odds, but if the French won, she and Louis would become prisoners waiting in the shadow of the gallows. Returning to the sloop, she noticed its name was *La Paloma,* the Dove. It was a symbol of peace. She prayed the sloop would sail her and those she loved to where they would find peace. She watched until the soldiers deserted the area for the fort and climbed aboard. Slipping the tie lines from the pylons, she shoved off and floated the sloop eastward along the shoreline until she was out of sight of the fort, then turned the sloop north and headed for the mainland. With all the confusion, she was sure no one had seen her take the vessel. But if they had, maybe they would think it was a dispatch to Saint Joseph's Bay for help.

Sneaking into the village, she entered her house. She placed the remainder of her food into one knapsack and stuffed two worn dresses, a pair of trousers, and a loose shirt into another. Before closing the second knapsack, she placed the box that held letters from her father on top.

Trudging back toward the sloop, she detoured into the church graveyard and stopped in front of her mother's grave marker. She ran her fingers over the rough, wooden cross and read her mother's name. Magdalena. Sadness filled her thoughts as she remembered how her mother, consumed by yellow fever, had passed away.

Her father had blamed the rough life of the settlement for her mother's death, and his grief had driven him to the sea. Before leaving for Havana, he had told Catana he was going to find a better life, then return for her. Now he was missing, and she had lost her chance to get information from Captain Carvajal. Turning toward the beach, she said an *Ave* for her parents and continued her trek to the sloop.

She climbed aboard and stored her knapsacks in the sloop's small cabin. It was only large enough for a small bunk, table, and chair. There were pegs on the bulkhead to hang clothes, and in one corner, a washstand with a bowl that was set in a depression so it would not fall to the floor in rough seas.

On deck, the golden sun embraced the world in a soft and peaceful glow. As Catana watched it dip farther toward the horizon, the shadows lengthened. Spanish boats crossed between the mainland and the island to reinforce Fort Principal de Asturias at Point Seguenza. Spanish frigates moved into battle formation. More frigates, plus the French vessels the Spanish had previously captured, ringed the inside the bay. They faced outward in order to fire against enemy ships attempting to force their way through the channel. Smaller vessels stretched out beyond the ring, prepared to fire on if a French ship successfully ran the channel gap, the same channel she and her friends were to sail through on their voyage south.

Catana grew nervous. Maybe the Spanish would take them for one of their defense vessels. However, what would they do when the *Dove* attempted to sail through the channel? She was so deep in thought that when something brushed against the back of her leg, she shrieked. Nervous and shaken, she spun around in time to see a cat dart through the open door into the cabin.

Catana crept toward the door, slipped inside, and closed it behind her, trapping the animal. The cat backed into a corner as Catana approached. It had a large frame but its ribs showed under matted orange fur. When she leaned forward to touch it, the cat arched its back and growled a low warning at her to come no farther. Catana backed slowly toward one of her knapsacks on the bunk. Without taking her eyes off the cat, she opened it, pulled out a piece of dried meat, and set it on the deck. Gradually, she moved toward the door, opened it, quickly stepped out of the cabin, and tightly closed the door.

Back on deck, she looked over the rail and noticed the tide was going out. It was time to sail for the island. She untied the mooring line and took the helm. Because she was not able to work the sails and steer at the same time, she needed to depend on the outgoing current to carry her to the island.

The water ran swiftly toward the channel between the two long, narrow islands and on toward the open sea. It would be a challenge to beach the sloop before it was swept out to sea. She prayed she could bring the shallow-drafted ship ashore without damage.

Pointing the bow at a southwest angle to compensate for the eastward flowing current, she held tight to the helm. Looking down the fifty-foot cedar deck, she aimed the bowsprit several more degrees west. The current was stronger than she expected. The shroud lines hummed in the wind, and the pulleys clanked against the mast. She scanned the area. All the Spanish ships sat in battle position, and all the batteries from Fort San Carlos and the fort at Point Seguenza were trained on the bay.

Catana grew tense with each passing moment. What if someone took her for the enemy and fired? She was coming up on the island fast. Turning the ship at a slight angle to the shore, she let a wave carry the sloop onto the sand. The ship came to a jarring halt and almost threw her off her feet.

Crawling to the end of the seven-foot-long bowsprit, she jumped onto the dune that the ship had nosed into. The sloop was listing heavily to the port side, its keel buried in the wet sand.

She looked for a way to secure the sloop. One large wave could lift her off and carry her back out to sea. It was dark and she found noting in which to secure *Dove*. Trusting in providence, she sat cross-legged on top of the dune to wait.

A full moon was rising. Soon it bathed the water and white dunes in its silver light. Scanning the gulf, she saw the dark outline of French warships looming against the moonlit sky, bobbing on their anchor lines. She and her companions were trapped between the French and Spanish fleets. If Louis arrived soon, they might be able to slip past the French in the darkness. They would leave their white sails furled so the moonlight would not reflect and alert the enemy. But if they were not here by dawn, they would have to remain hidden until dark and go out with the tide.

She climbed down the north side of the dune, sat facing the direction from which Louis would come, and watched the shadows for movement. The surf was much gentler on this side of the island and the soft sounds of the waves washing onto shore lulled her to sleep.

CHAPTER EIGHT

Once the moon rose, Louis set to work on his escape plan. During his stay at the fort, he had learned where the captain of the guard kept the master key to all the doors in the fort. In the confusion of eminent battle, it had been easy for him to slip into the office and "borrow" the key.

He had warned Catana it would be several hours after dark before it was safe to free Tokala and Jabulani. Inching along the arched passageway of stone, he drew close to the cell where Tokala was imprisoned and peered through the iron bar door. Torches, spaced far apart, dimly lighted the passage. The torch directly across from the cell door threw no light into the room. A ray of moonlight found its way through a small barred window, but there was only enough to see black images of men sleeping on the floor along the walls.

"Tokala," Louis whispered.

There was no response.

"Tokala," he whispered louder.

Louis noticed movement as one of the black images stirred.

"Tokala," he whispered a third time. "It is Louis."

The shadow rose from the floor and approached him. "I thought I was imagining things when I saw you working on the fort yesterday," the Indian replied in a hushed voice.

"I have come to liberate you and Jabulani and take you out of here. Catana should be waiting on the northeast end of the island with a sloop. How often do the guards make their rounds at night?"

"Since the French have arrived, they have been busy preparing for battle. They lock us in and leave us until we are due to return to work."

"That will give me plenty of time. Once I have freed you, we will find Jabulani's cell and release him."

"Our black friend is not in his cell," Tokala replied. "He and the men imprisoned with him have been assigned to an all night work detail. I overheard two guards talking. The Spanish think they will accomplish more if they work on the reinforcement of the fort twenty-four hours a day. The crews are smaller. However, they work us for ten hours then give us eight hours off to eat and sleep."

Louis groaned. This messed up his well thought out plan. "What are our chances of smuggling Jabulani away from the work crew?"

"They do not have as many guards posted, but they are alert and nervous. It is too risky."

Louis pondered the problem for a moment. "When the work party is returned, will they post a guard near the cell?"

"I do not think so. If the Spanish continue their present routine, I, and these men, will replace Jabulani's crew in the morning. This will allow them and their guards to eat and sleep."

Several men stirred in their sleep and one awoke. Louis lowered his voice for Tokala's ears alone. "When I unlock this door, do not say a word and do as I say."

Louis opened the cell door and spoke in a loud voice. "We need you for extra duty, red man. Come with me."

He locked the door behind the Indian and marched him down the passageway until they were out of sight of the other prisoners.

"I am taking you to join Jabulani's work crew. Once you all have been returned to his cell and the guards leave, I will come for you."

Tokala directed Louis to the work party and hid in the shadows while Louis distracted the guards by shouting at them. "I think I see the French ships moving this way. What are we to do?"

While four armed guards ran to the top edge of the fort wall and looked out across the water, Louis gave Tokala the signal to join the other workers.

"Sentry," one of the guards called out. "Do you see the French approaching?"

"No, they are all at anchor," a voice returned.

The guard peered across the moonlit water. "I do not see movement either." He turned and glared down at Louis. "You civilians panic for no cause."

"I apologize," Louis replied. "I thought they were launching an attack. Maybe what I saw were just moon shadows on the water."

"Nothing is going on out there. You should not be wandering around the fort at this time of night. Go to your quarters and let us get about our work."

Louis hung his head meekly and shuffled out of sight of the work party. He fingered the master key that lay heavy in his pocket. If anyone discovered that it was missing, the entire fort would be alerted. He would return it. But first he would visit Jabulani's cell to jam the lock on the door.

When he arrived, the iron bar door was wide open. He pulled a small pebble from his pocket and placed it in the latch. He closed and opened it several times. When he was satisfied it worked the way he wanted, he quickly returned the master key to where he had found it. He darted around the corner near the cell to hide and to wait.

As the grey of predawn grew lighter, Louis' nerves grew tighter than a bowstring. Would Catana still be waiting? What if she had been unable to sail the sloop to the island?

His heart jumped when he heard voices coming down the passageway. He stepped farther into the passage that was around the corner from the cell. When the guards stopped in front of the door, Louis eased a peek around the corner. Two guards shoved the slaves inside while a third slammed the iron bar door behind them. The door closed with a bang and bounced open. Louis held his breath while the guard glared at the lock, swore, and pushed the door firmly shut.

Once the guards disappeared down the passageway, there was silence except for ten prisoners preparing to go to sleep. Louis waited several minutes before he stepped out of hiding and pulled on the door. He called out to Jabulani and beckoned him forward. The black man looked at Louis with surprise, and then a smile spread across his face when he recognized his friend.

Mutters filled the small room when the prisoners realized the opening door could lead them to freedom. Louis held up his hand for silence. "I will leave this door unlocked if you vow not to try and escape until three hours after we have gone. Your best chance for a successful flight will be after the fighting commences between the French and Spanish. You will be able to escape unnoticed." He told them where to find the master key so they would be able to release the other prisoners in the midst of battle.

* * * *

Catana's eyes flew open when she felt pressure on her shoulder. It was broad daylight, and Louis looked down at her with a wide smile on his face.

She sat up straight and stifled a yawn. "What took so long?"

"It is a long story. I will tell you once we are underway."

"Where are Tokala and Jabulani?"

Two heads appeared over the rim of a dune. Tokala and Jabulani climbed over the crest and slid down to join Catana and Louis.

"*Gracias, Señor Dios!*" Catana said, making the sign of the cross. "You are all safe."

"Yes, for now." Louis replied. "But when the other prisoners escape from their cells and flood the island, there will be soldiers everywhere."

Tokala shrugged. "The Spaniards will be so busy preparing to fight the French they may not bother to go after them."

"I would not count on that," Louis said. "We should leave now."

Catana swept her arm toward the horizon. "If you have not noticed, the French are blocking us to the south and the Spanish are set to blow any unknown ship out of the water to the north. Only if we wait until dark can we slip by the French."

Louis rubbed his chin while thinking of a solution. "We could sail east."

"Sí, Saint Joseph's Bay," Catana agreed. "But if we are pursued, we will be arrested, unless…" With a smile, she continued. "Unless I can prove we are not fugitives. I must return to the presidio and the governor's office."

After Catana explained her plan, the four of them pushed the *Dove* into deeper water. The high tide lifted the ship, freeing her of the sand's hold. Hoisting a Spanish flag, they sailed northeast, avoiding the potential line of fire. They landed the sloop on the sandy shore half a league east of the colony.

"Sail on to Saint Joseph's Bay while I get the papers," Catana said. "I will meet you there. Meanwhile, think of a destination. South covers a lot of territory. I will also try and pick up several maps."

After the *Dove* was on its way east, Catana headed west toward Santa Maria. As she approached Fort San Carlos, she discovered it was under siege by Bienville. His men and hundreds of Indians came from three sides. Catana hid among the trees near the beach and watched as the French placed a battery on San Isidro Hill at the rear of the fort. Two cannons from Fort San Carlos barked at the cannon on the hill. At the same time, cannons from Fort Asturais on Santa Rosa Island fired at small French boats. They quickly took flight. The fighting was intermittent. She thought it better to wait and would attempt to approach the fort during a lull.

Several hours later, silence hung in the air. Now she would make her move. Catana approached the gate of the fort. The people of the village had taken refuge inside. To the guards, she was another civilian looking for safety. They recognized her and let her pass.

When she approached the building, she found it was deserted. She entered the governor's office and opened the bottom drawer of the desk. She grabbed the papers she had come for, several sea charts, a pen, and inkpot and headed for the door. She took several paces down the hallway when a loud voice shouted, "Halt!"

Catana came to a standstill and turned slowly. Captain Carvajal stood with his flintlock rifle trained on her.

"What are you doing coming out of the governor's office?"

"Governor Matamoros requested that I bring these charts to him."

The captain eyed her with suspicion, and she showed him the inkpot and pen. "He also wants me to write a record of the battle."

A cannon ball hit the wall behind her, and she ducked as debris rained down.

"Please, Captain, I must go before the fighting grows too intense." Her words fell on empty space. The captain was sprinting in the opposite direction to join his men. Once he was out of sight, she stuffed the papers, sealed inkpot, and pen into a waterproof pouch tied around her waist.

With the next lull in the fighting, Catana stole out of the fort and headed toward the village. The bombardment grew heavy. She found a safe place to hide until it eased and then started her way east toward Saint Joseph's Bay. Once out of range of the heavy fire, she slumped down onto a dune to rest and became engrossed in the sea battle unfolding on the bay.

Flags on the French warships signaled their ground troops, who surrounded Fort San Carlos. A French warship sailed through the channel and entered the harbor, followed by four others. Behind them were smaller ships. They all edged forward. Then the French warships dropped anchor near the line of Spanish ships. The French opened fire, pounding the larger Spanish vessels.

Hours passed and Catana's heart sank. The French were crushing the Spanish Fleet. Only two Spanish frigates remained in commission. Small boats dispatched from the large Spanish warships fled with survivors toward Santa Rosa Island.

Scanning the bay, Catana's eyes rested on one Spanish ship on fire then another. Several ships had sunk, and others were beached. At the hands of the French, her countrymen were dying in the sea and on land, and all she could do was watch.

Her heart sank further when she noticed the men at Fort Asturias strike their colors. The French warship, flying the admiral's flag, approached the Spanish flagship, and within minutes, the Spanish vessel struck her colors. A spark of hope flickered in her when she saw the Spanish flag still flew over Fort San Carlos, but before nightfall, that, too, came down.

* * * *

In the twilight, Catana turned east and continued her trek to Saint Joseph's Bay. Paralleling her were two small Spanish craft that had escaped. By the time she arrived, everyone in the Saint Joseph's settlement knew of the Spanish defeat.

Catana easily found the *Dove* anchored off shore and swam the short distance to the sloop. Climbing a rope ladder, she scrambled over the gunwale and onto deck. Louis intercepted her on the way to her cabin.

"Are you ready to get underway?" he asked.

"I think we will be safe here for several days. My people lost the battle, and I would like to learn their fate before we depart. Tokala and Jabulani will be in no danger with the papers. Come with me to my cabin."

"Speaking of your cabin, after we set sail for Saint Joseph's Bay, Jabulani opened your cabin door and a creature ran out so quickly that we could not tell what it was."

Jabulani appeared suddenly, grabbed Catana, and hugged the breath out of her. Stepping back, he held her at arms length. He had a wide smile on his face. "Whatever that creature was, it disappeared, leaving your knapsack torn to shreds. What food was in it is gone.

"Esmeralda!" Catana had forgotten about the cat. "It was a stray cat. I wonder where it went." She shrugged. There was no time to worry about it now.

"Jabulani, would you find Tokala and bring him to my cabin?"

All four filled the cabin. Catana asked Louis to sit on the bunk while the two slaves stood at the table. Catana placed in front of them the papers she had taken from the governor's office along with the inkpot and pen. "Gentlemen, these documents, when signed by the governor, make you free men."

Louis stood to take a look. "But they are not signed."

Catana pulled another paper out from underneath the stack. "This is what the governor's signature looks like." She painstakingly copied his name onto the papers and handed one to each slave. "Keep these with you at all times, for they show that you have been freed."

"What is that other document?" Louis asked.

"It is a Letter of Marquee. It is a rule of the sea that a Letter of Marquee should shown by the captain of a ship when—"

"I know what it is," Louis cut in. "But we are not privateers."

"We may have need of it some day," Catana replied. "I will put it in a safe place."

"I do not know the purpose of the letter." Tokala said.

"Privateers carry them," Louis explained. "It gives them the right to steal from ships belonging to the enemy. They can only attack foreign ships and must divide the loot with the crown. With this letter, the privateer is protected by international law and cannot be tried or arrested for piracy."

Tokala nodded with understanding. "It is good to have one of these letters."

Catana placed the Letter of Marquee in the box with her father's letters and put the inkpot and pen into a drawer in the table.

"Now that Tokala and Jabulani are no longer slaves, it will give us time to make plans. I would like to say farewell to Aunt Jacinta and Inez before we leave."

The tree men remained aboard the *Dove* while Catana returned to shore. Entering her aunt's house, she embraced Inez, happy her cousin was unharmed. When Catana attempted to greet her aunt in the same way, the cold stare she received from Jacinta froze her in her tracks. Instead, she gave the woman a forced smile and returned her attention to Inez. She decided to spend the night here and return to the *Dove* in the morning. There were several things she wanted to take care of before she returned to the vessel.

* * * *

The next morning, while Catana was in the town square gathering food to take aboard the sloop, a Spanish messenger arrived and informed the people that Bienville planned to ship the captured Spanish soldiers to Havana and transport the high-ranking Spanish officers to France.

Catana gave Inez the news as soon as she returned to her aunt's house.

"Juan will be sent far from me," Inez said in despair. "I will never see him again."

"It will not be for long." Catana replied. "Once the Governor of Havana receives word of what has happened, he will send the Windward Squadron to chase the French back to Mobile and New Orleans. The French are no match for our Armada."

* * * *

Later that afternoon Catana returned to the *Dove* to take the men food. As they sat on deck eating bread, cheese, and fresh fruit, Catana offered her latest plan.

"The governor and all the Spanish officials have been shipped to either France of Havana. This includes Carvajal, *gracias Señor Dios*. When the Armada arrives and regains Santa Maria de Galve, we will return to our homes in peace. If anyone questions us on our return, you, Tokala and Jabulani, have papers to show you are free men. The new officials will never know that we were fugitives."

Louis sighed. "Are you suggesting that until the Armada arrives we remain here on the *Dove?*"

"Sí," Catana replied, "until it is safe to return to Santa Maria." She smiled and popped a piece of bread into her mouth. "Soon everything will return to normal."

* * * *

When Catana returned to her aunt's house, she tried to comfort Inez, who was still mourning the loss of Juan.

"The Armada is on its way, that I am sure. A month from now you will be reunited with your love, and we will return to Santa Maria. Come, let us take a walk along the shore and enjoy the beautiful sunset."

They crossed the white dunes toward the beach and saw a man pull a small boat ashore. When he turned and ran toward the settlement, Catana recognized Mateo, a young Spaniard who had spied on the French.

"Maybe he has word of the Spanish Armada and has come to tell Governor Salinas." Catana said while crossing her fingers.

Intercepting the young man, Catana spoke. "Do you have good news?"

She looked into his sober face as he shook his head. "Monsieur Bienville has put Santa Maria de Galve to the torch. The fort, houses, and barracks, are gone. Everything has been leveled, including the stockade. They even burned the church. I watched as they rolled cannons into the sea."

Tears welled in Catana's eyes and trickled down her cheeks. "Why?"

"A Frenchman did not realize that I am a spy and told me that Bienville heard news that the Spanish are sending the Windward Squadron from Vera Cruz in order to reclaim Santa Maria. The Frenchman said Bienville chose to destroy everything rather than have the Spanish take possession."

"*Madre de Dios,*" Inez said ringing her hands. "What shall we do? Even if the Armada does come, we have no home in which to return."

Catana grew anxious when Mateo told them that the French planned to patrol the coast from Saint Joseph's Bay to Massacra. Would Saint Joseph's Bay be their next target?

After Mateo continued toward the governor's office, Catana took Inez by the hand. "Return home. I must inform my friends aboard the *Dove* of what has happened."

She borrowed Mateo's boat to row out to the sloop. Climbing aboard the *Dove,* she called the three men together and relayed the information Mateo had given her.

"Louis, will you go into what is left of Santa Maria and learn what the French plan? Mateo said there are still French troops there and a French flag flying."

"I will learn what I can and be back tomorrow."

Catana, Tokala, and Jabulani sat in silence as they watch Louis disappear into the twilight.

* * * *

Late the next afternoon, Louis returned with the news which buried Catana's last hopes of returning home. As they gathered on the *Dove*, Louis relayed what he had learned.

"Bienville conducted a court-martial. Remember the Frenchmen who defected to Governor Matamoros and sailed with Don Alfonso's scouting fleet?" The three listeners nodded.

"They were all hanged as traitors. This was before he torched the settlement."

"I wonder why Mateo never mentioned this." Catana said.

"It probably was not important information to Governor Salinas." Louis replied.

"Is there anything more we should know?" Tokala asked.

"After the fire, twenty-five French soldiers remained to fly the flag and hold the fort. They captured a small Spanish ship, and the captain said he was part of the Armada from Vera Cruz, but no other ships appeared. The French packed during the night to return west. When I left Santa Maria this morning, all that remained was the razed remnants to bleach in the sun."

Jabulani ran his fingers through his black, curly hair. "What of our future?"

"I say we sail south," Louis replied.

Catana shook her head. "There is nothing for us to the south"

Louis let out a deep sigh. "I cannot return home. I will be hanged as a traitor like my comrades. Stop and think about it, Catana. None of us has a home here."

Tokala swept his arm to encompass the deck of the *Dove*. "This is the only home we have now."

"Now that the French are gone, we can settle in Saint Joseph's Bay," Catana suggested.

Louis gave her an exasperated look. "Do you really want to do that, Catana? Although my countrymen are gone for now, they could return to Saint Joseph's Bay at any time and repeat what they did to Santa Maria. Would you want to go through that again?"

Catana shook her head. "You're right, Louis. It is probably best to sail south."

* * * *

That evening Catana returned to her aunt's house to inform Jacinta and Inez of her departure with the morning tide. Should she invite them to come?

She, and the crew of the *Dove,* chose Havana, where it would be safe, as their destination. Her aunt and cousin could stay in the second cabin that was larger than the one Catana claimed. The men could find shelter to sleep, either in the hold, or on deck.

When she finally gathered her courage to ask her aunt, the woman looked at her niece and spoke to her scornfully. "I would not cross the bay with you, let alone sail all the way to Havana."

"What will you do if the French attack Saint Joseph's Bay?"

The stony-faced woman tilted her head back, sniffed, and looked down her nose at Catana. "I would much prefer the company of the French than the four of you misfits."

Inez had come into the room and overheard the conversation. "Mother, I want to go with Catana."

"Absolutely not," her mother snapped.

While mother and daughter argued, Catana strode into the room she shared with Inez and placed her few belongings into her knapsack and slipped out the door.

CHAPTER NINE

The rising sun bathed the sand in its rosy glow as the four travelers weighed anchor and set a heading south. Louis and Tokala unfurled the sail while Jabulani took the helm. With the wind at their back, the *Dove* ran with the current. Her bow cut swiftly through the waves. Soon the sands of La Florida sank into the sea.

Catana stood at the bow, breathing in the tangy salt air. She had not felt so alive since before her mother's death. Her thoughts turned toward her father. Would she be able to find him once they were in Havana? Was there a clue somewhere in the letters that she had stored in her cabin? She turned toward her cabin and noticed the door swinging back and forth with the motion of the ship. As she approached it, a shrill scream came from inside.

Rushing to her cabin Catana was surprised, and then amused, to see Inez cowering in the corner of the room with a large, orange cat standing on the bunk. The cat's fur was standing on end, and she was ready to pounce onto her cousin. Esmeralda must have been spending her time in the hold of the sloop, and from the look of the cat, she had been eating well.

"Inez, what are you doing here? Does Jacinta—"

"She does not know." Standing, Inez faced her cousin eye to eye. "I stowed aboard so I could look for Juan."

"Your mother may seem unfeeling at times, but for you to disappear like this will worry her. She will think you have come to a disastrous end and are lying dead somewhere."

"I left a message with the priest. He is to give it to Mother when I am far enough away that she can do nothing to force my return."

"Why would the priest aid you in running away?"

Inez shifted from foot to foot before answering. "He does not know the contents of the message. I bent the truth a bit and told him that I was going on a special mission for our colony and that the message would explain everything to mother."

Catana rubbed the tense muscles in the back of her neck. *"Dios,* she is going to hate me even more for this."

"It is not your fault, Catana. It was my decision and mine alone. I said this in my message."

"Even so, she will not find me blameless. I will tell Jabulani to turn back."

Inez stomped her foot. "No!" The cat growled and arched her back further. "If you turn the ship around, I will jump overboard. I would rather drown than spend my life without Juan."

"You would?"

Catana jumped at the sound of Louis's voice behind her. Turning, she saw him leaning against the doorframe with a grin on his face.

"Louis, will you talk some sense into this girl? I do not want to have to answer to my aunt if anything happens to her." Catana turned back to her cousin. "Besides, I like you too much to put you in danger."

"What danger?" Inez asked. "Last night you invited both me and my mother to come on this voyage."

"Sí, but you would have your mother to keep an eye on you once we arrived in Havana. Louis, Tokala, Jabulani, and I may not be able to remain in Havana long if word goes before us that we stole this ship and freed two slaves."

"Juan will be there to care for me."

Catana shrugged. "We do not know that. He could have deployed to another fort or…"

Louis cut in. "Let her sail to Havana with us. We need someone to cook and sew for us. That will leave you free to help us sail the *Dove.*"

"I suppose you are right," Catana said. "There will be laundry to wash, sails to mend, and decks to scrub." Seeing the stricken look on her cousin's face, Catana added, "but we will all help you."

"Does this mean I can stay?

When Catana nodded, Inez rushed to her and gave her a hug. The sudden movement startled the cat, and she leaped into the air, darted past Louis, and disappeared out the door.

Shaking her head, Catana stared after the animal. "That cat shows bravery, but it runs like a coward."

The three voyagers stepped out into the bright morning sun, and Catana introduced her cousin to the others.

* * * *

It was not long before the crew of the *Dove* fell into their routines as seamen. Louis had sailed with his father often and was an experienced crewman on three-masted merchant ships. Catana, who had traveled with Louis on coastal voyages, learned to climb the rigging and trim the sails. Jabulani's experience came from working as a slave on an English ship as a helmsman, and Tokala learned seamanship quickly. Inez agreed she would be more comfortable doing simple chores and left the climbing of shroud lines and the furling sails to her crewmates.

Although they were shorthanded, the *Dove* was a small sloop. The vessel was fifty-feet long, not including her seven-foot bowsprit with a jib sail. Her one mast carried both a main sail and topsail, which gave her the speed to outrun many larger ships. Her shallow draft enabled her to sail close into shore. She had four cannons on deck. Two were on the starboard and two on the port. Catana prayed they would never have to use them. She knew nothing of firing the weapons.

The crew lacked an important ability; none knew how to navigate. They followed the western coastline of La Florida each day, and at dusk, they anchored the *Dove* close to the beach. Two crewmen rowed ashore to hunt for food and bring back fresh water. When night fell, the anchored ship rocked them to sleep.

On the third day, the sound of cannon fire thundered across the gulf. Louis quickly ordered Jabulani to steer the ship toward one of the many islands off the mainland's coast. While the *Dove* approached, the sun sank lower and mangroves cast long shadows on the water. They sailed to the leeward side of the island, drew close into shore, and hid in the darkness.

"Who do you think is out there?" Catana asked no one in particular.

Louis shrugged. "It could be either the British or the French. I don't want to take the chance of getting blown out of the water."

"We fly no flag," Tokala added.

"True," Louis replied, "but it sounds like a battle, and we could sail into their crossfire. We will be safe here."

The island was made up of small sand hills and a variety of vegetation. The water was deep along the shore, and when the *Dove* glided alongside a mangrove tree, Louis jumped ashore and tied the sloop to one of its mammoth roots.

"We will spend the night here and in the morning gather fresh supplies to fill the hold."

At daybreak, the sound of light thumping woke Catana. She looked out the porthole and saw that the movement of the waves was pushing the sloop gently against the giant mangrove tree. Rolling out of her bunk, she prepared for her trip ashore. Once everyone was gathered at the foot of the mast, Louis gave each of the crew an assignment. They climbed ashore with barrels and baskets to gather food and water. Toting a large basket between them, Catana and Inez went to look for fruit.

Catana scanned a small, sandy, clearing where flamingos and seabirds feasted on fish stranded in shallow tide pools.

"If the men follow the example of the birds, we will feast on fish this evening."

The crew had completed their tasks by late afternoon and agreed to remain on the island for another night. They made camp in sight of the *Dove* and each found a relaxing way to occupy their time. Tokala sat near the cooking fire whittling a small figure of a horse from a piece of wood. Jabulani repaired a strand of frayed roped and Louis had fallen asleep.

Catana felt restless and strolled to where Inez was mending one of Louis's shirts. "You know Louis was joking. You don't have to spend your time repairing his or anyone's clothing."

Inez shrugged. "I do not mind. It gives me something useful to do."

"Let us find some sandy beach and walk around to the other side of the island. I want to see if the ships that were fighting have gone."

Inez set down her mending. "I would like that. It will give us time to be alone and talk."

The mangroves continued to line the shore making it difficult to walk, so the two women turned inland. Sections of land were swampy, and they kept to the higher ground. The trees closed in around them. Strange vines twisted around their trunks and hung from their limbs. Catana was so engrossed in where she was stepping that when a vine brushed her cheek, she jumped and stifled a scream.

Inez stopped to wipe the perspiration running down her face with the sleeve of her shirt. "I do not want to go farther. We do not know what wild creatures are lurking around us. And what if there are snakes?"

The heat and humidity were sapping Catana of her strength. She was about to agree when she noticed an opening in the trees ahead. She pointed to a sandy hill in the center of a clearing.

"Let us climb to the top first. We should be able to see the other side of the island from there."

Inez shook her head. "It's getting late. I think we should turn back."

Catana grabbed her cousin's hand. "It will not take long, and maybe we can see an easier way back."

Atop the hill, the women were able to see both sides of the island.

"Look," Catana pointed out. "There is a trail not far from here that crosses the island. See? There is the *Dove*, and the trail will almost lead us directly to it."

Inez grabbed Catana's sleeve. "Over there," she said pointing to the other side of the island. "It looks like a beached schooner."

Catana peered at the ship, which was larger than the *Dove* and carried two masts.

"Come. Let us get a closer look."

Inez held back. "What if there are survivors?"

"Then we must help them. Come on."

They scurried down the hill, cut across an open area, and intercepted the trail. As they drew close to the shipwreck, they slowed down and approached with caution.

"I do not see anyone, do you?" Catana whispered.

Inez shook her head. The ship was lying on her starboard side with her gunwale almost touching the sand. One mast was broken, the sails were torn, and there was a gaping hole in the aft of her hull. The name *Sea Wolf* was painted across her stern.

Catana headed for the main cabin at the stern of the tilted deck. "The crew must have been taken prisoner."

"Or drowned," Inez added. "It is time to return to the *Dove*."

"I want to check the cabin. There could be something inside that will be of use to us."

"What would that be?"

"We cannot sail all the way to Havana by following La Florida's shoreline. This ship should have a map or chart Louis can use to navigate."

Inside the cabin, anything not nailed down was piled along the starboard wall. Catana made her way to the loose objects and sifted through them. She pulled a book out of the rubble. After scanning several pages, she looked up at Inez.

"This is a Waggoner, a volume of sea maps or charts. These maps have details on where islands, sandbars, and reefs are located. The book contains a wealth of information."

"Do you think there are any navigational tools in this mess?"

Catana looked further. "I don't see any. Wait, here's a box." She opened it. "It won't help us navigate, but will be useful. It contains medicine and herbs."

They continued to search but found nothing more they could use.

"It is growing dark," Inez reminded her cousin. "We better return to the *Dove*."

The two women climbed out of the cabin and jumped from the gunwale onto the sand. As they started toward the trail, Catana tripped over a rope and almost fell. Looking down she saw the ship's flag partially buried. Pulling it out of the sand, Catana and Inez stared at a skull and cross bones painted on a red background. Pictured next to the grinning skull was an hourglass.

"Pirates?" Inez asked.

Catana nodded. "Pirates."

She and Inez stepped over the piece of fabric onto the trail and walked briskly back to the *Dove*.

* * * *

It was dusk when they entered the camp. Louis, Tokala, and Jabulani sat around a fire roasting what looked like a large bird. Louis stood when he saw Catana and Inez approaching.

"We have been worried and were about look for you." He ushered them to the fire and gave a quizzical look toward the box Inez carried.

Catana flashed the Waggoner in front of him. "Inez and I are hungry. We will tell you where we have been while we eat."

Once everyone was settled around the fire and enjoying a hot meal, Catana explained how she and Inez found the beached ship, the medicine box, and the charts. Louis wiped his fingers on his pants leg and took the book. His eyes lit up as he turned the pages.

"All the islands and waters of the Caribbean Sea are here. There is Cuba, Jamaica, Santa Cruz, and The Tortugas, Martinique…" he continued to thumb through the charts. "…Tobago, Trinidad, Hispaniola, and La Florida."

"It also charts the small islands the Spanish list as useless. It looks like many of those islands are marked as destinations."

"Why would a ship want to sail to a useless island?" Tokala asked.

Louis slapped a mosquito on his arm. "The islands would not be considered useless to sea rovers. These islands have small rivers and rocky inlets. Pirates use them as hiding places for their ships. They stay in wait for a heavy merchant ship then attack."

"That would explain the pirate flag," Inez said.

Louis sat up straight and stared at Inez. "You found a pirate flag?"

Inez nodded.

"Tell us more about the ship that was wrecked on the beach." Louis continued.

"It is a schooner, and it is larger than the *Dove*," Catana answered.

Louis grinned. "A favorite ship of pirates because of its speed and shallow draft. A schooner, or sloop like ours, can dart in, attack, and sail to shallow water where the larger ships cannot go. The pirates will hide in a shallow cove until it is safe."

"You make it sound like you enjoy the idea." Jabulani mused.

"I am sure he does," Catana replied. "While we were growing up, Louis would tell me every pirate tale the seamen brought home from their voyages. There were stories of Black Beard, Black Bart, and the latest stories are of two women pirates out of New Providence. What are their names, Louis?"

"Anne Bonny and Mary Read," Louis informed everyone.

"If given a chance," Catana continued, "he would 'go on account' and become a pirate."

"It does sound like an adventurous life," said Louis. "But most pirates come to a bad end. The English are capturing and hanging anyone associated with piracy. The poor devils that manned that beach ship were probably captured by a British warship."

"That must have been the cannon fire we heard yesterday," Tokala said.

Louis nodded in agreement. "They are either on their way to prison and will be put on trial to hang, or they have already been hanged from the yardarm of the British ship."

Inez swallowed her last bite of meat and licked her fingers. "That was quite a feast, gentlemen. From now on, I will let you do the cooking."

Louis gave her a gracious bow. "I'm glad you enjoyed it, my lady. Tokala and Jabulani had a devil of a time catching that flamingo."

Inez's eyes opened wide. "Flamingo? We ate one of those beautiful birds?"

Catana put her hand to her mouth to hide a grin as all three men nodded in unison.

Louis stood and brushed sand from his breeches. "We will leave at daybreak. Other pirates may be nearby and looking for their companions. As romantic as all those pirate stories are, I do not want to have to face one in battle."

By the time the fire burned down to a pile of embers, the crew of the *Dove* was asleep on the beach.

CHAPTER TEN

Catana awoke abruptly when a cold, hard, piece of metal jabbed her in the neck. The outline of a man stood over her with the barrel of his flintlock rifle pressed below her left ear. Catana squinted up at the man holding the gun on her. The rising sun was in her eyes, and all she saw was a dark mass against the morning sky.

He motioned for her to stand. Catana slowly rose to her feet. She was afraid that if she moved too quickly, he would blow her head off. The man was almost as broad as he was tall. He had a full head of red hair that fell to his shoulders and a bushy beard of the same color that stood out in every direction. His blue eyes observed her coldly. He made a gesture to someone behind her. When she turned her head, she noticed Louis, Tokala, and Jabulani stood silently while another man trained a gun on them. The man holding the gun on her spoke. Catana recognized the language as an English dialect.

"He wants you to put your hands in the air and join us," Jabulani translated.

Raising her hands, Catana stepped next to Louis and glared at the second intruder. His blue-grey eyes locked on to hers and made her nervous. He was younger than his companion. His dark chestnut hair carried glints of gold from the sunlight and his sun-darkened skin suggested that he had spent months at sea. She dropped her gaze and turned to Louis. "Are they pirates?"

Shrugging, Louis spoke to Jabulani. "Ask them what they want."

The man with red hair answered, and Jabulani translated. "His name is Captain Jamie McDowell, and he is from the ship that washed ashore. He and his crewman want the return of their charts and maps.

"What good are the maps if the seamen no longer have a ship?" Catana asked.

"Let us see what we can learn from them," Jabulani suggested. "Maybe we can find a way to help them and keep the maps in return."

Jamie and the black man spoke, and Jabulani turned to the *Dove*'s crew to repeat the information. "They are unfortunate victims. Their merchant ship was taken over by pirates, and the pirate captain threatened to kill Jamie and his crew if they did not join them and 'go on account.'"

"So they were forced into piracy?" Catana asked.

Jabulani nodded and continued. "He and his crewman Orlando Cordova," Jabulani nodded toward the man with Jamie, "are the only survivors. Once Jamie's ship was under the pirate flag and had sailed into the gulf, a British ship attacked and crippled them. While the British soldiers boarded the ship to round up the pirates, Jamie and Orlando dove overboard and swam ashore to this island. Several hours later, their damaged ship drifted ashore."

"That does not answer the question of why they need their maps if they have no ship to sail." Catana said.

"Orlando is the ship's carpenter. They plan to repair her and return to their home port." Jabulani replied.

Catana shook her head. "Inez and I saw the hole in her hull. It is too badly damaged." Suddenly Catana realized that Inez was not with the group. She scanned the rim of the trees along the beach. Was her cousin hiding among them?

Jabulani placed his hand on Catana's shoulder. "Jamie agrees that it will be a lot of work before the ship is seaworthy, but they want to return home and to their former lives."

"Would you please tell them to put their rifles down?" Louis asked. "If they are the owners of the charts, we will return them." Jabulani spoke to the two men and they lowered their weapons.

"We could have put those charts to good use," Louis muttered. "Now it will be a guessing game for us to sail to Havana."

"Not if we ask them to join us," Tokala suggested. Where is their home port?"

"New Providence," Jabulani replied after speaking to Jamie.

"Is that a haven for pirates?" Catana asked.

"It was at one time," Louis replied. "The new British governor of the Caribbean Woodes Rogers has cleaned up the piracy."

With a bit of negotiating, Jabulani and the crew of the *Dove* convinced Jamie and Orlando to join them on their voyage to Havana, where the two men could find a ship to continue on to New Providence. Tokala started a cooking fire and everyone but Catana sat down to eat. She grabbed a piece of bread and fruit. "I must look for Inez." With all the excitement, no one seemed to notice that her cousin was missing. Where could she have gone? Her cousin often pushed Catana to the limits of her patience. But she loved Inez and managed to accept her in spite of her foolish actions.

"If you do not find her right away," Tokala said, "return and we will join you to look. I was the best tracker in my village and…" A sad look crossed the Indian's face, and he did not finish.

Catana thought of the trail and was soon following it toward the opposite side of the island. Along the way, she called out her cousin's name. There was no response. She hastened her stride. Inez must be along the trail somewhere. Catana knew how much Inez hated sloshing through the swampy areas. As she came around a curve in the trail, she and Inez collided. Catana lost her balance and pitched to the ground.

Bending over, Inez held out her hand to help Catana to her feet. "Are you injured?"

Catana pushed away her cousin's hand, jumped to her feet, and brushed the sand from her breeches. "*Gracias Señor Dios,* I found you. I have been so worried, especially since those men came into camp. Where were you?"

"What men?"

Catana pulled a twig out of her hair. "Answer my question first. Where have you been?"

"I was unable to sleep so at dawn I returned to the shipwreck to fetch the pirate flag for Louis." She held up the sand encrusted piece of fabric. "I think it will please him. He is such a fan of pirate lore."

Digging into her belt pouch, Inez pulled out a piece of paper and handed it to Catana. I found this on the ground underneath the flag. I don't understand what it says, but there are two papers. One, a map, and the other, a legal-looking document."

Catana studied the papers carefully. "I think this is written in English. The men who joined us this morning should be able to read it."

"Now it is your turn to explain. Who are these men you speak of?" By the time the two women arrived in camp, Inez knew the story of Jamie and Orlando.

Louis stood and approached them, and nodded toward Inez. "Thank heavens you are back safe. Jamie said that if we leave right away, and the weather remains good, we will make the southern tip of La Florida by nightfall."

"Inez has something that will interest you," Catana said.

"Later. We want to put the *Dove* to sea. Collect you gear so we can be on our way."

Once aboard the sloop, Catana and Inez went to the cabin they shared. Louis had rigged a hammock for Catana to sleep in while Inez used the bunk. Inez put the flag into her knapsack, and the two women stood in the light of the small window to study the papers. "I do not trust those two Englishmen," Catana said. "I think they are pirates, and this is a treasure map."

"You said they were forced into piracy and want to return to their normal lives."

"That may be true, but I still do not trust them. I think we should keep these papers a secret."

Inez flopped down onto her bunk and smoothed the folds of her skirt. "I think you are right. Greed for wealth can change many a man. Who is to say whether Louis, Tokala, or Jabulani would turn against one another if they gained great wealth? What do you think we should do with the papers?"

"We will put it in the box containing letters from my father." Inez nodded with approval.

As Catana shoved the box with the papers and letters under Inez's bunk, the *Dove* lurched forward.

"It feels like we are under way. I will check to see if the men need help."

"You go ahead," Inez replied. "I did not sleep well last night and would like to rest."

Catana stepped onto the deck. The main sail was unfurled and taunt in the breeze. Jabulani was at the helm while the remainder of the crew struggled to unfurl the jib sail.

"What is the problem?" Catana called out.

Louis answered. "The sail is hung up at the tip of the bowsprit. No matter how we tug the lines it won't come loose."

Catana climbed out onto the bowsprit frequently when the ship was at anchor. It was her favorite place to sit and enjoy the sunsets. She noticed the water was calm and the forward movement of the ship was smooth and strode up to Louis. "I will crawl along the bowsprit and untangle the rigging."

Louis opened his mouth to protest, but Catana placed her fingertips to his lips. "You know I have climbed out there often. The calm seas will not throw me off balance, and there are plenty of ropes along the way to grip."

Louis nodded, and Jabulani explained Catana's intentions to the English crewmen. Orlando gave her a boost.

Crawling forward, she looked down past the loose canvas flapping below her. The water rushed past and churned into white foam where the bow of the *Dove* cut through the waves. The motion was making her dizzy. She pulled her gaze away from the water and trained her eyes on the tip of the bowsprit where the canvas was tangled in the lines. It was a simple problem, and when she tugged at the proper rope, the canvas pulled loose. The jib sail unfurled with a snap and the ship shuddered as the bow lifted to the wind. With the sudden movement of the ship, Catana lost her balance and fell toward the foaming water. She grabbed a piece of line secured to the bowsprit, but it slid through her hands burning them. Holding on, she dangled from the bowsprit unable to reach high enough to grab it and pull herself up. She looked down at the water. If she let go and she fell, the ship would run over her. Catana's arms began to ache, and she closed the eyes to pray. She felt faint. This was the end. She was about to let go when an iron grip encircled her wrist. Everything went black.

* * * *

When Catana awoke, it was in her cousin's bunk. Her hands were wrapped in cloth, and Inez sat mending a shirt in a chair next to her.

"What happened?" Catana moaned.

Inez moved her chair closer to the bunk. "Orlando crawled out onto the bowsprit and hauled you back. He is a strong man. You were dead weight, but he was able to pull you onto deck. Once you were within reach, Louis helped him, of course."

"Of course," Catana repeated. "I feel like a fool. I have never fainted. Then I was rescued by a pirate."

"Now, Catana, we do not know if he is a real pirate," Inez interrupted. "He might be a victim of circumstance like Jamie said." Catana looked down at her bandaged hands. "The rope took some skin off your palms," Inez informed her.

Catana sighed deeply. "That will render me useless for several days."

Inez returned to her mending. "I would not worry. We have enough crew to sail us to Havana."

The *Dove* arrived at the southern tip of La Florida at sunset, and the crew dropped anchor to spend the night. In the morning, the clear water mirrored the cloudless November sky. Along the mainland, a series of mangrove-covered islands encircled the shore like a necklace. The water was low, and even with the *Dove*'s shallow draft, they had to navigate with extreme care. The crew kept the ship far from shore to avoid running aground on sandbars. In deeper water, bottlenose dolphins frolicked around the ship. Catana stood at the rail to enjoy their antics. When it grew close to sunset, they anchored.

Tokala came up behind her and pointed out a small group of sea turtles. "Those are loggerheads and can weight up to three hundred fifty pounds. They make a delicious meal." Turning toward Jabulani, the

Indian called out, "Turtle soup," and pointed to the creatures swimming past the *Dove.*

Before Catana realized what they were doing, the two men stripped off their shirts and dove into the water with knives in their hands. An hour later the crew of the *Dove* sat around the main mast ready to feast on turtle soup. The cooking fire burned in a low-sided box of sand fastened to the deck near where they sat. They watched the embers carefully because a fire aboard ship was a death sentence. While the turtle stewed in a large iron pot, Jamie passed around beer to drink with the meal. Tokala and Jabulani toasted to their freedom. The second toast came from Jamie for a successful voyage to Havana, and then Louis raised his glass to the thrill of adventure. By the end of the meal, the crew was in high spirits, and they failed to notice the storm coming in until the *Dove* began to rock violently.

Jamie dashed to his feet to put out the fire. "Batten the hatches," he shouted in English. Catana saw the men jump into action. Tokala and Louis seemed to know what to do although they may not have understood the orders. Everyone on the ship became busy and noisy as they shouted over the wind. Looking down at her hands, Catana felt helpless. She watched the crew draw ropes through screeching pulleys. Although the canvas was secured, the main mast creaked with the swaying of the ship.

"Pull up the anchor so we can ride with the wind," Louis called out to Tokala. The Indian, black man, and the two British men pushed on the horizontal bars of the capstan to wind the rope and raise the anchor. "Go to your cabin," Louis called to Catana.

She slipped and slid on the wet deck until she reached her cabin. Jerking the door open, she lunged into the room as the bow of the ship rose. Once inside, she plopped down next to Inez on the bunk. Her cousin looked as white as a sandy beach, and she tightly held the frame of the bunk with one hand while saying her rosary with the other. A blinding flash of light poured through the small window followed by a clap of thunder, which shook the timbers of the ship. A heavy downpour pounded the roof of the cabin while Inez recited *Aves.* They were on the last decade of the rosary when the waters grew calm and the ship bobbed in silence. Catana stepped out onto deck and strode to the rail. The moon broke through the clouds, and a gentle breeze took the place of the wild wind.

After conferring with Jamie, Louis called a meeting, and crew gathered at the foot of the mainmast. The men agreed that Jamie should be appointed captain until their arrival in Havana. Catana and Inez were skeptical, but Louis convinced them that Jamie was the most experienced seaman of the lot.

Once voted in, Jamie ordered everyone to check the sloop over for damage then to meet in the captain's cabin. Catana's duty was to look for broken lines. After her tour of the deck, she found two ropes that needed splicing and went to notify the captain.

She not seen inside the other cabin before and was surprised to see how much larger it was. There was a table, four chairs, two bunks, and two of the bulkheads were banked with cabinets. The back bulkhead had a porthole twice as large as the one in her cabin.

Jamie motioned for Catana and Inez to take a seat on one of the bunks. Jabulani, Jamie, Orlando, and Louis took seats at the table while Tokala stood duty at the helm. A lamp hanging from a cross beam swung with the motion of the ship and spilled its light onto the charts spread over the table. Each time Jamie spoke, Jabulani translated. "There are treacherous reefs and shoals in the Caribbean. As sailors, we will use our common sense, knowledge of the charts, and we will need a lot of luck. We do not have an accurate way to calculate longitude. This means where our ship is sailing in reference to east and west. The storm has thrown us off course. We will have to intercept a trade route."

Inez gripped Catana's arm tightly. "Are we lost?"

"Jamie is a captain," Catana replied. "He knows how to navigate. If we are lost, it won't be for long."

Jamie spoke again, and Jabulani explained. "We have no navigational instruments aboard this ship, but we have the use of these charts and the stars. With luck, we should be on track soon."

CHAPTER ELEVEN

Catana learned that Jamie was not as apt at reading stars as he thought, when the next day the *Dove* was drifting on the open seas, and he had no idea how far west the storm had driven them. Searching through the shelves in the captain's cabin, Orlando found a navigational instrument called a back staff. It seemed strange to Catana that Orlando seemed to know more about sailing than Jamie. He was able to measure the position of the midday sun, do some calculating and was able to tell them, within seven miles where they were in a north and south direction, but he had no idea how far off course there were to the west.

That evening Catana took a tray with three tankards of beer into the captain's cabin where Jamie, Orlando, and Jabulani sat at the table pouring over the book of charts. Setting the tray on the table, she leaned forward to take a look. She understood some of the symbols, but none of the words because it was written in English.

"These are not always accurate," Jabulani explained to her. "Orlando thinks that if we turn south we should run into land." His finger pointed to Mexico. "Our water supply is getting low, and he does no know how long before we intercept land."

Catana gave the three men a weak smile as she set tankards in front of each man. She departed the damp, hot cabin, feeling the need of fresh air and wondering if anyone on the ship knew what they were doing.

Standing at the bow, she watched the silver moonlight reflect off the whitecaps where the ship's bow cut through the water. An eerie green glow radiated from the foam. She had seen phosphorus often while swimming in the bay at night; it never ceased to fascinate her.

She heard footsteps behind her and turned to see Orlando approach. He joined her at the rail and peered out across the sea. They stood in silence. Catana wanted to thank him for saving her life but was unsure of her English. "Thank you," she finally managed to say in a soft voice.

"*De nada*," he replied and continued to speak to her in Spanish. "I learned your language from my father. He was Spanish."

"I thought you and Jamie were English."

Orlando shook his head and smiled. "Jamie is from Scotland and was at one time the captain of a merchant ship."

"And you?"

"I am from Ireland."

"How is that possible if your father is Spanish?"

A frown crossed Orlando's face. "He is dead now, killed in a battle at sea."

Catana opened her mouth to say how sorry she was but could not find the right words.

"My mother had wealthy relatives in London. I guess this inspired my father's desire to provide a better life for his family. He went to sea for the Spanish king under a letter of Marquee to protect Spanish treasure fleets in the Caribbean. With the payment he received, he planned to buy land and become the owner of an estate. For several years, my mother and I awaited his return. Then word came that he had been killed in battle at sea while defending a small fleet of Spanish ships off the coast of Mexico."

"Why would your father make such dangerous choice to acquire wealth?

Orlando shrugged. "I guess he had the call of the sea in his blood. When the British replaced the French as principal plunderers of the Spanish treasure ships in the Caribbean, he offered his services to the Spanish king. Spain believes it owns everything in these waters including the islands. I was a young lad at the time my father successfully captured or fought off many British ships."

Catana placed her hand over his. He was gripping the rail so tightly his knuckles were white.

"My mother was so distraught over the news of my father's death that she died of a broken heart several months later. That is when I signed on with a merchant ship and became a crewman under Captain Jamie McDowell. I had not used my Spanish language for many years until I became a crewman on a merchant ship.

Catana and Orlando stared at the water, each deep in thought. Finally, Catana broke the silence. "You never did tell me how you, a man from Ireland, had a Spanish father."

"He was a crewman on a ship that was a part of the Spanish Armada. The Spanish fleet departed England and proceeded on their journey back to Spain by sailing around the northern tip of the British Isles. When the fleet turned south along the Irish Coast, it was to remain far west of the Irish coast because of the treacherous currents and rocky shores. Somehow a third of the fleet was caught in a strong current, and the ships were dashed against the shore. Few Spanish sailors survived. My father was found washed ashore, almost dead. My mother told me how she and her parents found him and took him in. They lived in a small, remote, coastal village so no one, other then her family and the villagers, knew of his past. My mother and father fell in love and married a year later." Orlando cleared his throat. "It is time for me to take the helm. *Buenos noches, señorita.*"

Catana stood at the rail a while longer. Orlando was a quiet man. Jamie McDowell, on the other hand, was jolly and never ceased talking; yet, the two men seemed to have a special bond. The conversation with Orlando revealed a lot about the man. Her feelings of mistrust toward Orlando and Jamie began to ebb.

When she entered her cabin, Inez was asleep in her bunk. Catana swung into her hammock and let the motion of the ship rock her to sleep.

* * * *

"Sail ho," a voice shouted. Jumping out of her hammock, Catana opened the door and stepped out into the bright morning sun. Looking up, she saw Tokala perched on the yardarm of the main mast. He pointed toward the horizon. "There to the port bow."

Coming toward them from the southeast was a three-masted ship. "Looks to be a warship," Tokala called out.

"Does she have signal flags on her halyard?" Louis called up to the Indian.

Tokala shaded his eyes from the glare of the sun. "I think so, but all I can see are bright specks against the sky."

Louis dashed into the captain's cabin and returned with a spyglass. Climbing the ratlines, he joined Tokala. After he scanned the ship with the spyglass, Louis shouted down to the crew gathered at the foot of the mast. "It is a British brigantine."

Tokala and Louis skirted down the lines to the deck. "That ship is able to do combat on the open seas," Louis informed Catana. She squinted toward the approaching ship and studied it carefully. Its three masts carried numerous square sails, and the ship looked to be three times the size of the *Dove.*

"What are we to do?" Catana asked, looking from one man to another and then toward Jabulani, who stood duty at the helm. No one had an answer. She knew Inez was still in the cabin, oblivious to what was happening, and she saw no sign of Jamie's friend. "Where is Orlando?" she asked Louis.

"He was in the hold checking…there he is." Catana turned to see Orlando appear through a hatch. As he approached the crew, he dusted himself off and stopped next to Catana. "We have only a few supplies remaining," he said in Spanish. "Not even enough to attract rats"

"Rats?" Catana repeated.

"Every ship I have been on has had rats in the hold because of the food supplies. This ship has none that I have seen and…" His voice trailed away when he saw the anxious expression on everyone's faces.

Jamie pointed to the British ship in the distance and spoke to Orlando in English. The two men conversed in their native tongue for several minutes, and then Orlando translated Jamie's plan.

"So the British do not fire on us, we will pretend to be a crippled ship. When they come close, we will tell them that our ship's rudder was damaged in a storm and ask them if they can spare enough food and water until we can anchor at a port."

Louis nodded with approval. "We can also tell them we were blown off course, are lost, and ask them if they can direct us to the nearest port."

Catana crossed her fingers and prayed the ruse would work. She helped the crew adjust the rigging so the *Dove* gave the appearance of a crippled vessel. *Dove* rocked with the sweep of her sails in a motion that looked like her crew was unable to steer her. The sloop bobbed through the water at an angle to the wind, her stern faced toward the warship.

The British brigantine drew near. Suddenly a bright plume of smoke spurted from the warship's upper deck followed by the boom of cannons. The heavy ball plunged into the sea, making a tall white fountain in front of the *Dove*'s bow. The gun ports on the lower deck of the British ship swung open.

"Run," Jamie cried and grabbed the helm. Tokala and Louis let out the canvas. The sloop's full sail caught the wind, and she flew across the water.

Catana crouched below the gunwale and grabbed Louis when he came toward her. "Do you think we can outrun the British?" she asked in a breathless voice.

"We have a fast sloop. As long as we can stay out of cannon range, yes, I believe we can. I am needed on the ropes to keep the *Dove* close to the wind as possible and maintain our speed."

"What can I do to help?"

Louis shook his head. "Until your hands are healed, the best help would be to stay out of the way. Why not check on Inez?"

Catana stood up straight and put her bandaged hands on her hips. "You want me out of the way? I will have you know—"

"Not now, Catana. I have work to do." He turned to climb the shroud lines.

Catana stormed into her cabin and slammed the door. "If it were not for me, Louis would have never had this ship to sail."

Inez sat on her bunk in a dark corner, her eyes wide with fright. "Catana, what is happening? I was sleeping when I heard cannon fire and suddenly the ship lurched forward. I almost toppled out of bed."

Catana pulled a chair next to her cousin's bunk and sat down. "We were fired upon by a British ship. I don't understand why they did not give us the chance to explain that all we wanted was help. We flew no enemy colors."

Inez put a hand over her mouth. "Oh no."

"Oh no what?" Catana said with suspicion.

"It must have been the flag."

"The pirate flag? But how?"

Inez shifted uncomfortably on the bunk. I had nothing to do last evening. Everyone's clothes were mended, so to keep busy I washed the pirate flag."

"Why would that cause an attack on the *Dove?*"

"Because I hung it out the window to dry on a piece of line and—"

"And the British saw it this morning and thought we were pirates," Catana finished. "Is it still out there?"

Inez nodded.

Catana jumped to her feet, went to the window, and pulled in the flag.

"I intended to hang it out for a short time, only enough to dry," Inez lamented with tears in her eyes. "I forgot about it."

"It was long enough to get us into trouble. If Louis or the crew learns of—"

Inez gripped Catana's hand. "Please do not tell anyone. I feel such a fool."

With a sigh, Catana folded the flag and put it in the sea chest at the foot of the bunk. "The British will not take our threat lightly."

"What do you mean?"

"A flag with skull and cross bones sends the message 'death to you.' The hour glass on the flag means 'your time is running out,' and the color red shows that the pirates flying the flag give no mercy to their captives."

"How do you know so much about pirate flags?" Inez asked.

Catana slumped back down into her chair. "From Louis and his stories."

* * * *

By the time the sun dipped toward the western horizon and quenched its flames in the sea, the *Dove* had outrun and lost sight of the British warship. As darkness descended, Tokala shouted from his perch on the mast, "Land ho."

Catana came out on deck for fresh air and brought Inez with her. Scanning the horizon, she spotted the outline of land as it melted into the darkness. The moon was rising; its silver light reflecting off the water. Captain McDowell maneuvered the sloop between two dark masses of land and into a bay.

Jabulani approached the rail and stood next to the two women. "The captain said we will anchor here for the night. In the morning, we will sail around the island for a better look. He thinks he recognizes this bay. If so, he will know where we are."

Since they had taken flight from the British warship, the crew had no time to eat. Once they had anchored, they gathered around the mast and sat on the deck, to eat hardtack, cheese, and the last of their beer. Orlando made a place for himself next to Catana. "You ladies have nothing to worry about. Jamie thinks we are near Havana."

"What of the British ship?" Catana asked and bit off a piece of hardtack.

"Jamie does not think a warship like that will bother to pursue a small sloop like ours for long. Since we showed no colors, they probably think we are just fishermen." He rubbed his chin while in deep thought. "Although, I do not understand why they fired on us."

"What if they were on a secret mission?" Tokala asked, joining the conversation, "and they did not want anyone around. They could have shot a warning to scare us off."

"Maybe," Orlando said rubbing the back of his neck. "But if that was the reason, why did they come after us?"

Catana almost choked on her food and took a swallow of beer to wash it down. Standing, she gazed at Inez and then looked down at the crew. She had always felt protective of her sensitive cousin so spoke up. "Men, I have a confession. It was my fault the British came after us. You see, I hung Louis's pirate flag out my cabin window after washing it. The British must have seen it."

Silence hung heavy as the eyes of the crew were glued on her.

"I do not own a pirate flag."

"Yes, you do," Inez said and explained to everyone how she had brought it back from the shipwreck to give to Louis.

Louis smiled at Inez. "Thank you." A frown crossed his face when he turned to Catana. "How could you be so stupid?"

Catana clenched her teeth and managed to reply in a meek voice. "I am sorry. How could have I known we would encounter a ship?"

"Wait!" Inez said. "It was I who hung the flag out. I washed the flag so that when I gave it to Louis, it would be like new."

"You did that for me?" Louis asked.

Catana glared at Louis. When he thought she was the one who had flown a pirate flag he called her stupid. Now that Inez confessed, he seemed pleased. In the past he usually had less patience with her cousin's antics than Catana. Why was he so forgiving toward her now? A sudden thought flashed into her mind. Was Louis falling in love with her?

Catana's jaws clenched tighter when she saw Orlando put his arm around Inez. "Do not feel bad," he said in a comforting voice. "It was a simple mistake."

Catana looked at her cousin with a new attitude. She had not realized that the girl she had grown up with had turned into a lovely young woman. Running her fingers through the tangles in her hair, she looked down at her dirty shirt and realized that the men saw her as one of the crew, not a young lady.

She straightened her back and stuck her nose in the air. "Excuse me, gentlemen, I believe I shall retire for the evening." Without a look back, she marched to her cabin and slammed the door behind her. She heard the sound of laughter and wondered if it was at her expense.

When the sun rose the next morning, the *Dove* remained anchored in the cove. With her sails reefed, she faced the open sea. Catana was the first one awake. Strolling onto deck, she looked into the beer barrel and saw that it was empty. All the crew, except Inez, was probably sleeping off the effects of too much drink.

"I hope they all have horrendous headaches," she muttered to herself. She wondered why she was in such a hateful mood as she strode to the stern of the ship. Her eyes rested on the island. Palm trees swayed while the light green waters of the shallows shimmered in rhythm with the trees. The fragrance of tropical fruits and flowers drifted on the sea breeze. She recognized the smell of jasmine. It was so peaceful. Maybe she would take a swim before everyone was awake.

Dressed in a chemise, she inched her way out onto the bowsprit and dove into the water. Even at this time of year it was warm. Bobbing and diving like a dolphin, she was enjoying her swim when she noticed movement out of the corner of her eye. She stopped, and treading water, turned to take a better look. The British warship was entering the cove and sailing straight toward the *Dove.*

CHAPTER TWELVE

Catana swam toward the rope ladder that hung from the starboard side of the *Dove*, climbed onto deck, and ran to warn the crew. By the time everyone was awake and on deck, the British brigantine was two-thirds into the cove and preparing to turn her broadside to the *Dove* to fire her cannons.

Captain McDowell issued orders, and Orlando repeated them in Spanish. "We are going to make a run for it. Everyone to his stations."

Jabulani took the helm while the rest of the crew climbed the shroud lines to work the lines and canvas. The *Dove*'s sails dropped and bulged in the wind.

"Head for the enemy ship," the captain shouted. Catana had learned enough English to understand the order and stood wide-eyed as the sloop steered straight for the British ship.

The brigantine heeled to the starboard to avoid the collision. "They have dropped the wind from their sails," Orlando shouted. The *Dove* leaped forward and passed the British ship, which was forced to come about and resume pursuit after losing momentum. The sloop headed for the open sea, and the enemy ship followed.

"Catana," Louis shouted, "stand at the bow and keep an eye out for rocks and shallow water. Warn Jabulani if you see anything so he can steer clear."

Leaning over the rail, she peered ahead into the clear water and caught sight of a steak of light green. It was a reef, and the *Dove* was heading straight for it. She opened her mouth to shout a warning, but before the words came out, there was an ominous scraping of the keel against sand. The ship creaked, and her timbers shivered as its bottom grated against the sandbar. Suddenly the sloop lurched forward and was free. Her shallow draft slipped into deep water.

Catana turned toward the stern and crossed her fingers when she saw the British ship closing in on them. A man on the brigantine screamed a warning to the captain. Seconds later, Catana heard a scraping sound followed by a loud crack. The enemy ship had hit the reef. The crew of the *Dove* heard shouts and curses from the crippled ship as the brigantine's portside gunwales tipped slowly toward the water and men jumped from the ship. The captain shook his fist at Jamie and his crew as he called out across the water, "You have not seen the last of me."

When the sloop was a safe distance, Jamie ordered the crew to slow to half sail so they could watch the demise of their enemy. In minutes, the warship's tilted bow settled onto the long sloping reef with her stern sticking out of the water at an odd angle.

"Do you think he knows who we are and take revenge?" Catana asked Louis.

"We were close enough that I was able to get a good look at the captain. I am sure he was able to do the same. With an Indian and a black man aboard, it would distinguish us from most crews."

"I suggest we get out of here," Orlando shouted. "There may be other British ships in the area." The crew set their sails and the sloop sped forward. After several hours, Orlando gave the order to drop all their sails, and the *Dove* slowed as if her hull had slid into a sea of syrup. Halting, the ship bobbed on the waves, running broadside to the current.

Orlando conferred with the captain then relayed a message to the crew. "We will steer a course in the general direction of Havana, but still we have no navigational instruments to guide us. Captain McDowell can work us back to the trades so we don't miscalculate. He recognized the island we departed and said that we are three days from Havana. There is another island on the chart between here and our destination. We will stop there for food and water. Does everyone agree with the captain's plans?"

Everyone nodded in agreement. Catana realized they could survive without food until they reached their port, but not without water.

* * * *

When they came upon the island, Orlando announced, "You will like it here. There are streams to bathe in, a place to get a bit of exercise and rest, and plenty of fruit, fish, and fowl. We will anchor in a hidden cove. The captain will assign someone to keep a look out from a hill in the center of the island for any ships that may come our way."

With Jamie's instructions, Jabulani guided the *Dove* into a peaceful lagoon. Catana peered down into the water. It was so clear she could see the sandy bottom. There was a steep cliff on their port side as the ship steered toward the sandy shore. From its summit, a small waterfall dropped into a basin surrounded by tall trees.

Once the sloop was anchored, Tokala and Jabulani lowered a rowboat into the water and secured it with a rope to the port side of the ship. Louis and Jamie attached a water barrel to the end of a line and lowered it to them.

Catana looked at her hands, which had healed with only a few scars from the rope burns. She called to Orlando as he descended the rope ladder to the rowboat. "What can Inez and I do to help?"

Inez joined her cousin at the rail and added, "Will I have time while ashore to bathe and wash some clothing?"

"Do you have a mirror?" Orlando asked.

Catana shook her head.

"I have one in my knapsack," Inez replied.

"Bring it with you along with anything you want to wash."

Catana whispered to Inez to put on trousers. "You do not want the men looking up your skirt when you descend the ladder, and you can wash the dress you have on."

By the time Inez returned with her bundle of laundry, the men had the barrel secured in the boat, and they were waiting for the women to board. Jamie stood on the deck of the sloop and spoke in English. "I will remain aboard the *Dove*." Catana, having learned a little of his language, nodded.

As soon as the women were settled in the boat, two sets of oars dipped into the water. Orlando sat at the bow with Jabulani at the stern. Each dip of the oars took them closer to the beach.

"Did you bring the mirror, Inez?" Orlando asked.

Inez fished around in her knapsack and pulled out a round bronze piece of metal with a handle attached.

"Give it to Catana," he ordered.

Catana was puzzled as she took the object.

Orlando gestured to the crest of a hill. "I want you to climb to the top and keep a lookout for ships. If you see one, signal us by using the mirror."

The sand made a scraping noise on the hull of the boat as it slid ashore. Once beached and secured, Orlando gathered the crew and issued instructions. "Tokala and I will fill the barrel. Louis and Jabulani, you gather fruit and nuts, and if you find water birds or rabbits along the way, it would make a nice evening meal. Inez, the waterfall is nearby. You can bathe and wash your clothing there. Catana, you will be our lookout. You will have a panoramic view from atop the hill. Return here when you see we are ready to depart."

Catana opened her mouth to disagree, but Louis gave her a warning look, and she snapped it shut. She stalked away. She did not like the way Orlando was taking over. He acted as if he was in charge of the *Dove*'s crew. Yes, everyone agreed to let Jamie act as captain, and Orlando was his friend, but that did not give the Irish Spaniard the right to order the crew around.

Stomping up the hill, she reached the summit and turned in a full circle at the paradise surrounding her. Pride filled her as she looked out across the Spanish Waters. Her people were the first of the Old World to sail here. What stories must have unfolded on these waters in the past. Looking down onto the lagoon, she noticed the *Dove* looked like a toy ship from this distance, and the men on shore were the size of bugs. She found a shady spot beneath an oak tree and nibbled on a mango she had picked on the way to the crest of the hill. The late morning sun was warm, and she grew sleepy.

As her eyelids slid closed, the sound of a twig snapping behind her brought them wide open. She turned slowly toward where the noise had come from and saw a man with a bushy black beard and piercing black eyes staring at her. His tattered white shirt hung on him and holes covered his breeches. He leaned on his walking stick not saying a word.

Catana broke the uneasy silence. "*Buenas dias, señor.*"

He continued to stare at her and said nothing.

"Do you speak Spanish?" she asked in English.

He shook his head and came a few steps closer.

"I can understand English better than speak." She informed the man. She pointed to the *Dove*. "My ship. I am Catana. Who are you?"

He gave her a bow. "Pleased to meet you. I be Bartholomew Higgins. You can call me Bart. Who be y'er cap'n, and where'd you come from?"

"The *Dove* belongs to me and Louis, but we are allowing Jamie McDowell to captain our ship until we arrive in Havana."

Bart stepped back and scowled at her. "Now why would ye be putting a pirate like him as Cap'n?"

"Do you know him?"

"Aye that I do, lass. That man is nothing but a scallywag. He and Captain Cordova is the reason I am on this island."

"They marooned you here?"

"No. Jamie marooned me on a sandbar out to sea. One that would disappear at high tide. I was able to grab onto a large piece of driftwood, before I was to go under to Davy Jones's Locker and floated to this island."

"Why would Jamie do such a thing?"

The man smiled. "'Cause dead men tell no tales."

"So you know something that Captain McDowell does not want repeated?"

"You might say that, lass. If I be ye, I would watch my back around him. He will steal yer ship from under you once you hit port."

Catana shook her head. "If he wanted the *Dove*, he would have tried to take it by now."

Bart shrugged. "He probably needs ye as crew. He has no more love for Havana then the port has for him. He won't be hanging around there long, he won't."

Catana sank to the ground, her mind in turmoil. Was this crazy man telling the truth? "What about his friend Orlando? Is he also a pirate?"

Bart spit in the dirt and sat next to her. "I know no Orlando. He must have come aboard after I was marooned. What does he look like?"

He is taller then Jamie, attractive, with chestnut hair and eyes that sometimes look grey and other times blue."

"That be Captain Cordova yer describing. I never knew his Christian name."

That did not agree with Orlando's story. He said that he was a carpenter and that Jamie the captain. "Are you sure they are pirates? He told me that he and Orlando were forced into piracy when they were taken prisoner. The two men said that all they want is to return to their home port in New Providence and live in peace."

"Don't let em fool ye, lass. Jamie is nothing but a pirate, and Cordova the cap'n of the *Seahawk*."

Catana rubbed the tense muscles at the back of her neck with her fingertips. "That was not the name of the ship Inez and I found beached on an island north of here, but that is where we met Jamie and Orlando."

"It probably be another ship they stole. It was beached? Were there any other crewmen?"

"They were the only two."

Bart shook his head. "I wonder what happened to the crew of the *Seahawk*."

She heard a sharp whistle pierce the air. Looking down onto the beach, she saw everyone gathered and ready to leave the island. Turning toward him, she noticed he was chuckling to himself. "I cannot leave you here," she said.

"It's best you did, lass, 'cause I dare not show my face to Jamie or Cap'n Cordova. Especially the cap'n would kill me right off, and you, too, if he knew I had been talking to you." He laughed. "Dead women tell no tales."

"I could send someone from Havana for you."

Bart grew nervous and stood. "No, you must not do that. Tell no one you have seen me. I rather remain here with my monkeys than face anyone from Havana."

Catana heard the whistle again. She gave Bart an uncertain nod and ran down the hill, skidding on loose rocks and sand along the way. Running up to Louis, she whispered in his ear, "Meet me in my cabin after we get underway. It is important."

He gave her a quizzical look, shrugged, and turned to help Inez into the boat. Catana and Tokala pushed the small craft off the sand and into the surf where a wave freed it to the sea. The two pulled themselves aboard, and Catana joined Inez, who was sitting on the water barrel. Facing the bow, she watched Orlando work the oars and wondered who he really was.

"Do not shift your weight," Orlando ordered. "We could easily swamp the boat." Catana tensed when she noticed the waterline within inches of the boat's top rim. With worries of swamping the boat and of Bart's story, she felt as jumpy as a cat cornered by a dog by the time she climbed aboard the *Dove*. The hard work of loading the supplies from the boat to the hold of the sloop kept her busy, but she would stop periodically and look at her British shipmates in a different light.

It was night by the time they finished, and when Catana entered her cabin, it was too dark to see. She fumbled around until she found a lamp. Using her tinderbox, she managed to light the wick and jumped when a shadow moved toward her. Peering into the dimness, she recognized Esmeralda. She had not seen the cat in almost a week. Pulling out a morsel of dry bread from her trouser pocket, she set it on the table next to the lamp. The cat crept out of the shadows and stretched her neck toward the food. Esmeralda's green eyes were like glowing emeralds in the lamplight.

Catana sat in silence. When the cat finished the food, it looked up at her and slinked its way toward her. Stopping, the animal dropped down, rubbed her head against Catana's hand, and began to purr. She looked at the ugly ball of fur, and Catana realized she enjoyed the company of the beast. There was a knock on the door, and the cat scampered from the table and disappeared into the dark.

The knock came again along with a voice. "It is Louis. Are you in there, Catana?"

"Come," she called out.

When the door opened, she spoke. "Would you find Tokala and Jabulani and bring them here? Where is Inez?"

"Inez is fine. She was with me and stopped to talk to Orlando."

"Bring her, too."

"Jabulani is at the helm. Should I have Orlando take his place?"

Catana thought for a moment. "No, you can pass the message to him. I do not want Jamie or Orlando to know that I have called a meeting."

Louis returned within minutes with Inez and Tokala trailing behind. Once they were seated, she told them about meeting Bart on the island and the conversation they had. When she finished Louis shook his head. "I think the man was crazy with an overactive imagination."

Tokala agreed. "I have seen nothing to indicate that Jamie and Orlando plan to steal our ship."

"Nor have I," Inez added. "Now that I am learning to understand his language, I have gotten to know Jamie better, and I think he is quite a gentleman."

Catana did not know what to think. Bart did seem a bit crazy. Sitting back in her chair, she brushed an errant lock of hair out of her eyes. "You may be right. But we should not throw caution to the wind. When we arrive in Havana, I suggest we keep an eye on our British friends and a guard on the *Dove*."

CHAPTER THIRTEEN

"Land ho on the starboard bow," Tokala called from his perch atop the mainmast. He scurried down the ratlines to join the crew and handed the spyglass to Catana. "It is Havana. This is where we will make our home until Santa Maria is again under Spanish rule."

Catana trained the glass on a smug of clouds floating on the horizon. Cuba was dark green encircled by white sand. As they sailed through the turquoise water, Jamie pointed out the sandbars and coral reefs and guided Jabulani around them. "Keep west of the northern push of the Gulf Stream, yet stay far enough east to avoid the shallows," he informed the helmsman.

With Jabulani at the helm, Orlando, Louis, and Tokala on the sails, and Jamie barking commands, the ship cleaved her way through the water toward Havana. The tropical island's detail became more prevalent as the *Dove* drew closer to shore. Smoke from the burning chaff of sugar cane plumed into the air to join a halo of clouds nestled on the island's mountain peaks. Catana joined the men to reef the sails as they slid into the harbor.

The rosy hue of the setting sun turned the pale sand into a delicate pink and trimmed the crest of the waves with a warm glow. The sound of a joyful tune played on a guitar floated across the water, while taverns along the waterfront lit their lamps. As the *Dove* drew close to the docks, a mist crept across the bay following them. By the time they secured the sloop's line to a pylon, a blanket of fog covered the waterfront. Catana noticed the outlines of two men, floating ghostlike in the damp air on the cobblestone dock arguing.

Before Louis could take one step toward the gangplank, Catana grabbed his sleeve and whispered, "We must keep a guard aboard the *Dove*."

"Whatever for? Havana is known to be a safe harbor."

"What if Jamie and Orlando plan to steal her?"

"I think you are over reacting to a crazy man's fantasy."

Catana drew closer to Louis when she noticed Orlando nearby. "I do not want to take the chance of losing our way back to Santa Maria."

"If you are so sure, stay aboard and guard it yourself. I plan to enjoy the evening in a tavern with my friends. That includes Jamie and Orlando. Since they will be with us, you will be wasting your time, but suit yourself."

Catana's temper was rising, and she wanted to say something hurtful to Louis, but before she could think of anything, he ran off to join the other men and left her behind. *"El Diablo,"* she muttered. "Men can be so self-centered." She raced to her cabin to get her dirk. She would sit where she could see anyone attempting to come aboard. At any indication of foul play, she would slit a throat.

When Catana entered the cabin, she was surprised to find Inez dressed in a beautiful blue gown with a tight bodice. White lace fringed the low neckline that barely concealed her bosom. Her cousin sat at a table, looking into her hand mirror while combing her luxurious long hair. "I am going to look for Juan," she said simply.

"Tonight?"

"Sí. The fort is not far, and the commander there can summon him for me."

"Why not wait until morning?"

Inez stood and stamped her foot. "Why should I wait? Louis and the others have gone to a tavern. Soon each man will be with a woman, maybe bedding her. Meanwhile, I sit here and do nothing? No, I want to see Juan tonight."

Catana did not want her cousin to go out into a strange town alone, especially dressed like that. "I will go with you, but let me change into a skirt and blouse first."

Maybe Louis was right and there was no danger to the *Dove*. While Jamie and Orlando were with him, they could not steal the sloop.

Slipping on a white blouse with full sleeves and a red skirt, she wrapped a turquoise scarf her father had given her around her waist and tucked her dirk into the band. "I have no fancy dress like yours, but it will have to do. I am not meeting my true love." As they left the cabin, Catana had to admit her cousin looked beautiful. "Inez, before we leave for the fort, I want to stop by the tavern and let the men know where we are going."

When they arrived in front of the tavern, Catana shoved a reluctant Inez through the door. "With Tokala and Jabulani at our side," Catana confided, "no one would dare cause trouble for us. I want to speak to Louis privately." Taking up the lead, Catana pushed her way through the noisy crowd of men until she saw Louis and the crew at a corner table toward the back. "They would be on the opposite side of the room," she muttered. When several drunken sailors stood in their path, she grabbed her cousin's hand, pulled her around them, and plowed her way to the corner while several catcalls pierced the air.

Orlando slammed his tankard onto the table and shouted. "Quiet! These ladies are with us."

Catana looked around in surprise as the room grew silent, and the men opened a path in front of her and Inez. With every one staring at them, Catana felt self-conscious, and it seemed to take forever before they reached the table. As soon as the women were seated, the room became noisy again, as though nothing had happened.

"Why are you here?" Orlando asked.

"I must speak to Louis for a moment," Catana replied. "Would you gentlemen keep an eye on Inez?" When the men all nodded, Catana stood and pulled Louis to the side. "I will be unable to guard the *Dove* as I planned. Please watch Jamie and Orlando closely. Do not let them out of your sight."

"Catana, you are…" He stepped back and gave her a suspicious look. "Why are you not able to guard the sloop, and why is Inez dressed as if to go to a ball?"

"Inez insisted on finding Juan tonight. We are going to the fort." She noticed a hurt look in her friend's eyes. She had not realized how fond of her cousin he had become and placed a comforting hand on his shoulder. "Is it serious?"

"I have always known that her feelings were directed toward Juan. Now that it is time for them reunite, I realize that I have fallen in love with her."

"I think you should tell her."

"No, I want her to be happy. If Juan is the one she wants, it is best to say nothing."

Catana thought for a moment. "She is anxious to be with him."

"Take Tokala or Jabulani with you for protection."

Catana smoothed her skirts and looked toward the table where Inez and the men sat. "I do not think that will be necessary. The fort is only blocks away, and Tokala or Jabulani would rather spend time here than sitting around at the fort. Besides, I have my dirk and can take care of Inez and myself."

Louis gave her hand a squeeze. "That I have seen more than once."

Leaving the hot, stuffy tavern, the two women walked along the waterfront and soon saw the fort across a small field. When they approached the gate, two guards stood at attention in the firelight of torches lined along the walls in brackets. Inez fluttered her eyelashes at one guard and spoke loud enough for both to hear. "It is important that we see the commanding officer," she said in a sultry voice. "He is expecting us."

The guard looked at his companion, shrugged, and led the two women into the fort and escorted them into a small business office. An officer sat behind a writing table and looked up. Once the guard departed and closed the door behind him, Inez explained their visit.

"I am afraid Juan Muerte is not here," the officer said. "He has been invited to a fiesta at the home of Senor Hector Onrubia, one of our most distinguished citizens. I would go myself if I were not on duty. It is a gala affair. Juan was just commissioned an officer and—"

"Would we be allowed to join the celebration?" Inez cut in. "We are old friends of Juan from Santa Maria de Galva."

Catana tapped her cousin on the shoulder to get her attention. "I do not want to go to a fiesta."

"Please come. It will be a wonderful surprise for Juan, and I am dressed properly."

Catana looked down at her skirt and blouse. "Well, I am not."

"We will remain outside," Inez said. "I will have a servant send Juan out to us."

Catana rubbed her temple with her fingertips. The slight ache in her head was growing stronger. This was getting complicated. "Where is this fiesta?"

On the outskirts of Havana at Onrubia's hacienda," the officer replied. "You will need a carriage to take you there."

Catana sighed with relief. "You will have to wait until tomorrow when he returns to the fort."

"I know the man at the livery stable," the officer said. "He will provide a carriage to take you there."

Inez squealed with delight. "That is perfect. I have coin enough to rent one." Catana moaned as the pain in her head increased.

Twenty minutes later, the two women were seated in a coach drawn by four black horses. The driver had explained that this was the only vehicle available. All the others had been hired to take guests to the fiesta. It cost every coin Inez had brought.

The coach entered a torch lined drive and pulled up in front of a cobblestone walk that led to a massive white house. It had a row of columns that stood at attention across the front of the building.

Inez was first to alight from the coach and Catana trailed behind. A man bared the front door. "This is a private party. Do you have an invitation?"

Inez stood silent, then spoke in a voice of authority. "Do you know who I am?"

The man shook his head.

"I am the viceroy's daughter and have come to congratulate Juan Muerte, an old friend, on his good fortune. My father is quite proud of the young man and sent me to represent him because he had pressing affairs to take care of."

"I see, and who is this?" He gestured toward Catana.

"My maid, of course."

The man stepped aside to let the women pass.

"Come, Catana," Inez put her nose in the air, and they strode into the entry hall.

Catana was stunned by her cousin's actions. "Now that we are inside, what is next?" she asked, looking into Inez's flushed face.

"It sounds as if someone is making a toast in the dining room. Juan is probably in there."

They approached the doorway to the room and slipped inside unnoticed. Everyone's attention was on a distinguished-looking gentleman holding up a silver goblet. Catana had never seen so many beautiful women dressed in formal attire. "The man standing at the head of the table must be our host Señor Onrubia." Catana whispered to Inez.

"Sí, and there is Juan next to him. Does he not look wonderful in his uniform? He is the guest of honor, is he not?"

Catana nodded. "That is the impression I receive."

"*Dios*," Inez gasped and gripped Catana's hand. "A woman has taken his arm and smiles at him as if she owns him. I will…"

Inez started toward Juan, but Catana stopped her and whispered in her ear. "You do not expect Juan to be a guest of honor without an escort. My mother once told me it is the way of the Spanish Court."

Silence filled the room as Señor Onrubia tapped his goblet for attention. "My daughter," he announced nodding toward the young woman hanging on Juan's arm. Señior Onrubia cleared his throat.

"See," Catana whispered, "Juan is escorting the man's daughter as a courtesy."

"My daughter," Senor Onrubia repeated, "has agreed to become the wife of this fine young Spanish officer we honor here tonight. Ladies and Gentlemen, may I present my daughter Señorita Esperanza Onrubia and her fiancé Corporal Juan Muerte."

As cheers erupted from the guests, Inez pushed her way forward with fire in her eyes. She had taken several steps before Catana was able to grab her by the arm and pull her through the door and into the hallway.

"Let go of me," Inez said struggling against Catana's tight grip. "I will kill him. What of the promises he made to me?"

"It is best not to make a scene in front of him. It will make things worse for you. Come, we will return to the *Dove* and decide what to do next."

They walked out the front door and headed for their coach. Catana uttered words of comfort to her cousin who had broken down crying. Two guards stepped out of the shadows and blocked the path, their rifles trained on the women.

Catana's head pounded. Nothing had gone right since their arrival in Havana. Anger welled within her. "What is the meaning of this?"

"We have instructions to take you to our captain," the tall guard replied.

Catana stretched to her full height. "And what if we do not want to go with you?"

"We will be obliged to shoot you," the second guard said. He was a short, heavyset man with watery eyes. Catana did not doubt that the man would not carry out such orders.

With their rifles trained on Catana and Inez, the guards marched the two women to a garden behind the house. "What would a Spanish captain want with us?" Inez whispered.

"Quiet!" the tall guard snapped. "No talking."

Entering the garden, Catana froze when she saw the handsome captain in full dress uniform.

"Ah, I thought that was you," he said with a smile that did not reach his eyes.

"Captain Carvajal," Catana acknowledged.

"When I saw you enter the dining room I knew I must offer my greetings. How is our little thief—or should I say pirate—this evening?"

Catana and Inez stood in silence.

"Did you think I would let you get away with stealing a Spanish Navy sloop and assisting in the escape of two most dangerous prisoners?" He turned to the two guards and spoke in a soft but deadly voice. "Arrest them."

CHAPTER FOURTEEN

Louis felt relaxed after several tankards of grog. He was not used to drinking rum, and the amount he consumed deadened his pain of losing Inez to that Spanish soldier of hers. Maybe he should find a woman to bed tonight. There were a number of wenches in the tavern. But if he went off, he would not be able to keep an eye on Jamie and Orlando as he promised Catana.

Picking his tankard up to drain the last drop, he noticed a man pushing his way trough the room and heading straight for their table. The man summoned Orlando to the side, and they spoke in whispers. Jamie seemed to recognize the man but said nothing. Without a word to the other men at the table, the stranger turned and melted into the crowd.

Orlando motioned for Jamie, spoke with him and both men returned to the table. "Jamie and I have business to attend to," Orlando announced. "We will meet you back on the ship in the morning."

Catana's warning gave Louis an uneasy feeling. "Is there anything we can help you with?" he offered.

"No," Jamie answered abruptly. "We will take care of it on our own."

Once Jamie and Orlando disappeared through the door, Louis expressed his feelings to Jabulani and Tokala.

"Do you think they plan to sail away with the *Dove*?" Tokala asked.

Louis stood so quickly he lost his balance and knocked his chair to the floor. "I do not know. I think we should follow them in case Catana is right."

Leaving the tavern, the three men trotted along the waterfront. In the fog, they could barely see Jamie and Orlando ahead. They drew closer and slowed their pace to remain far enough behind as not to be noticed.

They passed several merchant ships sitting low in the water with their heavy cargos. The vessels strained at their mooring lines with the outgoing tide. It was a perfect time for Jamie and Orlando to sail away quickly. The two ships blocked the view where the *Dove* was anchored. Louis sighed with relief when he caught sight of their sloop bobbing alongside the dock.

"They are passing the *Dove,*" Tokala said. "I do not think they plan to steal her."

"Maybe not," Louis replied, "but they are up to something."

Moonlight reflected off the fog, making it difficult to see, but Louis, Tokala, and Jabulani managed to keep Jamie and Orlando in sight. They continued toward a spit of land reaching into the bay. A row of coconut palms stood at attention along its sandy shore. As Louis and his two companions drew closer to the trees, the air grew heavy with the smell of mud and marsh. The earth below their feet was swampy and sucked in their feet with each step.

Louis halted and held up his hand when he heard voices ahead. He spoke in a quiet voice so only Jabulani and Tokala would hear him. "We will hide in that clump of palmetto palms and listen to what they are saying."

Pulling a palm branch aside, Louis saw that Jamie and Orlando had joined five rough-looking men sitting around a campfire. Orland addressed a tall lanky man with hollow eyes and sunken cheeks. "I received your message, Damien. Thank heavens you were able to escape. How did you learn Jamie and I were in Havana?"

"Everyone in the brotherhood knows ye, sir. When one of 'em saw ye dock the sloop and go into the tavern, he came here to let us know."

"Are you the only to survive?" Orlando asked gesturing to the men around the fire.

"Aye, sir." Replied a small man dressed in fancy but tattered clothing. "This is all of us. The others are still in prison."

A man, the youngest of the lot, spoke up. "How is it, sir, that you got away and ended up here?"

Orlando and Jamie explained how they had joined two women and three men as crewmen on a sloop. "We must return to the *Seahawk,* and outfit her. To do this, we will need further use of the *Dove.* We will leave on her with the morning tide."

Jabulani translated parts of the conversation and, when the men around the fire changed the topic, he punched Louis in the ribs. "Catana was right. They plan to steal our ship."

The three men moved behind a line of trees. "What should we do?" Tokala whispered.

Louis thought for a moment. "Return to port and sail her out to sea before they have a chance to take her. Catana and Inez should be back from their visit with Juan by now."

The three men's whispers grew louder as they continued making plans, and their talking came to an abrupt stop when Orlando stepped out from behind a tree and spoke. "Will you join us, gentlemen?" The men from the campfire appeared out of the moon shadows to surround them.

"It looks like we do not have a choice," Louis replied.

Once everyone was settled around the fire, Orlando introduced his friends starting with Damien, the tall, lanky man. Next to him sat Percy, the man with clothing fancy enough to wear to a ball if it had not torn and dirty. William was heavyset with a thick red beard and long hair fastened back with a strip of leather. The creases around his sparkling blue eyes showed he laughed often. Tom held out his hand to greet the newcomers. He was the youngest, maybe no more than sixteen. The last to be introduced was Ben. He was a tall, rugged-looking man with bushy black hair. A scar ran along the corner of his left eye and down into his beard. Louis did not like the way his eyes shifted.

After the introductions Jamie stood. "Now that we all know one another, let me explain to our visitors from the *Dove* what this meeting is about. These men are crewmen from the *Seahawk.* The finest ship afloat, I might add. They were once pirates, but have sworn 'the oath.'"

"What oath is that?" Tokala asked.

"Not many years ago, pirates sailed freely upon these waters," Jamie replied. "Many a port welcomed them for they brought find goods into ports to sell at low prices."

"They could afford to," Louis muttered. "It was stolen merchandise."

Jamie continued as though he had not heard Louis. "'Twas till Woods Rogers arrived in New Providence."

Orlando continued the tale. "The British assigned Rogers as governor-in-chief of the Bahaman Islands. He brought a royal pardon for pirates who turned themselves in before September 15, 1718."

Jamie nodded. "Aye, they had to swear an oath to stop practicing piracy forever. After that date they would be hunted down and hanged."

Louis shifted to a more comfortable position. "Were you and Orlando pirates?

"We were accused by a British officer although it isna true," Jamie replied. "Captain Lancaster sent British authorities after us. He wanted to see Orlando imprisoned. To save the crew of the *Seahawk,* Orlando convinced us to turn ourselves in to Governor Rogers and take the oath."

Percy straightened a piece of lace at his wrist. "There was several among us who only pretended to take the oath."

"Aye," Tom agreed. "Bart, our boatswain did not want to give up his life as a pirate and attempted to start a mutiny."

"Captain Cordova, Orlando that is, put him ashore on an island," William said with a chuckle.

"The very island we stopped and picked up fresh water and food," Jamie added.

"Were you worried when we anchored that Bart would take revenge?" Louis asked.

"No," Orlando answered. "The man is a liar and thief, but most of all, he is a coward."

By now Louis was totally confused. Bart must be the man Catana had met on the island. He had told her Orlando left him to drown on a sandbar. If Bart was a liar and thief, had anything he said been true?

While Orlando and Jamie discussed their plans to retrieve the *Seahawk*, William leaned toward Louis and spoke in a quiet voice. "Not only did Bart try to start a mutiny, he stole our map and offered to return it if the captain turned the *Seahawk* over to him. Orlando would have none of it. That is why he marooned the scallywag. We searched Bart for the map before leaving him and found nothing."

Ben leaned in front of Louis and spoke to William. "You only know what the captain told you. I think Orlando lost the map and blames Bart in order to save face."

Before William and Ben had time to start an argument, Orlando spoke up. "At daybreak, if Louis will allow us to use the *Dove*, we will sail to Santiago de Cuba where the *Seahawk* is moored, and where the remainder of our crew is imprisoned."

"Aye," Tom agreed. "Once we retrieve out ship and crew, we can return to New Providence and have Governor Rogers give us a new copy of the map and deeds."

William slapped a mosquito on his neck and addressed Louis and his companions. "We was all captured in the beginning and made slaves. Those you see here managed to escape. I and the boys headed cross-country while Orlando and Jamie took to the sea. Figured it would confuse those who would come after us. We promised one another to meet in Havana. We thought you was never going to show, Orlando."

"Jamie and I ran into problems," Orlando replied. "Once we separated from you, Jamie and I stole a row boat and later that night found a ketch. On our third day at sea, we encountered a pirate ship. They picked us up because the captain needed extra men. She was chasing a French merchant brigantine. If we agreed to help the pirate captain seize the French ship, he would aid us in the rescue the *Seahawk* crew imprisoned at Santiago de Cuba.

"The French ship was a fully loaded warship with a full crew and not a merchant ship. They turned and attacked. When we lost the battle, Orlando and I dove into the water and swam ashore. The others aboard the *Sea Wolf* were captured. Most pirates do not know how to swim, but 'twas most likely they were too stubborn to surrender."

Orlando stirred the ashes of the fire with a stick. "It was a few hours later that the *Sea Wolf* washed ashore far down the beach. We made our way to her, searched everywhere aboard, and were unable to find her charts."

"Aye," Jamie said. "When we saw the fresh tracks leading away from the ship, we followed them to the top of the hill and saw your sloop down in the bay."

Louis sat for a moment in silence. "Now I understand why you need the *Dove*. Tokala, Jabulani, and I will do all we can to help."

Orlando cleared his throat. "Would you be willing to join my men and help us sail the *Dove* to Santiago de Cuba? Once we have the *Seahawk* and the crew freed, the *Dove* will be yours to do as you like."

For Louis, the thrill of adventure outweighed caution. "Are you in agreement, Jabulani and Tokala?"

The black man's teeth shone bright in the light of the moon as a wide grin crossed his face. "No man should be a slave to another. You can depend on me."

Tokala nodded. "And on me."

Orlando stood, grabbed Louis' hand, and shook it. "Good. We will leave on the morning tide. My men and I will come aboard at dawn."

Standing, Louis brushed the sand from his trousers. "It is time for me to return to the *Dove* and prepare Catana for the news."

"Tokala and I will come with you," Jabulani said, joining Louis. "We will protect you when Catana loses her temper." His hearty laugh echoed along the sandy beach.

As the three men started their walk back to the ship, Louis ran his fingers through his hair. "The Dutch, French, British, and Austrians are all at war with Spain. Now the Spanish can add us to the list." He quickened his pace, and his two companions followed on his heels.

Boarding the *Dove,* Louis headed for Catana's cabin. He knocked loudly on the door but received no response. It was unlocked. Opening the door, he slipped inside and held his lantern high to look around. Inez might have stayed with Juan, but where was Catana? The three men searched the ship from stem to stern. When they found no trace of her, they gathered at the foot of the mast. Tokala suggested they check the taverns and the fort. They strode down the gangplank into the dense fog that lay low along the waterfront. The taverns were closing and drunks were being turned out into the streets.

Louis and his two companions stopped several men to ask if they had seen Catana but with no avail. They approached the fort and Louis spoke to a guard. "Have you seen two women? One was dressed in a blue gown, and the other was in skirt and blouse."

"Sí," the guard replied. "They have been arrested and are now in the stockade." He gave the three men a suspicious look. "Are they friends of yours?"

Louis opened his mouth to say yes and to demand to see them, but before he could utter a word, Tokala spoke up. "Ah ha, someone has finally outsmarted those two wenches. It is about time. They have lied to us, stolen our coin, and heaven knows what they have done to others. We have been trailing them for two days. It is too bad some one arrested them before we could take revenge. Eh, Louis?"

Tokala's words confused Louis, but he nodded in agreement.

"Tell us," Tokala continued, "What have these women done to warrant arrest?"

"It is not my place to give you that information," the guard replied stiffly.

Louis caught on and joined in. "Come now, we deserve to know if it is a hanging offense. My friends and I would take delight in watching those two 'dance in the air.'"

"Pardon me?" the guard said.

"You know, watch them hang," Tokala explained.

The guard moved closer to the three men and spoke in a confidential tone. "As a matter of fact, it is a hanging offense. They are accused of piracy. One of the women stole a Spanish Navy sloop." The guard spit on the ground. "I heard that she and her accomplices, one a Frenchman, helped two dangerous criminals escape from a prison in La Florida."

Louis moved closer to the guard and spoke in a low tone. "They are more dangerous than we thought. How did you manage to capture them?"

The two women disrupted Señor Onrubia's celebration, a very important man in this area, this evening and threatened a Spanish officer."

Tokala sighed deeply. "It is something those two would do." He clapped the guard on the shoulder. "Good work. I am relieved those two are no longer a menace to honest men, and that they get the treatment they deserve."

"I did not put them under arrest," the guard explained. "It was Captain Carvajal."

Louis clenched his fist at his sides but kept a smile pasted on his face. "Since you have everything well in hand, my friends and I will be on our way."

Once they were out of hearing range of the guard Jabulani chuckled. "It will be amusing when we cheat the high-and-mighty Captain Carvajal out of a hanging."

"We will need the help of Orlando," Louis replied. "He is familiar with Havana and mentioned he knew his way around the fort.

Although Inez's heart belonged to Juan, Louis still loved her and could not help worry about her safety. "Poor Inez. She is innocent of all this. I wonder what the guard was talking about when he said she and Catana disrupted a celebration."

Jabulani shrugged. "We will learn their side of the story after they are rescued."

"By the way, why did you make up that story about us wanting revenge on Inez and Catana?" Louis asked. "I was going to try and convince the guard to let us in to see them."

Tokala shook his head. "I doubt he would have let us in." He seemed suspicious of us, and might have had us arrested as accomplices."

"I agree," Jabulani said, "because Captain Carvajal was behind the arrest, he will be on the alert for us. We cannot free the women if we are in prison."

Louis placed his hand on Jabulani's shoulder. "You are right. Come, men, let us return to the *Dove* and take her out of port before Captain Caravel sees her. We will join Orlando and his men and make plans to rescue the ladies."

CHAPTER FIFTEEN

Outside the cell door, light from a torch flickered and cast dancing shadows on the stalls. Catana sat on the floor of her cell, rubbing the muscles in the back of her neck. Although her headache was gone, her shoulders were stiff. Even with a layer of straw, the floor was hard and damp. She looked to where Inez sat in a corner wiping a tear from her cheek with the sleeve of her dress.

Catana crawled toward Inez and took her hand. "Do not worry. Louis will realize we are missing and come looking for us."

A rat, with a twitching nose and beady little eyes, scurried across the floor of the small, damp room and paused to look at them. Catana gave a shudder. "I wish Esmeralda was here. I hate rats."

The echo of footsteps came toward them, and stopped outside their cell. The large frame of a man blocked what little light there was, and Catana held her breath as the door of iron bars swung open. An armed guard stepped inside. "The Captain requests the pleasure of your company, ladies." He gestured with his rifle for them to stand. They were ushered to an office where Captain Carvajal sat writing on a paper with the scratch of a quill.

Looking up from his work, he grinned at the two women and bid them to come forward. "I have completed writing your confessions as traitors to the Spanish Crown. If you agree to sign them, I will be generous and sell you into slavery. If not, I will have you hanged and will display your bodies for the crows to eat."

Catana grasped her cousin's shaking hand and spoke through clenched teeth. "We will sign nothing."

"Suit yourself," the captain said. He stood and pointed to the paper. "I will keep this until the morning in case you change your mind."

"You cannot hang us without a trial," Catana said.

"Ah, my dear, that is where you are wrong. Pirates have been such a scourge that when we captured them we have the authority to hang them on the spot."

Inez rubbed her throat lightly and gave Catana a frightened look. "We have until tomorrow to decide?" Catana asked.

"Yes, the slave auction is to be held in the afternoon."

After Catana and Inez were returned to their cell, Catana looked around quickly before the guard departed with the torch. Her eyes fixed on a window high on the back wall.

The guard saw her gaze. "Do not attempt an escape. These cells are below ground. Although the window is at ground level, it is too small to climb through." He gestured down the passageway. "The captain has doubled the guard at the exits. In the other direction the passage comes to a dead end." He chuckled softly and slammed the door. Catana watched him take the last torch and disappear into the shadows.

In the darkness, Catana hummed while she tried to think of a way to escape. How long would it take Louis and the men to realize they were missing? When they did, would they have any idea where to find her and Inez? Her thoughts became jumbled, and she drifted into a light sleep.

When Catana awoke, she was able to see her surroundings in the dim light of dawn. Inez slept curled up in a corner along the back wall. Catana stood and checked the walls for a crack or weakness and found nothing but solid rock. She shook the bars; all were tightly in place. The window was long, narrow, close to the ceiling, and as the guard said, too small to pass through. She saw a chain embedded in the back wall and used it to pull herself up to grab a bar in the window. Peeking through, she saw that the window was only a few inches above ground. No way to escape there.

Inez stirred and then called out to Catana. "I thought I was having a bad dream, but it is true. We are prisoners."

"I am afraid so, and I have no plan for escape."

Inez sat up and pulled straw from her hair. "Should we sign the confession and stall for time?"

"I thought of that, but I do not trust Captain Carvajal. He might use the signed confessions as an excuse to hang us."

The two women sat in silence until they heard footsteps coming down the passageway. Catana recognized Orlando's voice. "I am ready to pay a substantial amount for your two prisoners. After what they did to me, they will wish had never been born when I get through with them."

"Aye, they be the scourge of the earth," she heard Louis say.

"For the right price, you are welcome to take them off my hands." It was Captain Carvajal.

As the men appeared, Catana whispered to Inez. "I do not know what the men are planning. I do not trust Orlando."

"But Louis is with him. You trust him."

Orlando was dressed as a dandy. He wore a white wig and tricornered hat and at his throat, a lace cravat. Catana's eyes scanned his red velvet coat, cream-colored tights, polished black boots, and returned her look to glare into his eyes. She saw Louis mouthing the words, behind Captain Carvajal's back. "Follow Orlando's lead."

Catana thought she understood what they were doing. "Why are you here?" she asked in a voice cold as a rock in winter.

"So you remember me?" Orlando asked in an amused voice.

"How could I forget a monster such as you?" Catana said and spat at him.

Orlando stepped back and laughed. "You have made a fool out of me for the last time. When I heard the news in town that you and your companion are to be sold at auction this afternoon, I knew it was my chance to give you what you deserve."

"No!" Catana cried. "Captain, you do not know this man. I would rather hang than be a slave to him."

"Please, señor, do not do this to us," Inez pleaded.

The Spanish captain rubbed his hands together, a delighted grin on his face. "This is better than I bargained for. Not only have I found a way to make you suffer, I will receive a rich reward. Guard, unlock the cell door."

Catana attempted to back into the corner of the room when Orlando stepped inside, but Orlando whipped out his hand and grabbed her by the wrist. His grip was like an iron manacle. He jerked her out of the cell and drew a pouch full of coins from his belt. "This should more than cover out agreed price," Orlando said, pitching the pouch to the Spanish captain.

Louis pulled his flintlock pistol and trained it on the two women. "I believe we can take care of this from here, Captain, if you would like to count your coins."

Captain Carvajal opened the pouch, and a wide grin crossed his face. "Thank you, gentlemen. They are now yours to do with as you please."

"Move," Orlando ordered the ladies, "or I will have my friend shoot, not to kill but to cause you great pain."

As the two men and their prisoners headed toward the main gate of the fort and were about to go through, a soldier called out. "Detain those civilians."

Orlando stole a look at the man who gave the alarm and swore. "It is a man from the fort at Santiago de Cuba. He has recognized me."

Guards with rifles bared their escape. "There are too many to fight," Orlando whispered. "Quick, in here." They followed him into a building along the wall next to the gate.

Catana stopped inside the door and looked at the variety of weapons in the room. "Where are we?"

"The armory," Orlando informed her.

He ran to a powder keg and used the butt of his pistol to break it open. Pouring a mound of black powder in a trail along the dirt floor, he gestured the others to follow him out the back window while the guards attempted to break down the locked door in front. Once outside, Orlando seized a torch from a bracket on the fort's wall. "Get behind those sacks of grain piled next to the wall. When I light the powder, duck." He threw the torch through the window and ran to join them.

Catana straightened up slowly to peek over the rim of sacks. The door broke open, and a cloud of acidic blue smoke billowed from the window. There was a shattering explosion. A shockwave of hot air swept over them like a tropical squall. The building shattered and fell in on itself. Smoke billowed high into the air while dark flames and scraps of debris flew from the destruction.

When the smoke cleared, Orlando led them around the damage and toward a hole in the fort's wall. Catana kept her eyes trained on the opening. She did not want to see the carnage that lay all around. Her adrenaline kept her running at top speed, but Inez was starting to lag behind. The Spanish soldiers were in hot pursuit and would soon be upon them. They followed Orlando around the corner of the livery stable a few paces outside the wall and ran into team of horses hitched to a supply wagon. Orlando leaped onto the seat and gathered the reins. "Get in," he shouted.

Louis grabbed Inez by the hand and pulled her forward into the wagon. Catana jumped in behind them, lost her balance, and fell heavily into the wagon bed as Orlando whipped the team of blacks into a full gallop. Pulling herself upright, she brushed her hair out of her face and turned to look behind. Through the dust, she saw soldiers shake their fists and then head for their horses.

"I will have to drive along the waterfront road in order to get to the *Dove,*" Orlando shouted over his shoulder. "The ride might get a bit rough."

Catana noticed how Louis held onto Inez to keep her steady and smiled to herself. She was happy for his interest in her cousin, but she worried that Inez would break his heart. Bouncing around in the cart, Catana gripped the side of the wagon tightly as they swung around a corner, toppling a food vender's booth. Vegetables spewed over the street as they raced on.

When they turned down the road paralleling the beach, Louis scanned the smoking fort. "The Captain has sent up a signal flag to the warship in the harbor. They plan to fire on us. Can you go faster?"

Orlando slapped the reins several times, but the animals were already at a dead run.

Catana watched with a frozen stare as sailors on a man-of-war opened her broadside ports and rolled out the cannons. A bright flash and thunderous sound were followed by eight cannon balls. They arched through the air toward them. Explosions erupted all around hitting buildings, the governor's palace, and several taverns. Catana crouched low and covered her head to protect herself from flying rocks and wood.

The wagon followed the road away from the waterfront and entered a grove of trees. Orlando pulled the team to a halt. "By the time the ship reloads its cannons and is ready to fire, we will be far out of range. Havana is another town in which we will never be welcomed, eh, Louis?"

He put the horses into a jog toward the spit of land where the *Dove* awaited them. By the time they were safely aboard, Louis and Orlando filled the women what had happened while they were imprisoned and their rescue plans for the crewmen in Santiago de Cuba.

CHAPTER SIXTEEN

It was late afternoon when the *Dove* anchored off the coast of Santiago de Cuba. The crew stood on deck while Orlando pointed out a hill behind the town. "The prison is inland half a league and at the foot of that hill. Before we attempt a rescue, we must take possession of the *Seahawk*."

Jamie picked up the spyglass and scanned the waters for the ship. "There she is off the starboard bow. I see two men on her deck. We will have to overtake whoever is aboard. Does anyone have an idea how we can seize her without attracting attention?"

Louis pulled Catana aside. "Remember the pirate story I told once, and how they stole a ship?" Catana thought for a moment then smiled.

When dusk fell, a small boat slid alongside the *Seahawk* with Catana, Inez, Damien, Orlando, and Louis dressed like native venders. Louis had shown the crew how to darken their skins with tannin by smearing on the dark oil. Waving grass hats and bandanas, they called to the men aboard the *Seahawk*. "We have fresh fruit for sale." A man dropped a rope ladder. Gathering baskets of fruit, the natives climbed aboard the *Seahawk* and were greeted by three men.

Catana scanned the ship for others. "Is this everyone? We have enough fruit for a full crew."

"Sí, señorita, this is all that is aboard for now. Others will join us in the morning to set sail with the tide. We will take all the fruit you have to sell."

Before the Spanish seamen realized, Orlando and his companions whipped out the pistols and knives they had hidden under the fruit and overcame the three men.

"What shall we do with them?" Louis called to Orlando.

Orlando searched them for weapons. "Put them in the hold. Make sure the hatches are secured so they cannot escape and warn others. We will deal with them before we get underway. The next step is to rescue the remainder of our crew."

"Do you have a plan, Captain?" Damian asked.

The question startled Catana and she whispered in Louis' ear. "Is Orlando truly the captain of the *Seahawk?* I thought it was Jamie." Bart had told her that Cordova was captain of the *Seahawk* while she was on the island but thought it had been one of his lies.

Louis looked at her and shrugged.

"Damian," Orlando said, "signal the *Dove* to come aside. Once my men come aboard, we will have a meeting and decide our next move."

The *Dove* slid alongside the *Seahawk*, and Jamie threw a line from the sloop to Orlando. When the two ships were attached, the men on the *Dove* climbed aboard the *Seahawk* and gathered at the foot of the main mast.

While Catana waited for the meeting to start, she gazed around at the *Seahawk.* She was larger than the *Dove.* Sleek, with a spear of a bowsprit almost as long as her hull, she held a parade of canvas that would make the ship swift. Turning to Jamie, Catana asked, "How large a crew will she take?"

"Sixty men, and she carries fourteen cannons. The *Seahawk* can slip in and out of channels where a man-o-war would flounder," he added with pride. "When we were a pirate ship, we darted in for an attack, did our damage, and withdrew so swiftly most ships did not know what hit them."

Catana remembered Orlando's story about being forced to become pirates when captured. If she asked Jamie, would his story be the same? There were so many lies floating around she did not know who or what to believe. "Why did you turn to piracy?

"That is a long story. It was because Captain Lancaster of the British Navy—"

"Attention, gentlemen," Orlando shouted.

"I will be telling you more, later," Jamie whispered in her ear.

"We have twenty-five of our men waiting to be rescued," Orlando continued. "Most of us are familiar with the prison. Once we are inside the walls, we will locate and free our men. Our greatest problem will be getting close enough to overpower the guards and gain entrance."

The men mumbled among themselves while Catana circled around to join Inez. Her cousin was standing at the rail deep in thought. Catana put a hand on her shoulder to comfort her. "Are you still brooding over Juan?"

"Spanish soldiers are such swine. I may not get revenge on Juan, but it would give me pleasure to see one or two soldiers squirm."

Catana thought for a moment. "Maybe you can have your wish. What if we use the same ploy as Orlando and Jamie did in Havana, except it is you and I who want to purchase slaves?" Catana presented her plan to Orlando.

"It will not work. Only the affluent can afford to buy slaves." He sighed and looked at them. "You ladies do not have enough coin, nor do you look the part."

"Stop and think, Orlando," Jamie said, entering the conversation. "They can dress like wealthy women and pretend to—"

"Be the viceroy's daughter," Inez said, finishing the sentence. "That is what I did at Señor Onrubia's ball in Havana. I have a dress that a noble lady would wear."

"Do you not remember? Your blue dress was ruined during our escape," Catana said.

"Of course I remember. But I also brought along my lavender trimmed in silver lace."

"Did you bring your whole wardrobe?"

"No, only those two good dresses. I wanted to look my best for…" Her voice choked up, and Catana squeezed her hand.

"That is fine for Inez, but what of you, Catana?" Orlando asked.

"We could steal a dress," Damian suggested.

"And draw everyone's attention?" Tokala asked.

Jamie stroked his beard and thought for a moment, "Unless you are willing to give her your dress, Orlando."

The chatting ceased as everyone stood in silence looking at the captain. Jamie drew Orlando aside and spoke in a low voice that Catana was unable to hear. She chuckled. "Orlando owns a dress?"

Inez shrugged. "How would I know, I—"

"Catana, please come here," Jamie shouted. She followed him into the captain's cabin, and he led her to a trunk in a corner. Opening it, he pushed aside some loose gear on top, and he pulled out one of the most beautiful gowns Catana had ever seen. It was ivory brocade trimmed in lace.

Jamie held it up next to her. "I have a feeling this will fit you, my dear. Try it on."

"Why does Orlando own such an exquisite dress?"

"'Tis part of the tale I was telling you earlier.

"The dress was to be a gift for Ana, Orlando's intended, but he never had a chance to give it to her."

"Did she die?"

"Nay, worse. She betrayed him to Captain Lancaster, the man who forced us into piracy."

She looked at the gown with apprehension. "Are you certain he wants me to wear this? Seeing it might open new wounds."

"Aye, I am sure he will not mind. It has been two years now. Not long ago, he told me that she had never loved him and betrayed him to get what she wanted."

"What was that?"

"Power and wealth. When she learned that Captain Lancaster had acquired a fortune and was popular with the English court, she agreed to marry him." Jamie handed the dress to her. "Enough talk for now. Let us see if you fit into this dress."

Jamie sent Inez into the captain's cabin to help Catana dress. Catana felt fortunate she did not have to dress like this everyday. First, she put on three petty coats and then struggled into the heavy dress. Inez pulled on the laces to tighten the bodice. The stays dug into her ribs and almost drove all the air from her lungs. Was it any wonder she preferred a simple skirt and blouse? Standing back, Inez observed Catana in the gown. "We must lace the bodice tighter."

Catana took a deep breath. "Why? It is already uncomfortable."

"It will push your bosom up and give you more cleavage. You do want to distract the guards, do you not?"

"Yes, but by talking to them."

"Believe me, cleavage is more distracting to men than words."

Catana felt self-conscious when she stepped onto deck. Darkness had fallen, and a full moon brightened the sky and reflected off the water. Standing in the light of a lamp hanging from the mast, she looked around at the faces of the men. They were staring at her. Jamie broke the silence. "'Tis an angel we have here. You look breathtaking, my dear. The dress fits you well."

"Quite," Percy agreed. Louis and the others nodded with approval. She was afraid of Orlando's reaction. Although Jamie claimed Ana no longer mattered to Orlando, did Catana's appearance in this dress remind him of what could have been? When he stepped into the circle of light, she saw no emotion on his face nor heard any in his voice when he spoke. His reaction confused her at first. Was Orlando hiding his true feelings for his lost love, or was he over the past? She tilted her head higher and strode toward the ship's rail, wondering why should she care. She was doing this to help him rescue his crew.

"We will board the native boat to go ashore. William, you and Tom remain aboard the *Seahawk*. Have her ready for a fast get away. When we return, we will turn the *Dove* over to Louis and his companions. We will have enough crew to run the ship or to fight, but not both. I prefer to run. Louis, I suggest you do the same."

William slapped Tom on the shoulder. "I guess it's up to us, lad, to ready the *Seahawk* to run."

Louis checked the *Dove* to ensure she would be ready to flee and then returned to the *Seahawk*. By dawn, a full plan had been drawn out and the landing crew boarded the small craft. The women descended the rope ladder slowly wearing full skirts with three petty coats. Inez was accustomed to such dress, but Catana felt awkward in her movements. Her tight stockings and stilted shoes did not help. When everyone was settled, the men rowed the native boat toward the docks of Santiago de Cuba.

* * * *

Later that morning Catana and Inez, masquerading as wealthy women in high society, climbed into a hired carriage. Jabulani, dressed in fine clothing, posed as their driver, and Tokala as their manservant. Orlando hid three flintlock pistols under Jabulani's seat and handed Catana a dirk before they departed toward the prison. She strapped it to her arm with a strip of fabric and covered it with her long sleeve trimmed in lace at the wrist. Since the carriage was open and the December sun hot, Inez convinced Catana to purchase two parasols.

"A waste of coin," Catana said looking at her parasol with distaste.

"We do not want our delicate skin to become burned now, do we? To portray a proper lady, one must speak as such, and proper ladies are concerned with their skin. When we arrive, do not forget to flirt shamelessly."

"I am not in the habit of such behavior. But if men's lives depend on it maybe you should give me a few lessons," Catana said with a bit of irony in her voice.

"I will be happy to. After all it will only be an act." As they rode, Inez instructed Catana in the art of flirting.

Once the carriage was outside of town, Louis, Orlando, and his crew followed behind at a distance with a supply wagon. Twenty minutes later, the carriage pulled up in front of the gates of the prison where a guard raised his hand to halt them. "What is your business here?"

Catana fluttered her eyelashes. "I am the viceroy's daughter and on a mission to relay an important message to the captain of the guard, or whoever is in charge here. Please direct me to his office."

When the guard learned who she was, he stood at attention. "Sí, señorita. His office is that building," he said, pointing to a stone structure a hundred paces ahead.

Jabulani wheeled the team of bays toward the prison building and brought them to a halt in front of the door. A guard hurried forward to open the carriage door for the ladies.

"My good man," Catana said, looking down her nose at him. "Please tell your commander to come here. I have a message for him and do not want to soil the hem of my new dress."

The guard hesitated. Catana leaned forward, exposing more bosom, and whispered in his ear. "For me?" Straightening, she winked at him. "You will not regret it…later."

The guard cleared his throat. "Sí, señorita. I will see what I can do."

"How I hate belittling myself like that," Catana said with shudder after the guard left. Tokala, who was holding her parasol to shade her from the sun, chuckled, and she jabbed him in the side with her elbow.

A large heavyset man moping perspiration from his forehead lumbered through the door. His heavy jowls and close-set eyes reminded Catana of a pig. The broken veins on his large nose and round cheeks indicated he was a heavy drinker. Catana smoothed her skirts and took her parasol from Tokala. "Help me down."

Tokala stepped out, placed a small carpet on the ground for Catana to stand on, and extended his hand to assist her down from the carriage. Drifting to the ground in a flourish of silk skirts, she beckoned the commander to come closer. Taking a deep breath, she felt as if her breasts would pop out above the neckline. The hair on the back of her neck stood up when the commander focused his eyes on her chest and licked his lips. "*Madre de Dios*, is that all men think about?" she muttered under her breath. Reaching out with her fingertips, she stroked the man's arm. "Can you see it in your heart to help a defenseless woman in need?"

The commander mopped his brow. "I must know what you want first."

"I would like to buy five of your strongest prisoners. My father, the viceroy, is in need of laborers to replace two who died under the whip."

The commander eyed her with suspicion. "Why would the viceroy want prisoners from here?"

"He has been to several slave auctions, but the choices are few. No one at the sales was strong and healthy enough for hard labor."

"Does your father not fear that these men would try to escape or kill him?"

"My father has many guards. If a prisoner misbehaves, the punishment is heavy. We have never had a laborer successfully escape. They are too afraid of the consequences. He has word that you have able-bodied seamen imprisoned here that would fit his needs. He is willing to pay well."

"If I were to sell you these men, how will you transport them to your father? You are not equipped to handle them."

"I have brought a wagon and some of my fathers guards. They wait outside the gate."

Catana pulled out a money pouch and opened it to reveal gold doubloons. "I believe we can arrange a purchase?" Catana saw greed in the man's eyes as he nodded. "Good, may I bring in the wagon and my men?"

"Guard," the commander shouted to the man on the gate, "signal the men outside to bring in the wagon."

Catana smiled as a large supply wagon drawn by a team of four horses lumbered through the gate. Orlando and Louis sat on the seat while Percy and Ben walked alongside.

Like a striking coral snake, Catana whipped out her dirk and pushed it against the commander's throat. "Do exactly as I say. You are going to take us to the prison and have the guard inside unlock the cells."

The commander opened his mouth in an attempt to cry out, but Catana pressed the point of the blade closer, pricking his skin and drawing blood. "If you do not cooperate, I will plunge this blade so deep into your throat that it will extend out the back of your neck. Now do as I say."

The commander's face was white with terror. "Are you mad?" he said in a rasping voice.

Catana nodded. "Mad enough to kill you if you do not obey. Now turn around and tell your guards to throw down their arms."

"Guards, drop your weapons and come here." The guards stood with puzzled looks on their faces. "That is an order! Do as I say or they will kill me."

One by one the guards dropped their flintlock rifles and approached the carriage. Once the guards were out of reach of their weapons, the men around the supply wagon pulled away a canvas cover and pulled out rifles and swords. Tokala and Jabulani grabbed the weapons hidden under the carriage seat.

"We will detain the five guards," Tokala said to Catana. "You and Louis escort the commander inside to release the prisoners."

Striding through the door of the building, Louis grabbed a torch from a bracket at the top of the stairs with one hand and held a flintlock pistol trained on the commander with the other. They entered a dark, damp building that contained the cells. Descending the stairs into further gloom, Catana plucked a second lit torch from the wall at the foot of the steps without lessening the pressure of her blade against the commander's side. The smell of human waste took her breath away and made her eyes water. A few high windows let in enough dim light to see into the cells. Two guards sat at a table playing a board game. They looked up when they heard the three visitors approach.

"Bring the keys to me, immediately," the commander ordered.

One of the guards stood. "Is there a problem, sir?"

The commander gave a startled jump when Catana jabbed him with the point of her blade. "The keys, hurry," he pleaded.

Louis waved his flintlock at the guards. "Do as your commanding officer orders."

The guard snatched the keys from his belt and handed them to Louis. Within seconds, the cell doors opened, and the crewmen of the *Seahawk* spilled into the passageway. Louis shoved the two guards and their commander into one of the cells and locked the door. "*Adios, amigos,*" he said saluting them. "Orlando has a wagon outside to take you to your ship," he announced to the freed prisoners. A cheer erupted from the men as they scurried up the steps and out the door. Louis and Catana trailed behind while the guards and the commander rained curses on them. "What language," Catana uttered and covered her ears.

Stepping into the bright sunlight, the released men ran to embrace their shipmates and pat one another on the back. Catana smiled.

Suffering in this miserable dress was worth watching heartwarming reunion. While Louis and Jabulani escorted the remainder of the guards to their cells, Catana climbed aboard the carriage. "Inez, loosen the laces on my dress before I die." Inez picked at what had become a tight knot and could not untie it. Catana handed her the dirk. "Cut the damn thing."

"If I do, the dress will become too loose and expose more than you will comfortable with."

Catana noticed Ben easing through the crowd with Jamie's coat thrown over his arm. As Ben neared the carriage, a man bumped him toward her, and Catana was able to reach out and snatch the coat. Ben's startled look amused her. She gave him a flirtatious smile. "Jamie will not mind if I borrow his coat until we return to the ship."

Ben returned her smile with a look of stone. "Jamie is attached to his coat, you know, and gave it to me to hold and keep it safe."

"It will be safe with me." Catana insisted and turned back to her cousin. "Now cut the laces."

Inez hesitated. "It will ruin the dress. Orlando—"

"I do not care about Orlando or his dress. I cannot bear it any longer. I will replace the lacings later. Now cut."

With a quick slice of the blade, the dress's tight embrace loosened and slipped lower. Catana quickly threw Jamie's coat on and buttoned it.

No one pursued them from the prison so Jabulani and Orlando put the horses at a leisurely trot toward the beach. Louis helped the two women into the native boat and took them to the *Dove*.

"I will return soon," Louis said as he headed down the ladder. "I want to check with Orlando and see what his plans are." Once the boat departed for the *Seahawk*, Catana headed for her cabin to change out of the gown. She did not want to further ruin the dress. She would return it before the *Seahawk* and the *Dove* sailed their separate ways.

She was pulling on her breeches and shirt when Inez came through the door. "Did you notice how brave Louis was?" she Inez said clapping her hands.

132

"Sí, very brave," Catana agreed, "as were all the men." She took Jamie's coat and hung it on a peg. "I will return this later. He will have no need of it until it grows cooler after sunset."

When Catana returned to the deck of the *Dove*, Orlando and Jamie stood at the bow and she joined them. "We have come to say farewell," Jamie said.

"Are you preparing to leave?" she asked. "I thought you would wait until the evening tide goes out."

"'Tis best we sail now," Jamie replied. "We dinna know how soon someone will discover the men at the prison and sound the alarm. 'Tis a good idea if you left right away too."

Catana brushed a tear from her cheek while emptiness filled her heart. Until now she hadn't realized how much she would miss the crew of the *Seahawk,* especially Orlando. "Where are you going?"

"Port Royal," Orlando answered. "We have business to take care of there."

Catana gave a start when Louis came up behind her and turned to face him. "Where can we go, Louis? We are no longer welcome by the ports in Cuba. After our visit to Havana, and freeing prisoners in Santiago de Cuba, we probably have a price on our heads."

Louis looked down at her and grinned. "We could always go on account and become pirates. We have the ship and a flag to start with."

Orlando stepped in. "It is a hard life, and you are not equipped for success. Pirates use large crews to overcome the ship's they attack. There are only five of you. Barely enough to sail, let alone attack."

"He is right," Catana agreed.

"Why not follow us a while until you have made a decision," Orlando suggested.

While the men talked, Catana noticed movement on the water in the distance. The harbor entrance was blocked by three man-o-wars set end to end. They sat with their broadsides facing the *Dove* and *Seahawk.* Catana took a deep breath. "*Madre de Dios.* The Spanish have blocked the channel. We are trapped"

CHAPTER SEVENTEEN

Orlando and the crew of the *Dove* boarded the *Seahawk* to warn everyone. The men looked to where Catana pointed and muttered in disgruntled voices. The three ships stood like menacing giants blocking their way to the open sea and freedom. "We should o' never attempted this rescue," Ben grumbled. "Now we are doomed."

Orlando held up his hand for silence. "We are out of firing range, and they cannot come closer because of the shallow water."

"But there is no other way out of the bay," a crewmember shouted. "If we try to ram through them, the *Seahawk* and *Dove* will be shot to pieces." The voices of the crew grew louder.

"Silence!" Orlando shouted over the arguing. "I have a plan. Calm down and I will explain."

He signaled for the members of the *Dove* to gather around him. "Fire is the greatest terror of seamen. Ships are built of combustible materials." He took Catana's hand and gazed into her eyes. "I know that you plan to use the *Dove* to return to Santa Maria when it is safe, but I need your ship."

Tears welled in Catana's eyes. Swallowing the lump in her throat, she spoke in a low voice. "You want to turn her into a fire ship?"

"That is correct," Orlando replied. "It is the only way I can think of to escape. When this is over, I will replace her. Meanwhile, you and your crew can join us on the *Seahawk*."

Catana looked at Louis, Inez, Tokala, and Jabulani, all of whom stood in silence. "Do you agree?" she asked.

"Orlando is right," Louis said. "It is the only way." Inez, Tokala, and Jabulani nodded in agreement.

Catana took a deep breath to steady her voice. "Before we start, Inez and I have a few belongings we would like to transfer to the *Seahawk*."

Orlando squeezed her hand. "Of course."

Entering their cabin with her cousin, she pulled the box with her father's letters and the map Inez had found from under the bunk. Snatching the gown she had worn earlier and the bag with her meager clothing, she put them in a pile in front of the door. She helped Inez pack her trunk, stuffing it with everything her cousin owned, including the pirate flag. "We will have several of the men come for this, Inez. It is too heavy for us."

As they were leaving the cabin for the last time, Catana remembered Jamie's coat and added it to her things. Swooping up her belongings, Catana stepped out the door with Inez in her wake.

After everyone had removed what he or she wanted from the *Dove*, the crew went to work turning the sloop into a fire ship. Orlando stood on deck of the *Seahawk* giving instructions. "We will look for empty barrels in the hold of both ships and use the wood to fuel the fire. I noticed three barrels of grog in *Seahawk*'s hold. We will place them at intervals on the deck near the main mast of the *Dove*. Place one barrel of gunpowder at her bow the other at her stern."

Orlando had the remainder of his men string hemp and extra canvas then slap pitch on them. When they were finished, Jamie gathered everyone around the foot of the mast on the *Dove*. "I need five volunteers," he announced. "One man to steer the sloop toward the warships, two men to light the fires, and one at the bow the other at the stern."

"It is my ship. I want to volunteer," Catana called out.

Louis grabbed her arm. "No, it is too dangerous."

"How many here are good swimmers?" she asked in a loud voice. Only Tokala answered.

"Anyone who volunteers will have to be able to swim back to the *Seahawk*. It seems only Tokala and I qualify."

"The lass is right," Jamie agreed. "Once the burning sloop is on a heading straight for the man-o-wars, the volunteers will have to jump ship and swim."

Catana folded her arms across her chest and stood tall. "That settles it."

Catana and Tokala remained aboard the *Dove* while the others boarded the *Seahawk* to set her sails to run. Tokala took the helm and turned the bow of the sloop toward the Spanish war ships. As the *Dove*'s sails took the wind and she bore toward the blockade, a man-o-war opened fired. Catana quickly took her torch and held it to a hemp line saturated in pine pitch. The fire started slowly and smoke filled the air. As the sun plunged into the sea, it painted the sky with brilliant reds and orange mimicking the flames that grew on the fast-moving sloop. Catana scanned the main mast of the burning ship, and her eyes rested on the yardarm. Something moved. Peering through the smoke, she recognized Esmeralda. She had forgotten about the cat.

Flames traveled along the pitch soaked ropes toward the barrels of gunpowder on each end of the ship. They were halfway to their target. Without further thought, she skirted up the shroud lines to rescue the animal.

"Get down you fool," Tokala shouted. "We are closing in on the warships, and the *Dove* will blow at any time."

Catana ignored him and reached to pluck the cat from the yard. Grabbing it by the back of the neck, she pulled, but Esmeralda had her claws dug into a piece of canvas. Catana yanked several times, and when the cat came loose, it tried to claw her. She held the struggling animal at arms length while carefully climbing down the lines.

Landing on deck, Catana saw Tokala motioning for her to jump, and then he dove into the water. The flames had reached the bow and caught hold of the sails that marched along the bowsprit. The *Dove* was only yards from their target. Flames ate at shroud lines she had descended and suddenly the canvas sheet on the mainmast flared up.

The huge spread of canvas floated down toward the barrel of gunpowder at the stern.

Holding onto the struggling cat, Catana rolled from the deck into the blackness of the water. She felt the pain of burns forming on the arm and hand that held the cat and let go. She swam for her life. Once Catana felt she was at a safe distance from the burning ship, she scanned the water for the cat but saw nothing. Her heart sank. Had she saved Esmeralda only to have her drown? She and the cat had acquired a strange connection. She loved the silly beast and admired Esmeralda's independence and ability to bounce back under adverse conditions.

A devastating roar echoed across the water as the sky lit up. She turned in the direction of the warships to see burning timbers flying through the night sky. The light of flames reflected off the water, and Catana saw the orange head of the cat bobbing on the waves. "*Gracias Señor Dios*,"she muttered with relief. Treading water, she reached out and grabbed the animal. Exhausted, the cat allowed Catana to hold on to her.

She found a piece of wood large enough to support her and set the cat on top. Using the wood to keep them afloat, Catana rested and watched the drama unfold. Reflection of the flames from the burning ships danced on the water. All three warships were engulfed in flame from stem to stern. Only one had her bow above the waterline, but she was sliding under. Catana flinched and almost lost her grip on the floating piece of timber when the Spanish ship suddenly flew apart in a roar of thunder. Thick plumes of smoke sailed into the air. With a groan from her timbers, the broken hull slid beneath the waves. In minutes, darkness surrounded her as the water quenched the flames of the sinking ships.

She scanned the direction in which the *Seahawk* was supposed to be and saw nothing. Panic gripped her. She was far from shore, and although she had the wood to hold on to, the tide was pulling her toward the channel and open sea. Holding her float in front of her with both hands, her arms outstretched, she kicked her feet to propel herself forward in the direction she thought the *Seahawk* would be. The cat seemed satisfied to remain aboard the piece of wood.

Peering into the night, she saw the black outline of the ship against the dark sky and she shouted. "Ahoy, man overboard." The ship floated toward her but looked like it would pass by her. She knew they were looking for her and ripped the sleeve from her white blouse, waved it in the air and shouted. The ship slowed, and she heard Louis' voice. When the ship was close enough, she grabbed the rope ladder and shouted to the men on deck. "I will need help up." Her burned arm had become so painful that she could barely use it.

Tokala climbed down to meet her. "I was afraid you did not survive. Of all the irrational things you have ever done, this tops them all."

"Just take the cat, please."

Tokala peered at the piece of timber she held to her chest. "You managed to rescue the thing?"

"Sí, now take her aboard so I can follow. Pick her up by the fur behind her head. I think the fight in her is returning."

Tokala grabbed the cat and ascended the ladder with Catana following slowly behind. A crewman she did not recognize grabbed her by her good arm and helped her over the rail. As soon as her feet hit the deck, Jamie shouted to the crew to get underway.

Dripping wet and hurting, Catana snapped at Tokala when he chided her for her actions. "Leave me alone. It was not an easy task to swim with a wet and angry cat. Where is Inez?"

"Captain Cordova has assigned a cabin to you and your cousin," he answered in a cool and formal voice. "Follow me, I promise to say no more about the cat."

Entering the cabin Catana noticed there were two bunks and sank down on the nearest one. Inez, sitting at a table mending one of her dresses dropped her sewing and raced to Catana. "I was so frightened for you." Inez grabbed Catana by her burned arm. In pain, Catana gasped and stood quickly. Inez gave a startled look at the red blisters. "I am so sorry I did not realize you were injured." She pushed Catana closer toward the lantern that hung over the table to examine her burns.

"When the blisters break, you will have to keep them clean. Stay here. I will get a medical kit."

Later, after Inez had slathered a salve on Catana's burns and bandaged her arm and hand, Catana changed into one of her cousin's camisoles and was asleep as soon as her head hit the pillow.

CHAPTER EIGHTEEN

Catana's burns were healing nicely by the time she leaned over the rail of the *Seahawk* to get a better look at Port Royal looming before them in the distance. Situated on a narrow spit of land, the settlement sat on the south side of Jamaica.

Jamie came to stand next to her. "Over twenty years ago, Port Royal had the largest number of pirates in all the West Indies," he informed her. "The town had carpenters, gold smiths, sail makers, a number of other merchants, as well as a large slave market. I was a young lad on a merchant ship and remember walking down Queen's Stead to Fisherman's Row." Pointing to a line of beach with a small docking area with two ships, he continued. "Back then, the wharfs were lined with large merchant ships, warehouses full of tobacco, spices, sugar, beef, wine, and beer. Port Royal had three churches, two prisons, and forty-four taverns. 'Twas when the British governors encouraged piracy."

"But why," Catana asked.

"Port Royal merchants became rich selling plundered goods they had bought from pirates, below market value. The city was full of gold."

Louis walked up and joined the conversation. "Imagine, Catana, this port was capable harboring five hundred ships and was a pirate's paradise."

"Aye," Jamie agreed, "and the pirates brought with them brothels, grog, and gaming houses. Them were great days back then."

"But look at it now," Catana said. "It looks like nothing but a small settlement. What happened?"

140

Jamie combed his fingers through his beard. "It all ended when an earthquake struck Port Royal. I was not there, but a man told me that the streets rose up then fell. Brick and stone buildings collapsed, and the earth opened up to swallow entire houses. The wharf and its ships, along with two streets full of houses next to the beach, dropped into the ocean. Then a great wave swept through the town. The man who told me said that he had fled inland and had watched as hundreds of people were swept out to sea. Many of those who survived died from injuries, disease, or fever. There were bodies everywhere. This is what remains."

The *Seahawk* slid along side the dock. Two of her crewmen jumped ashore and moored her with ropes at the bow and stern. Catana came ashore with Louis, Jamie, Orlando, and several of the crew. Stepping onto the cracked grey stone of the boat landing, she scanned the small buildings crowded together along the waterfront. White plaster was gone in places to reveal the timber beneath. They strode onto a street paved with broken paving stones. It was lined with houses where laundry hung from various windows. At the end of the street stood an empty structure, its windows gaping like empty eye sockets. Catana shuddered when she looked around and saw rats scurrying through a pile of refuse. "Why are we here?" she asked Louis.

"Orlando has business to take care, and Jamie and I came ashore to look around. Those of the crew who do not have watch are going to a tavern. Why have you come ashore?"

Catana shrugged. "I was following you."

"You should have remained aboard with Inez and the watch. The taverns are rough, especially for ladies."

Catana looked down at her clothing. She wore breeches and a loose blouse. "You want me to go back so you and Jamie can to spend your time in a Port Royal tavern?" She grabbed a wide brimmed hat from a windowsill, plopped it on her head, and stuffed her long dark brown hair beneath it. Grabbing Louis by the arm, she stopped him. "Will I pass for a cabin boy?"

Jamie stopped and turned to look at her. "Aye, lass. If no one knows you are a woman, you would be taken for a lad."

She fingered the hilt of the knife she wore in her belt. "If it gets too rough, I have a weapon."

"I would not count on that to persuade someone to leave you alone," Louis said.

"Aye, lass," Jamie agreed. "Everyone here carries a weapon and knows how to use it."

The small group turned down a side street. Catana noticed a sign above a tavern door and stopped to read it. A donkey pulling a creaking cart came around the corner, forcing her to jump aside. She almost stumbled over a one-legged beggar sitting in the doorway. She looked down the street and saw the crewmen from the *Seahawk* turn into the tavern and sighed with relief as Louis and Jamie continued on their way. Detouring around the donkey cart, she ran to join the two men.

"We are going into the Naughty Lady," Jamie said gesturing to another tavern several doors down. "You sure you dinna want to return to the *Seahawk?*"

"No, I would rather remain with you."

Catana followed Louis and Jamie inside. Everyone seemed to carry one kind of weapon or another. Several men stared at them as they entered; their eyes full of challenge.

Catana boldly strode behind her two companions to an empty table, sat down, and ordered a tankard of grog from a serving girl.

"Good girl," Jamie whispered. "You gotta show you're not afraid. "If you dinna, they will give you grief."

When the drinks arrived, Catana took a deep swallow of grog to settle her nerves and choked. Gasping for air, she set the tankard down. "*El Diablo,* what is this?"

Jamie took a long gulp and smacked his lips. "I think 'tis their own brew."

"It *is* stronger than we normally drink," Louis admitted, "but good."

Catana leaned over the table toward Jamie and spoke in a quiet voice. "Tell me, what is the special business Orlando has to take care of?"

"He is looking for information on Lancaster. Seems the man has been commissioned to a new ship. Orlando wants to learn where he has gone and shoot the ship out from under him."

Catana pulled her hat down farther on her head. "Is he still devastated about losing Ana to Lancaster and looking for revenge? He must still love her to chance going after the man and putting the *Seahawk* in harms way."

"'Tis not only because of Ana," Jamie replied. "Lancaster did more than lure Ana away from him. He was the reason Orlando and the men of the *Seahawk* were arrested for piracy and put into prison."

Jamie hailed a tavern girl to bring another round of drinks. The buxom woman leaned over Catana to fill Jamie's and Louis's tankards before topping off Catana's. Before the woman drew back, she pinched Catana on the cheek.

"I see ye have a fresh young lad with ye, gentlemen," she said winking at Catana. "Send him to my room later, and I will teach him to be a man."

When the woman continued on her rounds, Jamie and Louis roared with laughter. Catana, determined to keep her irritation under control, fingered the hilt of her knife. It was not polite to kill your friends. She waited patiently until the two men wiped the smirks off their faces. "Now that you have that out of your system," she said in a voice cold as a winter stone, "continue your story of Orlando and Lancaster."

"Orlando is not the only one who seeks revenge on Lancaster. The entire crew would like to reap revenge on the British captain."

"How did Lancaster manage to convince the authorities that the *Seahawk* was a pirate ship?" Catana asked.

"Orlando was a privateer at the time. He had a letter of marquee from the British ruler to defend the king's ships against the Spanish and French."

"Every nation has their privateers," Louis added. "Each country is to respect a letter of marquee."

"Yes, I know," Catana said, waving the remark aside.

"Aye," Jamie continued. "'Tis a rule of the sea that such a letter is shown or the vessel would be considered a pirate ship. Lancaster was aware that Orlando had rich holdings from the many French and Dutch ships he had captured. He also knew that Orlando loved Ana. Lancaster came after Orlando and the *Seahawk*. I guess he figured if he could discredit Orlando and his crew as privateers, he would receive the bounty Orlando had collected and keep it for himself."

Catana drew closer to Jamie and spoke. "How did Lancaster manage to trick Orlando? He is not easily fooled."

"The *Seahawk* was anchored in the bay here at Port Royal. Lancaster sent some of his men aboard one night and murdered the watch. As the crew of the *Seahawk* filtered back to the ship after drinking in a tavern, Lancaster's men captured them. Someone knocked me out as I climbed aboard with a couple of my mates. When Orlando arrived at dawn, his crew was either dead or locked in the hold. I canna describe how frustrated I felt when I heard my Captain's footsteps overhead and had no way to warn him. Because I was first mate, two British guards drug me out of the hold, stood me next to Captain Cordova, and arrested us as pirates."

"Why did Orlando not show his Letter of Marquee?" Louis asked.

"Lancaster came aboard as Orlando presented it to the British soldiers. Lancaster grabbed the letter and placed it in a brazier of hot coals at the foot of the main mast. Orlando and I watched as it burst into flame and the ashes scattered to the wind. Then, Lancaster made the arrest official. We were taken to court—I say it was a fixed trial—and Lancaster won custody of the *Seahawk* along with all our holdings. Ana followed the money and fell into Lancaster's arms, you might say. The British turned us over to the Spanish authorities in Santiago de Cuba."

"Why would they do that?" Catana asked.

"I overheard a guard say that Lancaster feared Orlando would make a plea to Governor Rogers and take the oath."

"The man who has been giving pardons to pirates?" Louis asked.

"Aye. Lancaster knew that the Spanish wouldna make any dealings with the British. We managed to escape, but from then on, we were fugitives and known as pirates. I, Orlando, and the men you met on the beach in Havana managed to escape, but we separated to confuse our pursuers. Orlando and I headed for New Providence and Governor

Woodes Rogers to ask for a pardon for the men of the *Seahawk*. The governor agreed when he heard our story. He was unable to grant freedom to the men imprisoned at Santiago de Cuba because they were under Spanish jurisdiction. He knew the goal of the *Seahawk*'s crew was to settle down and live in peace, and he regretted he could not help them."

"How would Rogers have known that?" Louis asked.

"Because of an earlier encounter with the British governor. A band of pirates who had taken the oath changed their mind and decided to take New Providence and return it to a pirate haven. The *Seahawk* happened to be in the area when the pirates attacked Rogers' ship, and Orlando came to the governor's rescue. Rogers invited us to New Province to give us a reward. When he learned that we planned to give up our lives at sea and settle down, he granted us a deed to land on one of the larger islands. Now that the *Seahawk* and crew are together we would like to see Lancaster get what he deserves before we set out to claim our land." Jamie drained his tankard. "'Tis time for me to go on duty. I think you should return to the ship with me, Catana. I dinna want you to be the cause of destruction to another port."

Catana sat us straight and glared at Jamie. "Do not put the blame all on me, I—"

"We will all return to the ship," Louis interrupted.

* * * *

When they boarded the *Seahawk,* everyone but the watch was asleep. The chilly breeze off the water reminded Catana that she had Jamie's coat in her cabin and offered to fetch it for him. He had the midnight to four watch and would be grateful to have it. Entering the cabin, the lamp burned low and, the room was steeped in shadow. It was not until she reached the peg she noticed the coat was missing.

"I could have sworn I hung it here," she muttered. "Maybe Inez took it." Her cousin was sleeping soundly, and Catana shook her awake. "Where is Jamie's coat?" Inez moaned. Catana shook her until she came awake. "Where is Jamie's coat?"

Sitting up, Inez mumbled, "Ben came for it several hours ago. He said he was taking it to Jamie."

"That is odd. Louis and I were with Jamie all evening, and we saw nothing of Ben."

Inez shrugged. "He is the one who took it."

Catana found Jamie at the bow looking toward the dock. "I am keeping an eye out for the captain. He and Ben are the only ones ashore."

"I did not bring your coat. Seems as if Ben took it. I swear he is obsessed with the garment. He refused to let me use it, and I snatched it from him to cover myself after the prison escape."

Jamie gave her a puzzled look. "What was Ben doing with my coat?"

"He said he was holding it for you."

"Now why would I let him do that? Ben and I barely get along. In fact, we dislike one another. Now he is missing and so is my coat."

Catana brushed an errant lock of hair from her cheek. "Is there something in your coat Ben would want?"

"Not to my knowledge. Unless he stole something from the captain and hid it in my coat. Maybe…ah, there is Orlando. Come, lass, I am anxious to know what he has learned of Lancaster."

As soon as Orlando stepped aboard, he spoke to Jamie and Catana. "I received word that Lancaster has sailed his new ship to Virginia in the colonies. He has two days head start. Do you think the crew is willing to follow him that far?"

"Aye, lad. I do." Jamie replied.

"When I return in the morning, I will call a meeting and the crew can take a vote." Orlando said.

"A vote is the fair way to decide," Jamie agreed. "But where will you be going in the morning?"

"Ana is at Lancaster's estate. When she heard the *Seahawk* was in port, she sent me a message and wants to see me."

"Does she know the reason we are in Port Royal?" Jamie asked. "Maybe it is a trick."

"I do not think so. The note says that she regrets making a terrible mistake and needs to see me. I plan to leave early in the morning, so I bid you good night."

After Orlando disappeared into his cabin, Jamie resumed his position as watch at the bow. Catana followed him, sat on the gunwale, and made herself comfortable.

"I hope the lad does not fall for whatever she tells him," Jamie said in a thoughtful voice. "I would hate to see his heart broken."

"I thought he put his feelings for her behind him."

"So did I, lass. But if he is responding to her note…" He shook his head. "I dinna know."

Catana stood and brushed dirt from the seat of her trousers. "We should follow him in case it is a trap."

"I dinna think it is a good idea. If he caught us, he would disown us."

Catana gave Jamie a wide smile. "Then we will be careful so he will not know."

CHAPTER NINETEEN

In the early dawn, Jamie and Catana peered through dense fog so they would not lose sight of Orlando. They took care to stay out his view in the event he looked back. "Orlando did no' hire a horse, so it must not be far," Jamie whispered as though afraid Orlando would hear hem.

They passed small shanties, and soon buildings gave way to open fields of sugar cane. After walking half a league, a mansion, flanked by pillars, loomed ahead of them. Only a low layer of fog remained, giving the building the appearance it was floating on a cloud. Jamie and Catana ducked behind the trunk of a giant oak when Orlando turned to look back before ascending the steps and walking to a massive wooden door. After several knocks, the door opened and Orlando disappeared inside.

The two observers drew as close to the mansion as they thought safe. Catana fingered the butt of her flintlock pistol that was tucked into the turquoise scarf wrapped around her waist.

"Let us check out the back," Jamie whispered. "Ana could have armed guards hiding there."

They stole to the edge of a flower garden and heard voices from the other side of a hedge. Peeking through the leaves, Catana saw Orlando and Ana sitting on a stone bench near by. Ana was a small woman with raven black hair and delicate features. Her liquid brown eyes looked into his as she spoke. Catana put her finger to her lips to warn Jamie to move in silence then pointed to the couple. Ana's voice carried in the air, and Catana was able to understand what she said. "It is so beautiful here, Orlando. My only pleasure in life is these lovely flowers."

Orlando replied in a bitter voice. "You have wealth and prestige. Is that not the reason you chose Lancaster over me?"

Ana burst into tears and clutched Orlando's hand. "I made a terrible mistake. It is you I truly love. Captain William Lancaster tricked me into believing that you were nothing but a pirate. He said that you attempted to murder him. Now I know he lied. Will you forgive me and take me as yours?"

Catana rolled her eyes, and Jamie shifted uneasily. Neither spoke in fear of being discovered. Catana strained to hear Orlando's answer.

Orlando stood and cleared his throat. "You are betrothed to Lancaster now."

"He will be gone for months. This will give us time to know one another better." She stood and threw herself into his arms. Orlando wrapped his arms around her and bent to whisper in her ear. The scene made Catana angry, and she drew back into the trees before she did something she would regret. Jamie followed. Men were such fools. Didn't he realize Ana was using him? It was his business, but whatever actions he might take would affect the whole crew. Besides anger, she felt hurt for some unknown reason. She shook her head when an absurd thought hit her. *Am I jealous?*

"If Orlando does as she asks," Catana said between clenched teeth, "he is a fool. I cannot blame Orlando for being deceived by her the first time, but if he allows it again, he deserves what happens."

"It only proves that love is blind," Jamie said with a sigh.

Catana turned and glared at Jamie. "Do you think he still loves her?"

"I thought he had gotten over his love for her, but by what we have seen—"

"What of the *Seahawk* and her men?" Catana interrupted. "What of your plans to settle on the island if Orlando decides to make a fool of himself with Ana?

"I dinna know, lass. Maybe Orlando does not love her, but maybe his idea to get revenge on Lancaster is to take Ana away from him.

"Orlando can go to the devil, if that is his plan." Catana turned her back on Jamie and marched toward the road. "I am leaving."

Jamie ran to join her. "My, your feathers are ruffled. I do not think the lad will go so far as to abandon his shipmates and give up his dream of becoming a landowner. Once Ana realized he has little to offer, she would run back to Lancaster. Are you upset, lass, that Orlando might still love the woman?"

Catana stopped and turned to glare at Jamie. "I do not give a fig what that man does as long as it does not endanger the *Seahawk* and crew."

She turned so quickly to continue down the road that she stepped in a rut. A sharp pain ran up her leg as she twisted her ankle and dropped like a sack of rocks onto the sandy soil. Jamie rushed to her side to help her up. When she stood and put pressure on the foot, she felt intense pain.

Jamie supported her to keep the weight off her injured foot. "Come, lass. We better get off the road before Orland starts back to the ship." Leaning heavily on Jamie, Catana hopped along until they were hidden from the road.

Jamie eased her down onto the ground and looked at her ankle. "It is swollen. D'ye think you can make it to the stream just ahead?"

Nodding, Catana got to her feet, and Jamie helped her to the cold, running water. She plunged her foot in to soak. In minutes, her ankle felt better, and she was ready to resume their walk to the *Seahawk*. Through the trees, Catana noticed Orlando pass on his way to Port Royal. Rubbing her ankle, she muttered. "I had hoped we would be back first. Orlando would have never known we were gone."

Jamie helped her to her feet. "We will make up a story of where we have been when we return."

Once Orlando was out of sight, they returned to the road. Catana limped along slowing their pace. The pain grew worse, and she was not certain how much longer she would be able to continue. They stopped to rest under a tree when an ox cart came lumbering down the road. Jamie hailed for the driver, and both travelers hopped into the back of the cart.

When they reached the docks at Port Royal, Catana noticed something strange aboard the *Seahawk*. Her eyes traveled up the main mast where she saw a rope dangling from the yardarm. It was in the shape of a hangman's noose. Slipping behind a cluster of barrels next to the ship, Catana and Jamie saw the deck was full of British soldiers. Orlando was tied to the foot of the main mast. Catana heard an officer dismiss most of the soldiers, and they disappeared toward town. The officer and six of his men remained aboard.

"What d'ye think they did with our crew?" Jamie whispered.

Catana shrugged. "We will have to sneak aboard. It looks as if they plan to hang our captain."

Jamie groaned. "Ana's note was a trap after all. The British officer that has Orlando captive is Captain Lancaster. The story that he departed for the colonies was a ploy to throw us off guard."

"If I had not turned my ankle we would have been here to defend the ship."

"'Tis better we were detained, lass." We would have been dealt the same fate as the rest of the crew, and not be able to help. We must find a way to stop those men."

"How will we get aboard? The gangplank is in view of the soldiers."

Jamie thought for a moment. "They have their attention directed on Orlando. D'ye think ye can climb over the gunwale at the bow?"

Catana peered in that direction. The ship was tied securely to a pylon at both the stem and stern. There was a small gap between the dock and the side of the ship. The gunwale was level with her shoulders. She would have to pull herself up and over using her arms. Staring at it for a moment, she replied, "I think so."

"I will go first and help you," Jamie said. "And try to be quiet."

Jamie ran to the bow in a stooped position. Straightening, he leaped, grabbed the gunwale, pulled himself up, rolled off, and was out of sight. As soon as he showed himself, Catana followed his actions. Leaping from the dock, she grabbed the gunwale. Jamie's strong hands grabbed her wrist and pulled her aboard.

Before Catana was able to draw her flintlock, Jamie shoved her down behind a coil of rope. "Someone is coming this way," he whispered in her ear.

Peeking from behind their hiding place, they watched a British soldier take an ax and cut the mooring line. With her eyes, Catana followed him to the capstan, where he and a second man hoisted the anchor. A third man cut the mooring line at the stern, and the *Seahawk* drifted out to sea at an awkward angle. The British men unfurled the sails, and the vessel was adrift in the current.

"*In el nombre de Dios*, what are they doing?" Catana whispered.

Captain Lancaster slapped Orlando in the face, laughed loudly, and then spoke in a loud voice. "You try to hunt me, Orlando, and fail. Once we are outside the harbor, I will hang you from the yard like a pirate, and then I will set the ship afire. Your crew will never escape the hold, and you all shall die. I and my men will board the *Seahawk*'s longboat where we will take pleasure in watching your demise before we head for shore."

Jamie cocked the hammer back on his pistol. "That son of a sea witch," he said through clenched teeth. "So the crew is locked in the hold. If we do not take action fast, our men will be burned alive."

Catana drew her pistol and pulled back the hammer, ready for an attack.

"There are seven of them and only two of us," Jamie whispered. "Once we get a shot off we will not have time to reload. If we can make it five to two, do you think you can run for the hatch to free the men?"

"Aye, Jamie." Catana took careful aim and slowly pulled the trigger. A thick cloud of sulfurous powder flashed in the pan and a pungent cloud of smoke filled the air as the pistol barked. Her aim was true, and her victim dropped to the deck. A split second later, a second British solder dropped. Smoke from Jamie's pistol swirled around his head, his forefinger still hooked around the trigger. Grabbing his pistol by the barrel, he held it like a club and knocked a third man to the deck.

That left four men to contend with. Catana sprinted toward a hatch, but on her third step, her ankle gave way, and she fell to the deck. Crawling, she reached the hatch and swung her pistol against the lock to break it. A sharp pain in her upper back brought her to a halt. A British soldier stood next to her with his rifle pressed between her shoulder blades. "Get up, missy, and keep your hands in the air."

Catana stood and hobbled in the direction her captor indicated. Only three British men remained, but they had the advantage. One held a gun to Jamie's head while Lancaster pointed his pistol at Orlando. Looking up at the noose hanging from the yard, she noticed movement on a lower boom. Esmeralda sat crouched, blinking her emerald eyes as she watched the action unfold below. Catana cussed under her breath. "After all the trouble I went through to save the cat from burning to death, she is in danger of her life ending that way after all."

The man holding a gun on Catana pushed her forward to join the group at the foot of the mast. She lost her balance as her ankle gave way, and she fell into the man holding a gun on Jamie. In turn, he tripped, fell, and hit the deck. In less than a heartbeat, the orange cat plummeted down and landed claws-first on Lancaster. The British captain dropped his pistol and grabbed at the cat on the back of his neck. Jamie scooped up Lancaster's gun and aimed it at the man who had been covering Catana. While Lancaster thrashed his arms to fend off the cat, Catana pulled her dirk from her sash and crawled to Orlando's side. With several slashes of the blade, she cut through the rawhide thongs that bound his arms and handed him her dirk to finish untying himself. In the confusion, Catana crawled to the hatch, broke the lock, and freed the crew. Once Orlando was free, he took control of the situation. He ordered Lancaster and his men thrown into the longboat and set adrift without oars.

"Why did ye not kill them?" Jamie asked.

Orlando chuckled. "I think the humiliation he will suffer is more of a punishment than death. When the story gets around that he was overpowered by a cat, he will never live it down."

"I am sure he will keep that quiet," Jamie said.

Orlando's grin widened. "Maybe so, but witnesses will tell the tale in taverns. Lancaster has the scratches to verify the story. If I know Ana, he will lose face in her eyes."

Catana stood in silence listening to the two men. Orlando put his hand on her shoulder and looked into her eyes. "Would you respect a man who was bested by a cat?"

Although his touch warmed her heart, she hid her feelings. Women such as Ana seemed more to his taste. To him, she was just one of the crew. "More than a man who was stupid enough to be bested by a woman, twice," she replied. Turning on her heel, she headed for her cabin to make sure Inez had not been hurt and to give Esmeralda a treat.

CHAPTER TWENTY

Once the *Seahawk* was under full sail, Orlando called the crew together for a meeting. Catana joined the group at the foot of the mainmast with Jamie next to her.

Orlando spoke in a loud, clear voice so that Jabulani at the helm, and the several crewmembers busy with the lines, could hear. "We will sail, without stopping, to New Providence. I want to speak to Governor Rogers about our land deeds before Lancaster poisons the governor's mind with his lies."

"I do not understand why you did not kill that son of a sea witch when you had the chance," Tom called out.

A wave of ayes rippled through the crowd.

"When I kill a man," Orlando continued, "it will be in a fair fight." A grin crossed his face. "I prefer to shoot Lancaster's ship out from under him. But that is for another day. Meanwhile, strike a heading for New Providence."

After the crew dispersed, Catana joined Tokala and Louis. "Since Orlando has offered land to all those who crew the *Seahawk*," Louis said, "I have been seriously thinking about accepting his offer like you and Jabulani, Tokala."

The news shocked Catana. "What of our return to Santa Maria?"

"Why not join us, Catana?" Tokala asked.

"I always thought we would return home someday."

Louis took her hand. "That is your dream. I no longer desire to return to Mobile or Santa Maria and the life I once led. Jabulani's dream is to live as a free man and own land. It is also true with Tokala. This is a chance to start a new life."

Tears welled in Catana's eyes. "I have no future here. I have my heart set on returning to Santa Maria. My father promised to return to me there. Inez has her mother to consider."

"Inez has also decided to remain here. We have grown close, and I hope to marry her some day."

"I understand," Catana said thoughtfully. She turned to leave, but Louis grabbed her arm. "If you remain here, we will seek out your father and you can be reunited.

"I have no idea where to look for him."

"You have his letters. Maybe there is a clue in them."

Catana shook her head with sadness. "The last one I received was two years ago. It was from Havana, but no one knew of him when I asked."

Taking her hand, Louis gave it a squeeze. "Think about it. We have several days before our arrival in New Providence."

When Catana entered the cabin, she bought up the subject. "Inez, are you truly planning to remain in the islands to settle down? What of our return to Santa Maria?"

"Is not it exciting? Louis wants me to be with him."

"What of your mother?

"She made a choice to remain at Saint Joseph's Bay. I am a grown woman, and I choose to remain with Louis."

* * * *

For the next few days, Catana had trouble sleeping. Her mind whirred with confusion as she tried to decide which path to take. Standing watch at the bow on the third morning of their voyage, Catana scanned the waters. As the sun rose ruddy in a sky full of mist, she noticed the sea was full of long swells. Into her second hour on watch, the trade winds died, and the air grew still. Looking east, she noticed a rolling mass of clouds on the horizon that towered like mountain peaks. She hunted for Jamie and found him in the galley eating. "There is a storm in the distance. It is heading in our direction." Jamie nodded and continued to eat. Catana continued. "We should notify the captain."

"We will let him sleep a bit," Jamie replied. "Orlando covered two four-hour watches last night because one of the crew was feeling poorly. I'll take care of it." Draining his tankard, Jamie stood and followed Catana onto deck. Looking at the bank of clouds, he rubbed his chin. "Normally we do not encounter severe storms this time of year, but this one looks evil."

Jamie shouted over the wind that had come up. "Jump lively, men. Furl the sails and close the hatches." Men dashed up ratlines; every yard of canvas was out. If they did not furl the sails quickly, they would pay the price with a broken mast.

"What can I do to help?" Catana cried over the howling wind.

Jamie grabbed her arm. "Go below. The crew will take care of the *Seahawk.*"

"But—"

"No buts. A good ship like this will ride the wind if we rig her tackles to the tiller. Once the storm hits, we all will go below to ride her out. Go now. Inez will be frightened, and you can comfort her." Rushing away, Jamie joined the crew to secure the ship.

Catana grabbed a line as the ship dipped, and the bowsprit touched the rough sea spraying the deck. A piece of canvas came undone and flapped wildly in the wind. If the whole piece tore loose, it would snap the bowsprit. Catana grasped the storm line and tied it around her waist to keep from washing overboard. She attempted several times to grab the line that twisted and coiled in the wind. With all her strength, she secured the canvas to the bowsprit with the line and sank to the deck exhausted. The swells were coming higher and more frequent. There was no way she would make her way across the deck to her cabin. The yaw and pitch of the ship was too violent. Pressed against the bulkhead with her storm line secured to the top rail she sat on the deck to wait out the storm.

The ship groaned and creaked. Walls of water crashed over the bow; the waves became mountainous. The *Seahawk* climbed with each swell then crashed abruptly into the valley. She attempted to stand, but her lower legs grew heavy as the ship rose with a huge swell. The weight left quickly as the ship plunged. As she slid to a sitting position, white foam spilled over the bow and washed down the foredeck. The wind tore and pulled at her hair, and she brushed the blowing strands out of her eyes. Catana gripped her lifeline so tight that her fingernails dug into the palms of her hands. The rush of water washed away anything not lashed down. Wiping saltwater from her eyes, she looked up at the blocks, halyards, and spars dancing in the wind and huddled farther against the bulkhead.

A sound of a loud crack brought her eyes to the main mast. Through the curtain of rain, she saw the top half of the mast plunging down toward the deck in a mass of ropes. The spar, shroud lines, sheets, and halyards came crashing down to the deck and trailed out over the gunwale on the port side. She sat helpless as she observed the destruction around her. Where were Captain Cordova, Jamie, and the crew? There was no sign of anyone. Were they below deck, or had they been washed overboard? What if she was the only one remaining aboard? "Don't panic," she told herself and remembered Jamie saying the crew would ride out the storm below.

When it grew too dark to see, the wind and rough seas grew more frightening. Several hours after dark the wind lessened, and the rain stopped. Although the seas calmed slightly, they remained rough. The ship rose and fell, but it did not seem so treating. Exhausted, Catana fell asleep.

A sudden jolt threw her head against the bulkhead forcing her awake. It was dawn. Wreckage littered the deck from stern to bow. Spars and ropes hung from the shattered mast. She heard voices. The crew scurried to and fro while Orlando stood on the bridge issuing orders to cut the ropes and to clear away the debris. The crew took axes and freed the top of the mast. She watched it slide into the sea, trailing long lines like arms on an octopus.

Catana tried to get to her feet to join them but was so weak she could not stand. The waves were high, but the sky was clear and a golden sun lifted out of the sea turning the water to burnished bronze.

"There be land ahead," one of the crew shouted.

"We still have a rudder," Orlando called out. "Jabulani, steer her for the island. The surge of the storm will carry us ashore."

Pulling herself up, Catana stood on wobbly legs and trained her eyes on the horizon. An island came into view through an early morning mist; a dark smudge in the distance. As the *Seahawk* drew closer, she saw clouds hanging over the mountains and a white curving beach glistening in a sheltered cove. Dark trees fringed the shore and rose in thick profusion up the slopes.

The crew shouted as they tried to control the path of the ship through the channel into the cove. Both Orlando and Jabulani fought the wheel as claws of stone reached out toward the ship. They were so close that Catana could see the masses of seaweed that choked the rocks.

A large swell lifted the *Seahawk* and flung her toward a reef, but the rocks disappeared below the boiling water and the ship rose high. Her keel scraped along the rocks and hit one so hard that Catana was thrown to the deck. The ship lifted with another wave, and the *Seahawk* darted between the headlands, through the channel, and into a quiet lagoon where the ship was protected from the full force of the heavy seas. Jabulani and Orlando held the wheel and pointed the bow directly toward shore.

Catana braced herself as the hull hit the sand. The deck trembled as the ship came to a sudden halt and canted to the port, throwing everyone off balance. The crew scrambled ashore and Catana was close behind. Soon everyone was assembled around Orlando while he gave instructions. "First, we will pump the bilges, then repair the storm damage to the hull, mast, and rigging."

Each man knew his job, and the crew disbursed to go to work. Inez caught Catana's eye and rushed to her side. "I was so frightened when you did not return to our cabin," Inez said with concern on her face. Catana took her cousin by the arm and led her to a fallen log. Signaling for her to sit, she explained why she had spent the night on deck.

* * * *

They were fortunate to have come ashore on an island with fresh water. By the time the crew found, cut, and trimmed a tree to replace the main mast, they had been ashore for over a week. Catana and Inez were unable to help with the heavy repairs but spent the days splicing broken lines.

On the evening before they were ready to continue their voyage to New Providence, everyone gathered around a blazing campfire to celebrate the resurrection of the *Seahawk*. Inez was deep in conversation with Louis, while Tokala, Jabulani, and Jamie sat with the crew drinking grog and telling ribald jokes. Catana's heart skipped a beat when Orlando approached her and sat down. She was in no mood to talk to him. The last time they spoke had been an unpleasant experience for her.

Orlando cleared his throat. "Are you still angry with me?"

Catana shrugged. She did not want him to know how emotionally confused she became when she was around him. "What makes you think I am angry?"

"It was the way you spoke to me. What were you implying when you said that I was stupid enough to be bested by a woman twice?"

Catana opened her mouth to answer, but thought it unwise and snapped it shut. She did not want him to learn that she and Jamie had followed him and knew of his meeting with Ana.

"I…I do not remember saying such a thing."

"You are upset about something. Louis told me you are not interested in a share of land. There is plenty for everyone."

"I have decided to take Louis's advice. Once all of you are settled, I plan seek out my father." She had no definite plans on how she would accomplish the task but did not think returning to Santa Maria and waiting for him was the answer.

"Let us help you. Then you and your father can join us on the island."

Catana shifted uncomfortably. "I would rather look for him on my own."

Orlando gave her puzzled look and was about to speak, but before he could utter a word, she stood and left.

Why did she feel so uneasy around Orlando these days? She grabbed a blanket and wrapped it around herself. To get her mind off

Orlando, she turned her attention to the full moon and thought how this was the perfect time for their departure. With a full moon, the morning tide would be at its highest point. This would help set the *Seahawk* afloat. The only thing the crew would have to do is untie the lines and give her a bit of a push. Soon she would be on her way out to sea.

At daybreak, everyone boarded the ship except three men. Each on a line, they would pull the ship into deep water when the tide was at its peak and would climb aboard when the *Seahawk* was afloat. Catana felt the motion of the ship as the water lifted and righted her. The ship slowly backed off the sandy shore as the tide turned and she floated free. The men on the ropes turned her so her bow pointed toward the channel. Jabulani, at the helm, lined her up to run her through the dangerous opening and onto the open sea. The crew swarmed up the shrouds and out along the yards to unfurl the sails. The canvas billowed, and it shown in the sunlight like a soaring gull. The ship surged forward, and Catana turned to watch the ship furrow the blue water with a line of foam. The roar of waves broke on the reef at channel entrance. The ship was heading toward an outcrop of rocks.

"Starboard the helm," Orlando shouted. "Hand over." The schooner spun on her keel, her top sails flapping in the wind. The ship slid past the booming surf pounding the rocks, and the open sea swelled under them. Flapping sails turned into the thumping of tight canvas. The *Seahawk* threw up her bow as the ocean slid under her. Catana had not realized that she was holding her breath and let it out with relief. They were on their way to New Providence, and soon Orlando and his crew would realize their dreams. Now she had to decide her future.

CHAPTER TWENTY-ONE

Before entering the harbor at New Providence, the *Seahawk* veered to the starboard to parallel the coast. Catana stood at the bow with Inez where Louis joined them.

"I thought we were going into port," Catana said when she noticed the change of direction.

"Orlando wants to anchor off shore in a cove east of the settlement," Louis replied. "Because we were delayed by the storm, Lancaster could have easily arrived first and turned Rogers against us."

"I am so tired of this ship," Inez said in a dejected voice. "I was looking forward to setting foot on land."

Louis slipped his arm around her waist and smiled down at her. "It will not be long, my dear. Orlando, Tokala, and I will be away a few hours. Once we know it is safe, we will put into port and go ashore."

Catana dressed in comfortable loose trousers and a blouse. She looked down at the turquoise sash cinched around her waist. "Let me fetch my flintlock, and I will go with you."

Louis grabbed her arm. "No. You might draw attention, and I am sure if Lancaster has told his version of the story around New Providence, it will include a description of you."

Catana was about to protest when Louis changed the subject. "Do you see those ships along the wharf?" he asked. "At one time, they would have belonged to pirates from all over the Caribbean. They attracted women of pleasure, con artists, and drug sellers to the island.

Such famous men as Henry Morgan and Edward Teach, also known as Black Beard, visited these shores."

"Aye," Jamie added as he joined them. "They are all dead, or have disappeared, now. When I was last here, the water along the shore was clogged with remnants of broken spars, casks, smashed fruit, and dead fish. Neglected ships sat in the bay with half-rotted hulls. When we went ashore, the heavy smell of rum and garbage permeated the air. Since the arrival of Governor Rogers several years ago, New Providence has been cleaned up."

Louis shook his head. "I understand there are still a number of pirates sailing the seas."

"Aye," Jamie replied. "Many took the oath but returned to their former ways. Others, such as Calico Jack, Anne Bonny, and Mary Read never bothered and are hunted in these waters.

"The two notorious women pirates are still terrorizing the seas?" Louis asked.

Jamie shrugged. "The last I heard they roam the Caribbean. They were last seen—"

"Jamie," Catana interrupted. "If I promise to keep out of the way, can I go ashore with you? I do not want to sit aboard the ship and wait. I could wear a hat and pretend to be a cabin boy, again."

"I dinna think Orlando wants anyone but Louis and Tokala to go with him. He believes the less that go the less chance one of us will be recognized. Why d'ye not stay here wi' me, lass, and we can play a game of chess and have a bit of rum while waiting in the captain's cabin?"

Half an hour later, Catana stood at the rail watching while four men at the oars of a small dinghy pulled away from the *Seahawk* and headed for the shore. Jabulani had been asked to join the landing party. Inez was in their cabin taking a nap, so Catana took Jamie up on his offer and joined him in the captain's cabin. A large smile crossed his face when she entered and sat across the table from him. He reached for the chessboard and handed her a full cup of Jamaican rum.

The two became so involved with their game that neither had realized how much time passed nor how much rum they drank. Catana was deep in thought, planning her next move, when a sharp rap on the door brought her out of her reverie. At Jamie's summons, Damien entered.

"Sir," the tall lanky man said, approaching them, "it has been over five hours since the captain went ashore, and now it is growing dark. I am concerned something has happened. I think we should take a group of men and look for him."

Jamie sat back in his chair thoughtfully. "I think it best that only two men go ashore, scout around, and return with whatever information they have learned. We dinna want to fall into a trap, if there is one. Nor do we want to alert Lancaster's men if all is well."

"Aye, sir," Damien replied. "Who do you plan to send ashore?"

Catana, feeling brave and uninhibited, answered him. "I believe Jamie and I will undertake that duty. You remain here and in charge of the *Seahawk*. If you see us returning in a hurry, have the ship ready to sail." Damian looked at her, turned to Jamie, and shrugged.

"Do as she says, man. You are in charge of the *Seahawk*. Come, lass, let's get under way." Damian stood with his mouth open in dismay as Catana and Jamie left the cabin.

Jamie grunted with each pull of the oar as he and Catana headed toward shore in a dingy. Catana took up a second set of oars and put her back into helping him. They were rowing against the tide, and by the time they beached the small boat, they had sobered up considerably.

"Now what is your plan, lass?" he asked as they strode down the beach toward the waterfront buildings.

"I thought that if we went into a tavern and mingled with the crowd we would hear the latest gossip."

"That's your plan? It dinna sound promising."

Catana stopped and put her hands on her hips. "Do you have a better one?"

Jamie shook his head and they continued in silence toward the buildings on the outskirts of town. Catana fingered her flintlock pistol stuffed into the sash around her waist, hidden by the generous folds of her oversized shirt. She pulled the wide-brimmed hat further down on her head.

Dusk was closing in, and a man was lighting the lamps along the pier. The cry of seagulls grew silent as they roosted for the night. Jamie guided Catana into a large common room at a tavern called The Bucket of Blood. As the made their way to an empty table in a dark corner, she collided with two sailors. They were arguing over a woman dressed in a gaudy dress. The collision almost made Catana lose her hat. Grabbing it, she pulled down further over her head.

"Watch where ye go, lad," one of the sailors warned. He sneered at Catana and stumbled on his way.

After she and Jamie were seated, Catana took a deep breath and let out a sigh of relief. Jamie ordered two tankards of rum. When the barmaid set the drinks on the table, Catana pushed hers away. "I do not want anything to drink. I have had enough for one day."

"Ye must drink some of it or it won't look right. Whoever heard of a sailor coming into a tavern and no' have a drink?"

Catana reluctantly picked up the tankard. The liquid was fire burning down her throat and her stomach. Tears came to her eyes, and she whipped them away with the sleeve of her shirt. She had the feeling she was being watched and noticed someone was standing close behind her. Turning slowly, she looked up into the face of a woman. Her bright red hair stuck out like she had come out of a strong wind, and as she leaned over, one of her heavy bosoms brushed against Catana's cheek. "Be needing a woman, lad?"

When Catana turned to Jamie for help, she saw his hand over his mouth and his shoulders were shaking in silent laughter.

"Me thinks ye won't regret it," the woman continued in a sultry voice and winked. "I know how to please a young lad, and I can teach you a thing or two."

Catana moved her chair to back away from the large breasts that strained to free themselves from the woman's bodice. The chair leg caught in a crack between two planks and toppled, spilling Catana to the floor like a sack of rocks. A roar of laughter filled the room as all eyes were trained on her. Once the noise died down to a few titters, the woman bent low, smiled broadly, and spoke in a loud voice. "I've had men fall for me before, but not so hard."

Another uproar of laughter filled the room, and Jamie came to Catana's rescue. "Leave the lad alone, miss. I think you have embarrassed him." Then he, too, burst into laughter.

A brawny sailor stepped out of the crowd and grabbed the redheaded woman by the waist. "Do not waste your time with an amateur when you can have a man like me. Come and let me show you a thing or two."

Catana picked herself up off the floor and with her back to the crowd readjusted her flintlock. It was fortunate the pistol had not fallen out. By the time she was settled back into her chair, the crowd had dispersed and had their attention on two sailors doing a jig on one of the tables.

"So much for staying inconspicuous," Catana said dryly.

"Think of the attention ye would have receive if y'er hat fell off."

"I do not want to imagine the consequences." Catana picked up the tankard and, forgetting the contents, took a deep swallow. She choked and sputtered until Jamie slapped her on the back so she could catch her breath.

"I am ready to return to the ship," she gasped. "This was a bad plan.

Jamie grasped her hand. "Do not be feeling sorry for yourself, lass. We came ashore to help Orlando and your friends."

Taking a shuddering breath, Catana straightened her back. "You are right. But I have no clue what to do next. We are not learning anything here." Scanning the room, her eyes rested on a familiar figure. She tugged on Jamie's sleeve to get his attention. "Is that our missing crewman, Ben?"

Jamie squinted in the direction she indicated and nodded. "Aye, and the lummox is wearing the coat he stole from me."

Lumbering to his feet, Jamie headed toward the truant crewman with Catana in his wake. Before they reached Ben, he ducked out the door. Jamie pushed through the crowd, flew out the door, and saw Ben rounding a corner into an alley. Catana was on Jamie's heels as they charged into the narrow passage between buildings. She plowed into him when he came to an abrupt halt. Seven men blocked their way, and seven flintlock pistols were pointed at them. Without a word, Ben stepped forward and relieved Jamie of his pistol. Catana was conscious of the pistol she concealed as Ben stepped in front of her. "I recognize you. You are one of the gerls from the *Dove* and the last one to wear this coat."

"Aye," she agreed. "And I see you now have it."

"That I do, lass, but it's missing something, and I want it."

Catana looked toward Jamie. He shrugged and spoke. "What are ye talking about, Ben?"

Ben pushed the muzzle of his pistol against Jamie's throat. "Don't be playing games with me."

One of the men with Ben looked around nervously. "I think we should be discussing in a more private place. Someone might come along and see us."

Ben jerked the pistol away from Jamie and pointed it toward the end of the alley. "You be right, Gus. We'll take them to the ship."

With two men in front, one to each side, and three behind Catana and Jamie, the small group marched down the alley until they came to the dock where a small sloop was anchored. Ben and his men herded their prisoners aboard. Catana wrinkled her nose at the odor of human waste mixed with the smell of rum that floated from the hold. The rotting deck boards creaked under their feet. She marveled that the vessel was even afloat. Ben stopped them at the foot of the ships main mast, picked up a piece of hemp line from the deck, and bound Catana and Jamie to the foot of the mast.

Ben held up Jamie's coat with one hand, waved his pistol at them with the other, and continued the conversation he had started in the alley. "I want you to be telling me what you scurvy people did with the map hidden in the lining of this coat. If you won't be telling me soon, you will be dancing the devil's jig from the yardarm."

Catana's eyes followed the direction Ben pointed his pistol and stared at the yard hanging high above their heads. "Honestly, I have no idea what you are talking about, Ben."

"Nor do I," Jamie added.

"The map, ye ijits. The one Orlando had in his desk and Bart took."

"Why would ye think it was in the lining of my coat?" Jamie asked with a grunt.

"'Cause that's where Bart hid it. Now it's gone and one or both of you have it."

Jamie thought for a moment. "Why would you or Bart want the map that shows the location of the land grant Governor Rogers gave us? Do you and your men plan to settle down and take up farming?"

"Don't try to fool me. I know it's the map to the treasure Henry Morgan hid on Isla del Espieritu Santo."

Jamie chuckled softly. "Sorry to disappoint you, but it is only a map to the island that Rogers gave to the crew of the *Seahawk*. If you and Bart looked closely, you would have noticed a letter attached that explains the map. That is why we have returned to New Providence. It is to have Governor Rogers issue a new map and letter to replace the missing ones."

Ben glared at Jamie. "You know Bart and I don't read. I think you are telling me a story."

Catana stood silent listening to the conversation and mulled over what they were saying in her mind. Was this the letter and map that Inez had found? Was that what everyone was looking for? If so, once she and Jamie got out of this mess—if they got out of this mess—she would turn it over to Orlando. They could leave New Providence and sail on to the island without the worry of running into Lancaster.

"I swear to ye on the pirate's oath that neither Catana nor I have the map."

Ben cleared his throat. "Tell you what I'll do. I'll give you 'till sunrise to remember where you put the map. No lies, no telling me it doesn't lead to Henry Morgan's treasure because Bart would not have risked becoming marooned for a piece of land." With a wave of his gun, Ben turned and strode away. His men followed like a pack of wolves.

Bound to the mast back to back, Jamie faced the bow; Catana faced the stern. Catana looked up at the yardarm, and tugged on the ropes that bound them. "It is your turn to think of a plan, Jamie."

After taking the sloop out into the middle of the bay, Ben left two men on deck to guard the prisoners. At first, the guards stood with flintlock pistols trained on the two prisoners. As the evening wore on the guards grew restless. The tall one, who had an ugly scar that ran down his left cheek, put his pistol in his bandoleer. "I don't think we need to be holding our guns on 'em, Pete. They're not going nowhere."

Pete, a short man with a toothless grin, nodded and slipped his gun into a sash tied around his waist. "How much longer do we have to be on guard?"

"Ben said two hours and then he'd send Gus and Mick out so we can have a few drinks, too."

While the two guards were engaged in conversation, Catana worked her dirk from her sleeve to her hand and began sawing at the piece hemp line that was bound around her hips. She was thankful the pirates had not searched her for weapons. The awkward angle made slow work. The guards were far enough away that Catana was able to speak to Jamie in a low voice without being overheard. "It sounds like the crew is already celebrating our demise."

"Aye, that is good, lass. How are you coming with the ropes?"

"I think I am halfway through. By the time they change the watch, I should be able to have the ropes loose enough to step out. The way the men are laughing and carrying on, the new guards will not be alert, and we should overtake them easily."

Catana continued to cut. Her hand was cramping, and she prayed she would not drop the dirk. It almost slipped out of her hand when the last strands of the rope snapped. It was completely dark now with only the light of a lamp hanging from one of the shroud lines at the bow. The prisoners were in deep shadows. The guards were not watching them closely and seemed more interested in going off duty.

"It's been more than two hours," Pete grumbled. "I'm getting mighty thirsty."

"Do you think they forgot about us?" the tall guard asked. "Go and remind Gus and Mick that it's their turn to guard the prisoners. I can watch these two on my own."

Pete scurried off toward the captain's cabin and the noisy crew, while the man guarding them leaned against the rail to wait.

Catana freed her arm and proceeded to attack a second strand of rope that crossed her chest. "Pete has disappeared into the cabin," she whispered. "I think I can have us free before he or the others return. What shall we do once we are out of these ropes?"

"The element of surprise works wonders when you lack numbers," Jamie replied. "The crew has been drinking heavily and willna expect trouble. Our greatest concern is the sober guard."

Catana sliced through the second round of rope and slipped out as the coils fell to the deck. With the stealth of a cat, she made her way toward the cabin and slid behind a water barrel. Picking up a discarded pulley, she tossed it toward the guard. When it hit the deck, the guard swung toward the noise and turned his back to where Catana hid. She bolted from behind the barrel like a fired cannon ball, hit the guard in the back of his knees, and knocked him to the deck, giving Jamie time to pull out of his ropes and dash to her aid.

The guard lay sprawled on his stomach and was attempting to get to his feet when Jamie landed with both knees on the man's back. Catana pulled her flintlock from her sash, brought it up, and slammed the butt of the gun onto the back of the guard's head. A loud groan escaped the man's lips before he went limp.

"That takes care of one," Catana said breathing heavily. "What of the others?"

Jamie stood and dusted off his hands. "We will lock them in the cabin. They are so engrossed with drinking they willna realize they are prisoners until morning.

"What about Pete?"

"I think he joined the others and forgot about his partner." Jamie went to the rail and looked out across the water at the distant lights on land. "We are too far from shore to swim, lass. Best we take their dinghy." After Jamie and Catana lowered the small boat into the dark water he pointed the bow toward the string of lights that lined the shore.

Settling onto the bench at the bow, Jamie took up the oars. "I hate the idea that those poor excuses for seamen got away with threatening us."

Catana looked down at her dirk. "We can do something that will make them think twice before they mess with us again."

"What do you have in mind, lass?"

"Row to the stern of the ship. We will cut their anchor rope." Taking her dirk, Catana cut through the anchor line. Once the ship was loose, it swung around with the current barely missing the dinghy.

"Grab the other set of oars," Jamie shouted.

Catana took the oars in hand and set her back into helping Jamie row. The bow of the dinghy rose with the forward motion as they headed for shore. Once they were clear and on their way, Catana chuckled. The pirate sloop was drifting sideways toward the open sea. "They will awake in the middle of nowhere, or if they go aground on a sandbar, they will be out of commission for several days."

Catana and Jamie did not have to row long before the hull scraped the sands of the beach. Climbing out, they pulled the small craft above the tide line and trudged through the sand toward the docks. The tide had carried them farther down the beach than they expected and Catana felt exhausted. "I need to stop and rest for awhile."

They slumped onto a dune and sat listening to the waves roll ashore. "I know where the map and letter are," she said over the roar of the surf. She pulled a stem of oat grass from the sand and thoughtfully chewed on its end. "I did not realize it was the map that Orlando lost." She continued to explain how Inez had found it and they had put the two documents in the box containing Catana's letters. "As you see, it is not necessary for Governor Rogers to issue new documents."

"Aye, this is good news. Now, if Orlando, Louis, Jabulani, and Tokala are safely aboard the *Seahawk*, we have nothing more to worry about and can be on our way with the morning tide."

CHAPTER
TWENTY-TWO

After Orlando, Louis, Tokala, and Jabulani departed on a *Seahawk* dinghy, they landed on the beach at New Providence and pulled the small boat beyond the tide line, hiding it in a cluster of oak shrubs.

"I pray Lancaster has not come near the governor," Louis remarked as he sat down to catch his breath. "I am more than ready to claim our land and settle down in peace."

"Aye," Orlando said, joining Louis on the sand. "I am tired of these games with Lancaster. Mind you, if he comes looking for trouble, it will be my pleasure to cut him down a peg or two."

Tokala sat next to Orlando and clapped him on the shoulder. "What happened to the revenge you wanted?"

Orlando shrugged. "He is no longer worth pursuing. I prefer to concentrate on our visit to Woodes Rogers and regaining the deed to our land.

Jabulani sat and took a deep breath of air. "Ah, to have land and freedom, what more could a man want?"

Once rested, the four men stood and strode down the beach toward the waterfront of New Providence. "There is always gossip floating around the docks," Orlando said. "If we keep alert, we might learn something."

Jabulani rubbed his stomach. "I am hungry. Can we stop at an inn and eat first?"

The men wove through barrels of rum, bundles of colorful cloth, and various items sitting on the dock that stevedores were unloading from a merchant ship. "At one time most of this would have been pirate booty," Orlando informed his companions. "Now that Rogers has cleaned up the Caribbean, there are no longer stolen goods for sale in New Providence.

"A pity," Louis said. "I heard the pirates sold their items at a low cost and there was a better variety."

"True," Orlando replied, "but it put a number of reputable merchants out of business."

Entering a small tavern, the men made their way to a table next to three men eating their mid-day meal. Once the tavern girl had delivered their orders, Louis and his companions sat eating in silence. A man at the next table spoke in a gravely voice. "When we are finished loading the ship, there is not another due until tomorrow."

A large man with close-set eyes replied. "Aye, and the cargo for this vessel will not be ready for two days. The merchant traffic has been slow."

The smallest man in the group spoke next and Louis was surprised at his deep voice. "'Tis because of those bloody papists. Those sons of dogs are threatening to regain their hold on the islands and return the Caribbean to Spanish waters."

The big man laughed. "Let them try. Governor Rogers will force them to back down."

"Aye," the man with the gravel voice replied. "But with the governor spending all his time cleaning the waters of pirates, he does not have the men to fight the Spanish if they come in full force. He will need help from British warships, and there has not been one around in weeks."

Orlando leaned over his table and spoke in a low voice. "If Lancaster's warship had been here, everyone would have noticed."

"Do you think it is safe to visit the governor?" Louis asked.

"Aye," Orlando replied. "When we finish our meal, we will go to his office."

* * * *

The governor's office was in a large building at the end of the town square. Rogers' secretary, a man who reminded Louis of a crane, led them down a hallway to a large oak door. The four visitors remained out in the hall while the governor's secretary went into his office to announce their arrival. The secretary reappeared and ushered them inside. The governor, a tall and distinguished-looking man, stood behind his desk with a smile on his face and extended his hand toward Orlando. "It is a pleasure to see you again, Captain Cordova."

Orlando grasped the governor's hand and shook it. "It is my pleasure to see you, sir." He introduced his companions and relayed the purpose of their visit.

"I am sorry that I cannot help you, gentlemen," the governor said with regret. "It is too late to lay claim to the island. The Spanish are in position of La Isla del Espiritu Santo. I have neither the men nor time to fight and recapture the island. The Spanish are gathering a fleet in Havana and plan to attack New Providence."

Louis looked at Orlando. His friend's reaction mirrored his own. Their dream to become landowners was now impossible.

The governor sat down in his chair, and his face showed no emotion. "I sent a message to have British warships come to my aid, but I do not know if they will arrive in time.

"Orlando," he said in a voice hard as stone, "I received information that you are wanted by the British as a pirate. It is difficult for me to believe that you broke your oath after all the help you have given me." He gave a deep sigh.

Orlando took this opportunity to explain to the governor what Lancaster had done. Rogers thought about what Orlando had said for a moment. "I never did like Lancaster and his pompous ways, but if I allow you to break your oath, and I do not order a punishment, it would ruin my reputation. Other pirates would feel they have the right to go back on their oaths without retribution."

"But, sir," Orlando pleaded. "We did not break our oath."

"I realize that, son, but the British military does not. Unless we conduct a trial and find you innocent, I have no choice but to imprison you."

Louis felt a hard knot tighten in his stomach. First they lost their land, now they would be imprisoned for piracy.

The governor cleared his throat. "Does anyone know that you have come here?"

"No, only my crew," Orlando replied.

"Where is your ship anchored?"

"It is hidden in a cove. The four of us came ashore quietly. We wanted to be certain Lancaster was not in New Providence."

The governor stood. "This is good. If you return to your ship immediately and sail away, this meeting never happened and I have no idea where you are. Do you understand?"

"Aye, sir," all four men said in unison.

"Then take leave of me before someone realizes you have come here."

Louis followed Orlando out the door with Tokala, and Jabulani close behind. They ambled along the docks as to not draw attention and headed for their dinghy. They were passing a line of pine trees along the beach when six British solders emerged from the woods with six flintlock rifles trained on the four men. Louis realized immediately that to try to fight or escape would be certain death.

When a voice came out of the trees, Orlando's face drained of color. "Lancaster," Orlando said between clenched teeth

"Where is the rest of your crew?" the British captain asked, stepping up to Orlando. Louis shook with anger when he noticed the sneer on Lancaster's face.

Orlando answered in a calm voice. "Our ship sank in a storm. We four are the only survivors."

Lancaster's eyes narrowed with suspicion. "How is it you are here in New Providence?"

"The *Seahawk* went down in a shipping lane and a merchant vessel picked us up," Orlando replied.

"How fortunate," Lancaster said and lifted his rifle a little higher. "I sailed my private schooner here days ago with the hope you would come. My wait was not in vain. I have special plans for you and your friends. It is too bad the others died and cannot be with you." The British captain gave his men a knowing nod, and before the prisoners took their next breath, the butt of a rifle smashed into each head.

* * * *

Louis thought fireworks were going off in his head as he slowly came awake. His eyes fluttered open to a dimly lit room. He lay on a stone floor with piles of straw along the edge of a stone wall. The smell of ammonia mixed with dung made his stomach churn. When he tried to sit, a streak of bright light flashed before his eyes, and a sharp pain ripped trough his head. He closed his eyes and lay still. To move was to hurt.

Hearing a rustle in the straw, Louis slowly opened his eyes and made out the form of Tokala sitting, holding his head. Louis's mind swirled in chaos. What happened? Where was he? The curtain of confusion slowly lifted. The last thing he remembered was a rifle butt hitting him in the back of the head, then nothing. He tried to speak. "Tokala, are you all right?"

The Indian groaned. "I will be fine. "Orlando is coming around, but Jabulani is as still as stone. I am afraid he has been badly injured."

It took several hours before the men were able to clear their heads, to sit, and to talk. Jabulani still lay unconscious, but he moaned softly. The dim room turned pitch black. Since the men could not see and were too weak to stand, they lay down to sleep.

Louis opened his eyes and saw the light of dawn creep through a small window. The pain in his head had lessened, and he was able to sit up and survey the room. The window was inches below an eight-foot ceiling. The only exit was a heavy wooden door bound in horizontal iron straps near the top, in the middle, and near the bottom. It would be impossible to break through.

176

Orlando stirred and came awake. "How is Jabulani?"

"I think he is better," Tokala said and sat up next to the black man. "He seems to be sleeping peacefully. Rest will help him heal faster."

Louis jumped when the door hinges creaked, and the door slowly swung inward allowing in more light and air. An arm quickly deposited a loaf of bread and jug of water, slipped out of sight, and the door slammed shut. Tokala crawled to the offering, picked up the bread, and threw it down in disgust.

"Infested with weevils," he grunted. Returning to his companions with the water, they each drank a share and saved some for Jabulani.

On the second day of imprisonment, Lancaster came to visit. The four prisoners were setting against the wall on a pile of straw and in deep conversation plotting to escape when the door flew open. Lancaster stood in the frame with three armed guards behind him.

"I see you gentlemen are feeling well enough to go to work," the British captain said with a sneer.

"Where are we?" Orlando demanded, choking down his anger.

"You will learn soon," Lancaster replied. "Guards, take these men to the building site and turn them over to my overseer, Mr. Hastings." Lancaster stepped aside to let the guards through the doorway. With three rifles trained on them, the four prisoners had no choice but to allow the guards to prod them down a stone hallway and out into the bright midmorning light.

It was a short walk to where men worked under the supervision of a bull-like man holding a whip. If any of the workers hesitated in their duties, or stopped to rest, they felt the sting of the whip.

"Mr. Hastings," one of the guards shouted, "the captain has sent four more workers."

The big man lumbered toward Louis and his friends. Standing with his arms crossed in front of his barrel chest, he glared at them and then spoke.

"Do you see those guards around the perimeter of the construction area? If you make one twitch to escape, they have been ordered to shoot."

Louis scanned the area and noticed men of various races and colors lugging heavy rocks up a ramp and placing them atop a stone wall while others set them in place with mortar.

The four new prisoners were put to work hauling heavy stones up the ramp. For Tokala and Jabulani, the work seemed easy. Orlando wavered at times under the weight, but Louis, who was the smallest of the group, struggled and felt the bite of the lash often. As the sun sunk behind a line of trees, even Jabulani was struggling.

Soon it was too dark to work and the crew of prisoners was herded through a tunnel into a large cave-like room. Seven guards trained their rifles on the thirty workers as they lined up in front of a man next to a large pot sitting on a small table. The man slopped a ladle of gruel into a wooden bowel and handed it to each man in turn. After they received their evening meal, they silently walked to a long table with benches lined on each side. Sitting, they stared at the wall like zombies. Louis and his companions were last in line, and the men at the table made room for the newcomers.

Once the last ladle of food had been doled out, the cook hefted the pot from the table and strode out the door. The guards kept their weapons trained on the prisoners while backing out of the room. The door closed with a bang and Louis heard the bolt slide into place.

The room erupted with the sound of voices. Some swore. Others muttered of their unjust fate. Louis got the attention of a dark skinned man across the table from him. "Can you tell us where we are?"

The man spoke with an accent Louis did not recognize. "We are on an island Captain Lancaster claims as his. Most of the men here once called this our home. He has enslaved my village and put us to work building a fortress.

"Where are your women and children?" Orlando asked.

"They work outside the fortress walls raising crops and preparing food for this evil man and his army.

"If you are a native of this island," Louis asked, "can you tell us about the lay of the land? We plan to escape, and it would help us."

The native smiled sadly. "I will talk to you after the meal. Someone will be here soon to collect the bowls. What is not eaten when they arrive will be taken away."

178

The men quickly returned to eating. The gruel was tasteless but contained no weevils, and it filled the emptiness in a Louis' stomach. He was taking his last bite when he door flew open. Soldiers entered and stood guard while two men collected wooden bowls, spoons, and cups.

Louis settled next to Orlando in a corner of the large room. Tokala and Jabulani joined them after relieving themselves in a trench of water running along the edge of a wall. The four discussed the information they had learned from the native. It was difficult to determine where he had gone. The only light in the room came from four torches set in brackets on each wall. Louis looked up when a shadow blocked out what little light there was. The native hunkered down and spoke in a low voice. "My name is Madri. We will talk so no one will overhear. There may be those who would tell the captain.

Orlando nodded. "It would not surprise me if Lancaster planted spies."

Madri made himself comfortable on the straw. "My island has good land for farming to the north. This part is covered in trees and rocks. The shore is made up of high cliffs with sharp rocks at the bottom. We are imprisoned at one of the many caves that honeycomb the hills."

"Where are we in relationship to the sea?" Orlando asked.

"Not far. The captain builds his fortress atop a cliff that overlooks the water. The tunnel to this cave comes out in the center of his fortress. At this stage, he has the perimeter walls completed. We are erecting the walls of what will become his living quarters."

Louis rubbed his temple where a dull pain was growing sharper. "Are there no other tunnels out of the cave?

"There is another way out," Madri replied, "but it runs underwater and no one knows how far."

"Has anyone ever tried to escape?" Louis asked.

Madri shook his head sadly. "Mr. Hastings threatened that anyone who tries will pay with torture and the life of their families. I have a wife and three young children. No one wants to take a chance."

Orlando placed his hand on the natives shoulder. "Thank you for the information. With it, my friends and I might devise a way to escape.

If we succeed, we will do what we can to rid this island of Lancaster and return your home to you and your people."

After Madri departed, the men of the *Seahawk* put their heads together to plan their escape.

CHAPTER TWENTY-THREE

Back in New Providence, Catana and Jamie returned to the *Seahawk* and were disappointed to learn that Orlando, Luis, Tokala, and Jabulani were still missing.

"It is late," Jamie said. "There is no one available this time of night to question. Tomorrow we will visit the governor. He might know something."

"What if the governor responsible is for the men's disappearance?" Catana asked. "We could fall into a trap."

Jamie thought for a moment. "You may be right. Let's get some sleep. With a fresh mind in the morning, we will think of a way to get information without putting ourselves in jeopardy.

Inez was in a state of anguish when Catana entered their cabin. Sobbing, she flew across the room to embrace Catana. "Louis is dead. I just know it. How can I possibly go on without him?"

Catana hugged her cousin and stepped back. "There has been no word of anyone killed. Jamie and I will continue our search in the morning."

"I want to come with you. Waiting here is unnerving."

"I promise Louis and the men will be back with us soon. Now try and sleep. We will need all our wits for tomorrow."

Catana slept fitfully. She should not have made a promise she was not sure she could keep. Would the governor be able to help, or was he under the influence of Lancaster?

At dawn, a seed of an idea grew in Catana's mind as she lay in her bunk. By the time the sun rose out of the sea, the idea burst into full bloom. Sliding from her bunk, she woke Inez. "Get dressed. Put on your finest so we can call on the governor."

Catana went to a trunk in the corner of the cabin. Orlando had offered it and the contents to the two women when he assigned them the cabin. Where he had gotten it, she did not know. Pulling out a corset, she looked at it and sighed. *The things I must endure to gain information.*

Inez slipped into a buttercup frock that set off her dark hair while Catana donned a mint green one. Both dresses were tight in the bodice, full in the skirt, and trimmed with ribbons and lace. Inez handed Catana her parasol. "Do not forget, proper ladies must protect their skin from the sun."

Catana grabbed it and charged onto deck to look for Jamie. He stood at the rail staring across the water toward the island. Tapping him on the shoulder, she batted her eyelashes at him when he turned to face her. "Would you mind rowing us ashore? Inez and I are going to visit Governor Woodes Rogers."

"Not alone and dressed all fancy like that, you willna."

"I have an idea how we can get information without exposing ourselves" Catana replied in a serious tone.

"And what might that be, lass?"

While Catana explained, Jamie nodded. "Aye, it might work, but I will send a couple of the crew with you for protection."

Catana hesitated. "I will agree only if they stay outside."

Jamie remained aboard to keep the ship in readiness in case they had to flee. He assigned Percy, who insisted on dressing in a flamboyant outfit of tight, buff colored breeches, red brocade coat over a snow-white shirt with lace at the cuffs and a cravat. Catana had seldom seen him dressed less than perfect. The second escort was Tom. Both Catana and Inez enjoyed his easygoing ways.

When the dinghy's keel scraped onto the sandy shore Tom jumped out and pulled the small craft by a rope until there was dry ground under foot. Percy stepped out carefully so he would not get his shoes wet and the two men assisted the women from the boat.

As they strode toward the governors house Catana gave instructions to the two escorts. "Remember, gentlemen, stay out of our way unless Inez and I come under attack."

"Aye, miss," Tom replied. "And I…" Tom's voice faded as Catana and Inez picked up their pace and hurried across the green. The governor's house was two stories high; walls covered with white wash. Above the front door, a balcony framed the second story windows. The rail of the balcony supported a flagpole flying the British Union Jack.

The two women stepped onto the porch, and Catana took a deep breath before knocking. A man dressed in a servant's uniform opened the door wide enough to expose himself.

"We have come to see Governor Rogers," Catana informed him.

"Is he expecting you?"

"No," Inez replied, "but we are in need of his help."

"We think the governor can assist us," Catana added.

"Very well, ladies. I will check with Governor Rogers and return shortly."

After the servant closed the door, Catana paced back and forth on the stone porch "I hope he agrees to see us. Everything is such a mess. Orlando is pursued by the British, you, Louis and I by Captain Carvajal and the French, and the Spanish are at war with everyone. I only wish—" The door opened before Catana finished what she was saying.

"Governor Rogers has agreed to see you," the servant said. "Follow me."

The servant led them down a hall, past several doors, and into a library. Books lined two walls from floor to ceiling. Under a window on the back wall, a man faced them from behind a large desk. He rose as they entered, offered them a seat on a settee that faced him, and sat once they were settled. He was a rugged-looking gentleman who looked as if he spent his younger years at sea. The two paintings of sailing ships that flanked the window at each side enforced Catana's impression of him.

"Good morning, ladies. I understand you are in need of help."

"Yes, sir. Do you know Captain Lancaster and Captain Orlando Cordova?"

The governor gave the two women a suspicious look. "I have heard both names."

"I and my cousin are in a quandary," Catana said and wrung her hands. Inez nodded in agreement. Catana continued. "Captain Lancaster has disappeared, and we have had no word from him in weeks. Have you any idea where we would find him?"

The governor leaned forward over his desk. "Why would this concern you?"

"Captain Lancaster is married to Ana, Inez's' sister, and she is in a panic thinking something has happened. He departed home several months ago in his new warship for New Providence."

The governor shook his head. "I have not seen the man in over a year."

"Oh dear, Ana will be so disappointed when we tell her the news, Inez."

"I would not worry, ladies," the governor reassured them. "What I know of Captain Lancaster, he can take care of himself. He could have returned home and is now in the arms of his wife. What does this have to do with Captain Cordova?"

Inez spoke up. "Orlando and Lancaster had a falling out. He is also missing. We are afraid they encountered one another and fought. Orlando could have been killed."

"Or Captain Lancaster," Catana added. "I do not understand why men fight over foolish reasons. Although, it was Orlando's fault."

"How can you say that?" Inez spat. "Captain Lancaster had no call to put Orlando on the defensive and brand him a pirate. He is no pirate."

Catana stood, put her hands on her hips, and glared down at her cousin. "Are you sure? Captain Lancaster seemed to know what he was talking about when he made the charge."

Inez stood and glared back at Catana. "Of course I am sure. Lancaster only made those false accusations to—"

"Ladies, ladies," the Governor interrupted. "I can assure you Lancaster has done nothing to Orlando. Granted, the British want him for piracy and if he were to step into this room now, it would be my duty to arrest him."

"Was he here?" Inez asked in an anxious voice.

"That I cannot say. I did hear he was on the island not long ago but has left." The two women looked at each other in puzzlement.

"I am sorry I cannot help. I have told you all that I can."

Catana gave him a slight nod. "Thank you, sir. Come, Inez. Why you chose a man who is an enemy of your sister's I will never know."

Once they were outside the governor's house, Inez broke into tears. Catana put a reassuring hand on her shoulder. "At least we know Lancaster has not been around. That means Orlando is here somewhere and the men were not arrested. I am sure the governor would have said as much if they had been."

"But we still have no idea where they are," Inez said with a sniff.

"My mind was so occupied with the meeting that I forgot to eat. Let us find Percy and Tom and look for a place. I'm hungry"

"I am not going into a tavern dressed like this," Inez replied.

"There are places a woman can go to eat without entering a tavern. Jamie told me of a place along the town square where wealthy go to dine. I have a few coins. Percy and Tom are dressed properly to go into such an establishment. Once we have eaten we will think of what we should do next."

The two women searched the shops and found no sigh of the men. "When I told them to stay out of sight they took me at my word," Catana mumbled. "We will eat without them, and look later."

Catana and Inez entered an arched doorway into a dinning area set up with tables covered in fine linen. Inez's eyes grew large as she looked around. "I have never been in such an elegant place."

Their silk skirts swished with each step as they entered into the dining room. As they glided toward an empty table near a large window overlooking the street, a gentleman dressed in black formal attire intercepted and escorted them to the table. Catana took a chair where she could look out across the green.

"Look at this, Catana, the table is set with real china and crystal. I feel like I am in a real court."

Catana turned her attention to her cousin and looked into eyes that sparkled with enjoyment, not tears.

"Would you ladies like a glass of wine with your meal?" Catana looked up at a striking young man who stood waiting for an answer.

"Yes, that would be fine," Inez answered in a haughty manner then leaned over the table after the waiter left and spoke to Catana in a low tone. "My mother once told me that when she visited with royalty in Spain, they had servants waiting on tables much like this."

Catana turned, scanned the room, and noticed two richly dressed men at a table. There were couples at three tables, and in one corner, two men and a woman sat dining and talking. She wore enough gold to fill a small treasure chest. Everyone in the room was attired in the latest fashions from Europe.

The young man returned with crystal glasses of ruby red wine on a tray and set one before each of the ladies. He recited a list of culinary delights. Catana and Inez decided on red snapper and sipped their wine while waiting for their order.

Catana licked the last drop of wine from her lips. "I almost wish it was a treasure map."

"What map?"

"The one you found next to the beached ship. Remember? The one in the box with my father's letters."

"I remember. But how do you know it is not a treasure map?"

Catana told her cousin of her adventure with Jamie and how Ben had kidnapped them. "So you see," she ended, "it is the map Orlando has been searching for. Ben thinks it leads to Henry Morgan's buried treasure.

As she was explaining to Inez who Henry Morgan was, she sensed a presence behind her. Turning, she looked up into Ben's smiling face and felt cold hard steel pressed to the back of her neck.

"Make one bloody move and I will shoot a hole right through ye, lass."

Catana smiled sweetly at him. "Why not join us for a glass of wine. Inez, do you remember Ben? He was a crewman when we were on the *Dove*."

Looking over the old pirate, Catana noticed how well dress he was. He wore a lace cravat loosely tied at his neck. His red waistcoat was trimmed in gold braid and he wore a leather belt with a large brass buckle. His black leather sea boots looked new. A smile played around her mouth as she wondered where he had stolen his outfit, "Come, Ben, join us." She said again and motioned to an empty chair at their table. "Mayhap we can settle our differences peacefully."

"I'll listen to what you have to say, but no tricks or I will blow ye away."

Catana held up her hand, "No tricks, I swear."

Ben kept his eyes on Catana and slid into the chair across from her. There, he kept his flintlock trained on her from under the table. "If I did not want the whereabouts of the map, I would shoot ye on the spot. It took us all day to get our ship back into the water. We thought our goose was cooked when Lancaster's schooner came into view. He must have been in a hurry to get to his island, for he did not notice us and sailed on by. If he had come after us, we were too helpless to defend ourselves."

Catana sat in silence for a moment before speaking. "From which direction was Lancaster coming?"

"I seen his schooner tied in a cove off New Providence several days ago. We was able to avoid him until you—"

"Where was he going?" Inez cut in.

"To his island, I told ye."

"Where is his island?" Catana asked.

"Now, why should I be telling ye that?"

"We need to know," Inez pleaded. "We think Lancaster has kidnapped some of our crewmen."

Ben chuckled. "That's why he didn't bother with us. He already found himself some slaves."

"Slaves?" both women responded at once.

"Aye, that scurvy son of a sea witch is building a fortress on an island. He has enslaved all the natives there and is trolling other islands for unsuspecting men to work on his building."

"How do you know this? Catana asked.

"Seen it for myself, I did. Ole Ben here gets around."

Catana stood quickly. Ben raised his flintlock and pointed it at her heart. "Don't be making any moves or ye be dead."

Catana sank back down into her seat. "Tell us, please, where is the island?"

"I'll be making a deal with ye. Give me the map and I will lead ye to Lancaster."

"No tricks?" Catana asked.

"No tricks, lass. I swear on the brotherhood of the coast." Catana ordered a meal for Ben, and as they ate they put together their plan.

CHAPTER TWENTY-FOUR

After Catana, Inez, and Ben finished their meal and stepped outside, Tom and Percy appeared with pistols drawn. Catana realized that no one in the crew except Jamie knew of Ben's treachery. "Easy men, it's only Ben."

"Aye," Tom replied squinting at the pirate. "I didn't recognize you dressed in those fancy duds." Both men returned their weapons to their belts, but Catana could tell by their faces that they did so reluctantly.

"Ben has information that will help us." Catana said.

Percy leaned toward Catana and spoke for her ears alone. "I do not trust him. When he was with our crew, he stole from me."

"He is our only lead," Catana whispered back. "We have no choice but to trust him."

Clearing her throat, Catana spoke loud enough for everyone to hear. "Ben has his own ship and crew. He has offered to lead us to where Lancaster is holding our Captain, Louis, Tokala, and Jabulani as slaves."

"Aye, I'm anchored off the point where ye…well, you know the place, lass. Have the *Seahawk* meet us there and I will lead the way."

* * * *

On boarding the *Seahawk*, Catana sought out Jamie and explained her pact with Ben. The Scotsman sputtered and fumed until Catana made him realize it was their only hope.

189

She entered her cabin to change into trousers and a loose-fitting blouse. Inez had already put on a simple cotton dress. Going to the wooden chest, Catana pulled out the box with her father's letters. Opening it she found the map with a letter attached.

"If those papers are so important to Orlando, why are you giving them to that scoundrel?" Inez asked.

"Would you rather have Louis alive and without land than lost to us?"

"Alive under any circumstances," Inez replied. "But what will Ben do when he learns it is a map to land, not a treasure?"

"I will assure him this is the map he was seeking. I am not responsible for what he thinks it is."

"If Louis and the men did not see Governor Rogers, then they were unable to receive a new map."

Catana shrugged. "There is no reason we cannot make a copy. We will keep the letter. I have learned some English, and it looks like a deed to the property. Ben's interest is the map. He will not want the other document."

"Once he has the map, what if he attacks us instead of leading us to the island?"

"I do not think Ben and his crew is a match for the *Seahawk*. His best interest would to abide by our deal."

As promised, Ben's ship was waiting at Dolphin Point. They followed in the wake of the *Vengeance* toward the west. It was not until the next morning that Catana saw the pirate ship drop anchor. She ran to the captain's cabin, snatched the spyglass from the table, and ran to the starboard rail. In the distance, she saw a dark smudge and trained the glass on it. It was an island, but was it *the* island. The *Vengeance* bobbed in the water while the *Seahawk* plowed up next to her.

"That is Lancaster's island," Ben called out and pointed to the spot on the horizon. "Now give me my map."

"How do we know it is the proper island?" Jamie called back.

"If you train your glass on the starboard side of the land, you will see that it drops as a sheer cliff into the sea. Lancaster is building his fortress atop that cliff."

Catana handed the glass to Jamie who studied the island carefully. "It seems he is telling the truth," Jamie said thoughtfully.

Catana pulled the map from her belt pouch. Looking at it, she asked Jamie, "how are we to get the map to Ben?"

"We will hook the two ships at stem and stern with grappling hooks, and he can come aboard the *Seahawk*."

The sea was smooth as glass and soon the two ships were bound as one. "I'll be wanting the lass to bring the map to me," Ben called.

It took several minutes for Catana to convince Jamie it was safe for her to board the *Vengeance*. Holding a rope secured to a yard, she climbed onto the rail of the *Seahawk* and swung onto the deck of the *Vengeance*, landing in front of Ben. She pulled out the map and unfolded it. "Is this the map you have been seeking?"

Ben looked it over carefully. "Aye, lass, this be the one."

"Can you give us more information about the island and its layout?"

"This is all I will do for ye. I know little about the place and plan to go no closer. You and your shipmates are on your own. Now I will bid you farewell and be on my way."

After Catana returned to the *Seahawk* and the *Vengeance* sailed away, she picked up the spyglass to study the island.

"'Tis best we sail out of sight," Jamie said, coming to stand next to her. "If we can see them, they can see us. We will sail south until we can no longer be seen, then we will turn and steer a course to the other side of the island."

According to a sketch on their charts, it was a small island with a rugged coast and many coves. Jamie studied the shoreline on the west side and noticed an opening in the cliffs. Looking at the chart, he pointed out channel that led into a cove. "We will hide the *Seahawk* there."

"What if Lancaster has men guarding the entrance?" Catana asked.

Jamie lifted the spyglass. "I dona see a sign of anyone."

Catana took the glass from Jamie and trained it on the passage through the cliffs. "Ben said that Lancaster sailed here in a schooner. Do you think it is anchored in that cove?"

191

Jamie shrugged. "I saw no sign of it on the east side of the island. If we find it, we must capture the crew without firing cannons. The sound would alert everyone on the island."

"Aye," Damien added joining them. "It will be dark when we enter the cove. We can sail close and capture the ship before they realize we are there."

Night shrouded the entrance to the cove as the *Seahawk* approached. A quarter moon, rising from the sea, shed no light. Catana heard the waves crashing against the rocks on both sides as the *Seahawk* slowly slid between the high walls. White caps cast an unearthly glow from the phosphorus in the water.

The map indicated it was a straight passage, and Jabulani lined the ship up to the center and held her steady. The space between the walls was barely wide enough to navigate safely. Catana climbed forward on the bow and positioned herself between the bowsprit and starboard rail to watch for darker objects in the dark sea. The tide was coming in, and the wind had picked up. The crew shortened the sails. Griping a lantern in one hand, Catana eased up the bowsprit as the ship cleaved her way through the water and left a trail of phosphorous foam. When the ship was well over the water, Catana peered into the darkness for rocks. The ship creaked and groaned as the tide carried it farther toward the cove. She held the lantern in front of her. The light reflected off claws of stone reaching out from each side toward the ship. They were so close that she could see the masses of seaweed that choked the rocks. The keel scraped along a rock, and the whole ship shuddered, shook itself free, and slid into deeper water. It seemed forever before the cliffs fell away and the *Seahawk* glided into the cove. Catana quickly doused the lamp.

The moon was higher and shed a ghostly light on the water. There was no sign of Lancaster's schooner. Taking the *Seahawk* as close to shore as they dare, they anchored for the night.

Jamie gathered the crew at the foot of the mainmast. "In the morning we will go ashore and learn the lay of the land before we make plans for a rescue."

* * * *

The crew spent three days learning the topography of the island, but they were unable to gain knowledge of the layout inside the fortress. All they knew was that it was a large area enclosed by a stone wall atop the cliff on the eastern shore. They watched from a hidden area among the pines while a small group of men, guarded by soldiers, filed out of a heavy wooden door set in the wall. Catana split away from the others and, undercover, followed them to a steep hill where men worked digging out large rocks and putting them into carts. The horses that pulled them were small and underfed. Catana could not imagine how the poor animals were able to pull something so heavy up a hill to the fortress walls.

Catana stole from the scene to find Jamie and Tom, who were scouting nearby, and led them to where the slaves labored. Jamie lifted his spyglass and scanned the prisoner's faces. "I dona recognize any of them."

A shot rang out. Catana covered her mouth to stifle a scream. Jamie moved the spyglass in the direction of the sound. "A guard shot one of he prisoners."

"Can you tell why?" Catana asked in a whisper.

Tom stretched his neck to get a better view. "It looks like the prisoner made an attempt to run."

"Is he dead?" Tears welled in Catana's eyes.

"I canna tell, lass. He isna moving. Those guards are savages," he added through clenched teeth. "One of them knocked the poor lad in the head with the butt of his rifle. My guess is that he is dead."

"Look," Tom pointed to the workers "The carts are full and everyone is leaving."

Jamie, Catana, and Tom watched in silence while the horses struggled up the slope toward the gate of the fortress. The slaves trailed behind the carts, and the guards followed with rifles.

When the massive wooden door slammed shut behind the last man, Catana rushed to the prone body on the ground. She put her fingers against his neck and found a faint heartbeat. "He is still alive," she announced. "We must hide him and find Damien. He has the most knowledge in treating wounds."

They made a litter by lacing vines between two strong branches. Jamie and Tom lifted the wounded man while Catana slipped the litter under him. They drug the man to the shelter of the trees where no one would see them.

"I will look for Damien," Tom said.

Jamie gestured toward the south. "He and Percy went in that direction. Catana, do you think you can check the wound? It does not look as if he is bleeding heavily."

Catana removed her dirk from the sash around her waist and cut the man's shirt away from the wound. The musket ball had entered his left side but was not deep. "Damien should be able to remove that without a problem," she muttered under her breath. Tearing a strip of cloth from the man's shirt, she handed it to Jamie. "Will you take this to that stream nearby and wet it for me?"

When Jamie returned, she applied the cloth lightly to the wound. She administered more pressure to clean away the dry blood and the man moaned softly but remained unconscious.

Minutes later, Tom appeared with Damien close behind. Hunkering down, Damien examined the wound. "I do not think the ball has gone deep enough to hit anything vital. I will need to remove it before it becomes inflamed. What worries me is that such a wound should not render a man unconscious for so long."

"That would be from the blow on the back of his head." Catana said. "A bloody guard struck him with his rifle once he was down."

Damien gave Catana a wary smile. "It sounds like you have been learning English from Ben." He prodded the wound with his fingers. "It would be best if I could remove this before the man awakes. Catana, hand me your dirk and find something in which to fetch water."

Catana searched the area and found a powder horn a guard either discarded or lost. She washed it out in the stream, filled it, and returned to her companions. The amount of blood that poured from the hole in the man's side made Catana feel faint. She managed to hand the horn of water to Damien with a steady hand. He washed away the blood and packed apiece of cloth into the wound.

"Press on this, Catana, until I can bind it." He tore several strips of cloth from the remaining material of the wounded man's shirt, tied them together, wrapped it around his waist several times, and tied it tightly.

With Damien in front and Tom in the rear, they carried the wounded man on the litter, while Catana and Jamie followed. They made slow progress, and it was not until sunset that they boarded the *Seahawk*.

* * * *

The man did not regain consciousness until midmorning of the next day. Inez was with him in the captain's cabin when he showed signs of reviving. Inez called for Jamie, and soon the whole crew was crowded around the captain's door. Catana pushed her way through to her cousin. "Has he said anything?"

Inez shook her head.

Jamie came barging through the crowd and ordered the men on duty back to work. "Damien, do ye think he is strong enough to talk?"

"I would give him some time and a bit of rum first."

Catana and Inez went to their cabin to wait. Catana's heart was pounding in anticipation to learn if Orlando, Louis, Tokala, and Jabulani were alive and in the fortress. Esmeralda lay in a patch of sunlight in the floor, and Catana sank down to stroke the ugly orange cat. It seemed to calm her nerves. It was Inez, more than the wait that made her edgy. Her cousin's nerves seemed tighter than a bowstring, and her tension was infectious.

There was a loud wrap on the door. Inez screeched, and Esmeralda jumped to her feet, hissing. "Come in," Catana called, keeping her voice steady.

Jamie entered. "I was able to learn that the captain and others are imprisoned in the fortress. The wounded man is Spanish and knows little English. I need you ladies to translate when he feels well enough to talk."

"How soon will that be?" Inez asked in an anxious voice.

"Damien thinks that after a meal and a little more rest he will be able to answer all our questions."

It was evening before Jamie summoned the women. "Bring paper, pen, and ink. He will draw a diagram of where the men are being held. He said there are tunnels and caves throughout the underground area in the cliffs."

Catana and Inez spoke with the injured man for more than two hours. When they came away, they had the information they needed to plan their rescue. He had drawn a sketch of the interior of the fortress and had given it to them.

Catana handed it to Jamie. After studying it at length, Jamie sighed deeply. "It dosna look to be an easy task. Lancaster has been through. I see little chance of rescue. I think the first thing we must do is find a way into the fortress."

CHAPTER
TWENTY-FIVE

There were two ways into the fortress. One was through the heavily guarded door. The other was an underground tunnel submerged in water. "No one has been able to hold their breath long enough to successfully swim the length," Juan, the injured man, told the ladies. "I have heard there are certain areas along the way where there are air pockets during low tide, but no one has ever escaped."

Catana found Jamie pacing the deck. She stopped him to relay the information. While they stood at the rail looking toward the island, she added, "Juan also said that Lancaster left the island several days ago in his schooner to join his crew on his new warship."

"With him out of the way," Jamie grumbled, "we might be able to outsmart the guards and the overseer, but how I would love to get my hands around that man's neck and squeeze the life out of him." Jamie strode to the captain's cabin mumbling. "We must find a way inside the fortress."

Catana stood at the rail staring at the island. Not able to think of a plan she sighed deeply, turned, and ambled to a wooden barrel where apples were stored. There were only a few left in the bottom, and she had to bend over its side to reach one. Grabbing a piece of fruit, she stood upright and a thought struck her. She ran across the deck and burst into the captain's cabin. "Jamie I have an idea how we can get into the fortress. How many empty barrels do we have aboard?"

After Jamie gave orders for the crew to search the *Seahawk*, the men collected five empty barrels and gathered at the foot of the mainmast. Catana stood on a barrel and addressed the men in a loud, clear voice. "Before we attempt my plan, let me explain how it will work. When Louis and I were in Santa Maria, we experimented with something we had read about and were able to remain underwater for a long period of time. I had forgotten about it until today. Damien, fetch me a glass bottle and I will demonstrate."

When Damien returned, she took the bottle and slammed it against the mast breaking off the neck. She led the men to a water barrel, and they gathered around. Holding the broken bottle, she continued to speak. "Pretend this is an empty barrel. When I plunge it into the water only a portion fills leaving an air pocket at the top." The men took turns to look closely at the bottle with the trapped air. "If we do the same with the barrels, we can travel under water through the tunnel until we are inside the fortress."

"I dona think it will work," Jamie said. "Did ye ever try to sink a barrel of air? It would have to sink far enough to go through the passage."

"Louis and I weighted our barrel down. The deeper we wanted to go, the more weight."

Damien ran his fingers through his hair. "The plan sounds a bit loony, but it might work. How will we be able to see where we are going?"

"It will be a bit tricky," Catana replied. "If we go while the tide is coming in, the water will carry us through the passage. Juan said the other end opens into a pool in a large cave."

"Is the passage large enough to accommodate the size of the barrels?" Percy asked.

Catana turned to Juan and asked the question in Spanish. He answered and Catana translated for the crew. "A prisoner tried to escape. After he swam a short distance into the tunnel, his lungs burned, and it grew too dark to see. He turned back. He told us the opening was taller than a man and wide enough that he could extend his arms full length on each side. He was a large man so that would give us the room we need.

"That is only from that end." Catana continued. "I am a good swimmer and will check the tunnel from this end."

Later that day, Juan rowed Catana to the base of the cliff where the opening to the cave was submerged. She filled her lungs with air and dove into the water. The water was clear and she had no problem finding the opening in the rocks. It was larger than she had imagined. Twice the size of what Juan had described at the opposite end.

She was in an entirely different world under water. Sun reflected off the coral-covered walls. Tropical fish in blues, yellows, and iridescent colors swam along side of her, then, as one, they darted away. Colors faded to blue then purple until everything was black. She had been so mesmerized by the beauty that she hadn't realized she was running out of air. In a heartbeat, she reversed her direction and focused on swimming toward the light. Her lungs ached, and she grew dizzy. More than anything, she wanted a deep breath of air. A few more seconds and she would be out of the cave. As soon as she was clear, she shot for the surface and gasped for air. Juan pulled her aboard the rowboat where she rested trying to catch her breath. On her return to the ship, Catana assured the crew the tunnel was large enough on this end. Lowering her voice for Jamie's ears alone, she added, "I hope it remains that way all the way through."

Early the next morning, Jamie brought the *Seahawk* as close as he dare to the underwater cave, and the crew prepared for their dive. With only five barrels, Janie ordered Tom to remain aboard ship. They were about to lower the barrels into the water when Damien spoke up. "Do you have a plan of escape?"

"Aye," Jamie replied. "'Tis simple. We will overpower the guards, release our men, and return the way we came."

"Jamie, are you forgetting that we have five barrels, and on the return, there will be nine men?" Percy asked.

Silence hung heavy in the air. Fingering his beard, Jamie spoke. "Seems we were so caught up on getting into the fortress that we dinna think about getting out."

Catana cleared her throat. "What if we took turns? If each of us is able to hold our breath to the count of forty-five while swimming under water, and then traded places with the person in the barrel while they swam, all nine should be able to travel back through the cave to the *Seahawk*. It will be difficult because the tide will be against us on the way back."

Damien shook his head. "I do not like that idea. Will two fit into each barrel?"

"I do not think they are large enough," Catana replied, "but let us give it a try to be certain." After trying several ways to fit two men into a barrel, they realized it was useless.

The five crewmen's heads bobbed on the surface of the water next to five barrels. "Damien," Catana called out. "You can remain in your barrel the entire way back. We will only need four of us to change places. Is that agreeable with all of you?"

"Aye," four voices responded.

Using links of chain, they experimented until they found the right weight to hold the barrel down enough so that only an inch of the wood rim remained above water.

Since Juan knew what to expect on the other end of the underwater passage, it was decided that he would lead. Catana would follow second, then Jamie, Percy and Damien. Catana tied a rope around the lead barrel and ran it through the chain attached to each of the wooden containers. They would traverse through the underwater passage like camels in a caravan.

Juan gave the signal, and the crew dove to swim up under the lower rim of the barrels. Catana could see clearly in the pristine water where the sun reflected off the white sandy bottom. Pulling herself under the rim, she surfaced inside her barrel. The water came to her chest but the remainder was air. She felt the tug of the rope and moved with the motion. "*Madre de Dios*, I hope this works," she said aloud. Her voice sounded strange as it echoed in the thick air.

At first, light reflected into the barrel from the sea floor, but as they continued, it grew dimmer and soon was black as pitch. With the pull of the rope in front, and the push of the water from behind, they moved swiftly and reached their destination in a shorter time than Catana expected. She was able to make out a dim light on the sand beneath her. There was a knock on her barrel, signaling her to leave it and swim to the surface. They were in a large pool inside a cave. Jamie's head popped up next to her like a cork. Then Percy and Damien appeared. Juan had already climbed onto a stone shelf that surrounded the pool and held out his hand to help Catana up. At the end of the cave near an opening, a burning torch in a wall bracket threw enough light for them to see.

Once everyone was out of the pool, Juan led them to the opening. "This tunnel takes you past a second cave where the prisoners are kept, and than it continues on to the yard. A heavy wooden gate with bands of metal is set in the perimeter wall and is the only way out of the fortress. Beyond the gate are the guards.

"Do they have guards on duty within the cave?" Jamie asked and Catana translated.

"Only when they bring in our meals," Juan replied.

"Is the door to where the men are held, locked?" Catana added.

"Sí, at all times." Juan answered. "Only when the men are taken out for a work detail or when the guards bring our meals do they unlock the door." Catana relayed the information to her companions.

Jamie rubbed his chin while he pondered the information. "So, we willna be able to gain entrance until a guard unlocks the door? Men, did you bring your knives?"

"Aye," everyone replied.

"The guards will have guns," Catana reminded him. "Knives or dirks cannot compete with flintlocks."

"That is why we must make a surprise attack, lass."

Juan spoke to Catana and she in turn informed the others. "Since today is Sunday, and Lancaster's men claim to be Christians, there is no work detail today. When the guards come with food, it will give us our opportunity to attack. There is a small barred window in the door. We will let the men know we are here so they can prepare to flee."

They slipped silently down the passageway. Jamie stealthy made his way to the large wooden door and called out Orlando's name while

Catana and the others remained hidden in the shadows. The crew watched while Jamie spoke through the small window then returned with a wide grin on his face. "All four of our men are in there and will be ready when we make our move."

Catana and the rescue crew waited for what seem like an eternity before they heard a noise in the distance. Through dancing shadows cast by the light of three torches on the wall, Catana saw the uniforms of five British soldiers. One carried an iron pot, the others flintlock rifles.

The rescue party stood tense in the shadows as one soldier unlocked the door and the small group of armed men disappeared inside closing the door behind them. Jamie motioned to Catana and the men. They edged toward the door with knives and dirks drawn.

"Now!" Jamie cried.

Jamie threw the door open, and he and his crew rushed into the room. At the same time, Orlando and Louis dove to where the four guards stood behind the table and knocked it over. One of the guards sprang back, bumping the others. Entangled, they fell to the floor. Tokala rammed the man with the pot and spilled the mushy substance onto the floor. In seconds, the cave was filled with fighting.

Catana charged a guard who retrieved his rifle and caught him in the upper arm with her dirk. He dropped his weapon and staggered back, blood seeping onto his uniform. Catana grabbed his rifle and knocked the man unconscious. Orlando sprang past her and struck the barrel of the rifle pointed at her as a guard pulled the trigger. The lead ball whizzed past her ear.

Other prisoners joined the battle, overcame the guards, grabbed the flintlocks, and charged from the room. Jamie, the last one out, slammed the door locking the guards inside. Juan led the way to the pool. The escaped prisoners followed and gathered around the still water.

"How many men do we have here?" Jamie asked Orlando.

"At least twenty."

Jamie shook his head. "Our plan willna work for this many." He showed the prisoners the barrels and explained. "We dona want to leave ye behind. Are there any suggestions?"

"We will go out the main entrance," Orlando replied.

"But there are too many armed guards," Louis protested, "and the gate is locked from the outside."

"How many rifles did we acquire?" Catana asked.

"I have one," Tokala answered.

"And I," shouted one of the prisoners.

Catana glanced at the one she had taken from a guard. "With mine that makes three."

"What good are they?" a man called out. "They have been fired and we have no shot."

"I did not get a rifle, but I did get a horn full of powder," Jabulani said holding it in the air.

Jamie scrubbed his fingers through his hair. "Did any of ye manage to grab led balls?"

They all stood shaking their heads. Orlando stepped forward and faced the crowd. "We will trick the guards into opening the gate and rush out with rifles if front. By the time they realize they are not loaded, we will have overpowered them.

Damien nodded. "I would rather take my chances that way than get back into one of those barrels."

With Orlando in the lead, they ran down the passage past the door where the five guards were imprisoned and into the bright sunlight. They came into a yard surrounded by a ten-foot-high stone wall and faced a large wooden gate, the only way out.

"Whyna climb over the wall to the back." Jamie suggested. "Are there guards patrolling that section?"

Orlando shook his head. "No, but they have no reason to. On the other side of that wall is a hundred foot or more drop onto sharp rocks and the sea. Lancaster had that wall built flush with the edge of the cliff. That leaves us with going through the gate."

Catana strode toward the gate and called out, "Guards, open up!"

There was no response. She called again. "Let us out!"

A voice called back. "What is a woman doing inside the fortress?"

"My friends and I came from the village to entertain the guards. We are now ready to return home."

More silence. Catana and the men waited. Jamie, Orlando, and Louis trained the unloaded rifles on the door. Slowly it opened and two guards appeared.

"Let us through or we'll blast ye," Jamie roared. Before he finished the order, the guards stepped back, swung the door shut and locked it.

Louis shrugged and looked around. "Does anyone else have an idea?"

"How many guards were out there?" Damien asked.

Catana scanned a pile of construction materials against the wall. Quickly she climbed high enough to peek over the edge. She held two fingers up and scurried back to the bottom. "A third man is headed toward a cluster of buildings on our left."

"He is going for reinforcements," Juan informed everyone.

"It will take too long for us to scale the wall," Tokala said. "Several of us might make it to the line of trees, but the guards could shoot us as we came over and we do not know how long it will be before others with loaded rifles will be here."

Catana grabbed the powder horn from Jabulani and ran to Louis. "Do you remember when we almost killed ourselves playing with gunpowder years ago?"

Louis gave her a puzzled look, then his eyes lit up. "Yes, but how…"

"We will use the rifle barrels."

Catana and Louis swiftly broke the stocks from the barrels. Rummaging through the pile of rubble, Catana found six small pieces of wood. She plugged one end of the barrel with wood, poured gunpowder into the metal tube, and plugged the opening with another piece of wood. Attaching a strand of hemp to each end, she had Louis help her hang it on the top hinge of the massive wooden door. Repeating the procedure with the second barrel, she hung it on the lower hinge and jammed the third loaded barrel through the handle of the gate.

"Get a torch," she called to no one in particular. A native rushed to her side to hand her a burning torch. She motioned for everyone to take cover and called out to the guards. "Open the door. We surrender."

Footsteps on the outside of the gate drew closer as she touched the flame to the hemp line attached to the mouth of each barrel. The fire crept along the twine as Catana ducked behind a pile of rocks. The gate ripped apart with a thunderous blast and flames erupted. A fragment of wood flew past Catana's head, and everything around them was engulfed in a billow of smoke. Through the cloud of smoke, Catana saw what was left of the shattered door hanging from one hinge.

A group of soldiers who were running up the hill from the left came to an abrupt halt. Orlando, his crew, and the escaped prisoners rushed through the opening and turned right.

Dusk was closing in and a storm was approaching. The pursued men slipped and slid down the rocks. Catana lost her balance and fell. Scrambling to her feet, she followed her companions. When they entered a grove of trees, Orlando halted everyone and ordered Juan to lead the natives to the *Seahawk.* He and his men lay in ambush for the soldiers. Catana joined Louis behind the trunk of a large tree. "I count thirteen soldiers coming our way," she whispered. "There are only seven of us."

"They think we have gone ahead," Louis whispered back. "Once they pass by, we will attack them from behind."

They waited in silence. The smell of rotted vegetation hung heavy in the thick air. In the distance, a flash of lighting split the sky, and thunder rolled across the hills.

Catana grabbed a thick tree branch that lay on the ground at her feet with hope that it would make an adequate weapon. As the soldiers approached, she crouched and, once they passed, let out her breath.

Orlando gave a hand signal. With rocks and branches as weapons, the crew moved as one to attack. Orlando, Louis, Jabulani, and Tokala closed in on four soldiers lagging to the rear and knocked them unconscious. Swooping up the rifles of the fallen men, they and the crew pursued the nine remaining soldiers.

Two British soldiers turned to face them while seven continued to charge ahead. Orlando and his men ducked behind the trees as two rifles barked at them. It alerted the other soldiers. Orlando took careful aim and shot one of the charging men in the knee. Tokala's shot missed its mark, but Jabulani's was on target, and the ball ripped into the man's chest. Louis exchanged fire with a soldier. The soldier missed. Louis hit the man in the shoulder.

Catana made a quick calculation in her head and decided there were six more flintlock rifles to deal with. The remainders were useless except as clubs. If she could get one or two soldiers to fire and miss, it would improve their odds.

She jumped out from behind the tree and called loudly, "Here I am." A rifle went off as she ducked for safety. A searing pain ripped through her left side. She felt unsteady for a moment but took a deep breath and regained her composure. When a small blossom of blood appeared on her blouse, she pulled her turquoise sash up to cover it. *No need to worry the men*. It hurt, but she would be fine.

Louis must have realized what she was doing and threw a rock behind a second soldier. The man spun around, pulled the trigger, and shot into the trunk of a tree.

"Damien," Orlando whispered loudly. "Take Percy and tie up the soldiers we have downed. I do not want any surprise attacks from them. Use vines that are hanging from the trees." A shot rang out but missed the retreating men.

Catana watched with curiosity as Orlando and Louis cut a piece of vine and stretched it ankle high between two trees. Orland stepped out into the open and waved his arms to get the soldiers attention. When the six men saw him, they bolted in his direction. The lead man tripped over the vine. Those following were unable to stop in time and fell over him. In the confusion, Orlando, Tokala, Louis, and Jabulani dove on top of the fallen soldiers, and within minutes, all the British soldiers were tightly bound. With the return of Damien and Percy, the crew learned that the only soldier dead was the man Jabulani shot in the chest.

"We will leave these men here," Orlando announced. "Their companions in the cave will untie them when they find a way to escape."

As Orlando and the crew continued to the *Seahawk*, the clouds grew heavier, blacker, and thunder rolled across the heavens. Rain fell gently all around, the drops pattering on the leaves. By the time they reached the lagoon, the sky had opened up, and the rain lashed their faces.

Catana pressed her hand against her aching side. When she looked at her palm, it was soaked with a mixture of water and blood. Peering across the dark water, she looked for the ship and saw the silhouette and white sails of the *Seahawk* in a brilliant flash of lighting. Then she passed out.

CHAPTER
TWENTY-SIX

Catana's eyes fluttered open. Orlando looked down at her with concern in his eyes. "Why did you not tell us you had been shot?"

"We were all so busy and it…Am I badly injured?"

"It is only a flesh wound, but you lost a lot of blood. After you passed out, we brought you aboard ship. Damien bound your wound."

Catana tried to sit but felt dizzy and fell back onto the bed. "How long have I been unconscious?"

"It is midmorning, and you are in my cabin. I…we were afraid we were going to lose you."

Catana noticed the concern in his voice. Did he care what happened to her? Up to now his attitude toward her seemed so indifferent. She did not understand why. He easily joked and laughed with the other crewmembers but seldom with her. Maybe she would figure it out at a later time. For now they had to concentrate on their escape.

Questions came flooding into her mind when she realized the *Seahawk* was still at anchor. "Why are we not at sea? Lancaster's men could attack at any time.

Orlando rubbed the back of his neck. "Juan, Madri, and ten of the villagers returned to the fortress during the night. They plan to gather all the British soldiers we tied up in the woods, those locked in the cave, and Hastings, the overseer, and transport them to a near-by island in the village canoes. The island is not far, but it is too far for them to swim back and take revenge on the village women and children."

"That does not explain why we are still at anchor," Catana said.

"We are waiting for their return. Juan, Madri, and several other natives want to join our crew and go after Lancaster to make certain he never bothers their island again."

Orlando slumped down in a chair. Catana felt sadness in her heart when she noticed the haggard look on his face.

"Do you realize we have nowhere to go?" he said in a low voice. "We are fugitives. The British think we are pirates, the French consider us their enemy, the Spanish at war with us as well as all of Europe, and I doubt the Dutch would welcome us." Orlando stood and took Catana's hand. "I thank the Lord that you will be all right. If anything—"

A loud rap on the door interrupted him. "Captain, Juan, and the others have returned," Jamie said as he stepped into the cabin.

Orlando smiled at Catana and released her hand. "I must go now." As he stepped out the door, he called back to Jamie. "Make ready to sail, but before we lift anchor, I want all the crew at the foot of the main mast for a meeting."

Because of Orlando's attention and kindness a warm feeling filled Catana's heart. Was he beginning to look at her as a woman instead of just one of the crew? She sat up slowly. The pain in her side was only a dull ache, "Where do ye think ye are going, lass? Jamie asked.

"I want to attend the meeting."

"Well, get your sea legs first. After I have the ship ready and the crew gathered, I will come back for ye."

Once Jamie was out the door, Catana slid her legs around and sat on the edge of the bunk. When she tried to stand, another bout of dizziness hit her, but once it subsided, she got to her feet. She walked slowly out on to the deck and supported herself against the starboard gunwale until she found a barrel to sit on. Louis saw her and brought Inez with him to join her.

"It is good to see you up and about," her childhood friend said. Inez nodded in agreement and took Catana's hand.

Silence fell over the crew when Orlando stepped in front of the crowd to address them. "We no longer have a port where we are welcome. Nor do we have a country under which we can claim to sail. Does anyone have a suggestion?"

"We can always go on account once more," Jamie shouted.

"Piracy?" Orlando responded.

"Oui," Louis agreed. "We will sail under the flag Inez brought aboard."

"Returning to the brotherhood will put us on the defense," Tom called out.

"We are already on the defense," Jamie replied. "'Tis best we return to the sea and go on the offence."

Murmurs filtered through the crew, and Orlando called for silence. "What say you, men? Are you all in agreement with Jamie?"

Everyone cheered.

Louis bent down and spoke to Catana. "Do you also agree?"

She hesitated and then answered, "Yes. I once thought of pirates as cutthroats, but now I wonder how many were driven to that way of life by people like Lancaster."

"If everyone agrees, so do I," Inez said.

Each person in turn stood before Orlando and placed his left hand on the captain's cutlass, right hand over his heart, and pledged loyalty to the *Seahawk*, the captain, and the code of the brethren.

When it came time for Louis and Inez to swear, Catana stepped in behind them. She was the last to take the oath.

Later that afternoon, Orlando presented a code of conduct he had written and read it to the crew. The articles listed the rules they would follow while aboard the *Seahawk,* and they covered everything from how pilfered cargo would be divided to what punishments would be issued for what crimes. Those who knew how to write signed their names. Those who did not placed an *X* on the paper.

While Catana added her signature, she overheard Jamie speaking to Orlando. "If we plan to face Lancaster and his warship, we will need more firepower. Four cannons and one swivel gun at the stern is not near enough."

The *Seahawk* did not get under way until the evening tide. If luck were with them, they would be through the channel before dark. Jabulani was at the helm and had the ship lined up to run her between the cliffs and out to the open sea. Tokala climbed the shrouds to unfurl the main sail while Tom and Damien worked the jib. Suddenly the sails flew out and filled with a loud crack. The *Seahawk* leaped forward like an arrow released from a bow and drove straight through the water. Catana held tight to the rail and listened to the surge and break of the waves along the walls of the channel. The booming surf against the rocks echoed on both sides. Soon they were through the passage, and the open sea swelled under the ship. The flapping sails turned into tight canvas. They sailed into the Florida trade lanes to prey on unwary ships and stayed clear of New Providence, which was Woodes Rogers' domain.

* * * *

It was a week after they had gone on account. Catana had the early morning watch and sat atop the yard on the main mast. She scanned the sea for a ship that could supply the *Seahawk* with more cannons. The waters around them were empty; a great desert of pink and gold hues as the sun rose. She noticed a dark blotch along the sharp horizon and lifted the spyglass to her eye. "Sail off the starboard bow," she called to the men on deck.

Orland climbed the shrouds to look. "She is too far to see her colors," he called down to the crew. If we sail toward her we will be able to make out her flag by midmorning."

An hour later, Catana determined that it was a merchant ship, and she flew the French flag. As soon as Tom climbed the mast to take over the watch, Catana scurried down the lines to relay the information to Orlando, who was at the stern inspecting the swivel gun.

"Captain, she is a French merchant ship. I do not think we should attack. It is much larger than the *Seahawk* and will blow us out of the water."

"She may be a monster of a ship," Orlando replied, "but she is a slow and lightly armed. From past experience, a ship like that will surrender when under attack. They carry a small crew of nineteen or twenty."

"I think a ship loaded with valuable cargo would have more protection."

Orlando moved the swivel gun back and forth to make certain it operated smoothly. "Most merchant ships would rather fill their space with merchandise. The greater the cargo, the greater the profits."

Orland had the crew take a vote, and everyone agreed to attack. They would fly the French flag and approach their prey from behind. The *Seahawk* continued her heading toward the French merchant ship. When she was within an hour's distance of their victim, a small island appeared to their port. The sloop slid into a cay where the crew watched for their victim. They waited until the slow, lumbering ship plowed well past them, and then they went into action. The *Seahawk* darted from her hiding place and followed the French ship at a safe distance. Catana trained the glass on her stern and read the ship's name, *Bon Ami*.

The sloop closed in on the slower ship and when they drew close the *Seahawk* pulled down the French flag she was flying and replaced it with the pirate flag. Jamie called across the strip of water that separated them. "We order ye to surrender." The crew of the *Seahawk* gathered on deck behind Jamie. All thirty-five waved cutlasses and shouted to terrorize the men on the merchant ship.

"Send us your captain," Orlando shouted, "or we will come aboard and kill everyone. We give no quarter."

Catana watched in amazement as crewmen on the French ship lowered a longboat and ferried their captain to the *Seahawk* without a shot fired. She was at the rail, ready to board the *Bon Ami*, when the captain of the merchant ship stepped aboard and raised his hands in surrender.

Orlando stepped up to meet him. "We only want your cannons. My men will go aboard your ship and transfer what weapons you have to the *Seahawk*. Once this is done, you may continue to your port. Louis, take the captain to my cabin and offer his a glass of wine."

Jabulani guided the sloop carefully alongside the French ship. Once they were side by side, the crew of the *Seahawk* threw grappling hooks onto the *Bon Ami*, bonding the two ships together. The deck of the sloop came even with the cannon ports on the second deck of the merchant ship. Ascending ropes and using boarding axes, the pirates climbed to the deck, swarmed aboard the French ship, and surrounded the crew.

Catana followed Orlando and Damien down a stairwell onto the second deck where four cannons sat in silence. Damien shook his head. "This will not be easy." Orlando sent Catana for help. Topside she recruited everyone not assigned to guard the French crew and brought them below deck. With hatchets, the men enlarged the cannon ports to fit the weapons through. It took them several hours of struggling before they had the cannons safely aboard the *Seahawk*. Orlando, true to his word, returned the French Captain to his ship, and the *Seahawk* set sail for the cay where they would outfit their ship.

* * * *

Three weeks later the crew of the *Seahawk* was on the beach of a small island. They sat around a campfire after adding six more cannons. They now had five cannons standing at attention on the port side of the main deck and five on the starboard. Catana took a deep breath savoring the aroma of the turtle soup Inez was stirring over the fire.

"Ye know we are running out of supplies," Jamie announced to the crew.

Orlando stood to speak to his men. "Since we now call the sea our home and are low on supplies, we will be obliged to confiscate ships, be they English, Spanish, French, or Dutch."

Percy spoke up. "We need clothing too. My coat is threadbare."

"We also need medical supplies." Damien added. Everyone started talking, naming one need or another.

Orlando raised his hand to signal silence. "When we take a ship from now on, it will be for all we can plunder."

"Aye," Jamie agreed. "What say ye, men?"

"Aye," the group echoed.

* * * *

The *Seahawk* bobbed on the glassy water of the lagoon. Not a breath of air stirred her sails. Catana sat on deck slapping mosquitoes as she watched the land bob up and down with motion of the ship. Her stomach felt queasy. She had been sailing on ships for almost eight months, been through rough seas and numerous storms, but this was the first time the motion of the ship made her sick. The winds had been calm for two days and they had not been able to pursue prey. She started to close her eyes to doze when she noticed a sail flutter. She sat up alert and called out. "Louis, I think a wind is coming up." He and two crewmen sitting in the shade of a bulkhead looked up. The main sail slowly billowed.

Jamie stepped out of the captain's cabin and shouted, "All hands on deck." Men scrambled to set the sails while others turned the capstan and raised the anchor. Three hours outside the lagoon the watch alerted the crew there was a sail at two o'clock on the starboard side. As the *Seahawk* drew closer, Orlando peered through the spyglass and took a deep breath. "She looks to be a slave ship."

"Should we bother to attack?" Louis asked. "She has nothing aboard that will be of use to us."

Jabulani glared at his friend. "If that is a slave ship, do you not think it is our duty to free the poor souls aboard?"

"Jabulani is right," Orlando agreed. "Run up our pirate flag, man the guns, and prepare to overtake her." Each cannon required four to six men to load, arm and fire. They had fourteen cannons but only enough men to fire half, because the swivel gun also needed to be manned."

As the *Seahawk* approached, the slave ship tried to flee. "Fire several warning shots at her," Orlando ordered.

Before they got off their first shot, the slave ship made a hard turn to the starboard, exposing her broadsides. A flash of light and loud boom sounded from one of her cannon ports. The ball arched through the air, missing the bowsprit of the *Seahawk* by inches. A plume of water sprayed into the air drenching Catana while she stood at the bow. She quickly ducked behind the gunwale.

"She's not going to give in easily," Orlando shouted. Turning to Jabulani at the helm, he issued further orders. "Bring the *Seahawk* around and lay us under the slave ship's stern."

The fleet little schooner swung around as another shot flew over them. It gave them time to move in before the slave ship was able to reposition herself for another shot. The sloop sailed up behind the larger ship and ducked under her stern. There was a grinding crunch as the two ships came together. Orlando threw a grappling hook. It skidded across the deck of the slave ship, and when he jerked it back, it lodged firmly into the ships stern rail. Another hook flew onto the ship's stern, and soon manila lines bound together the vessels. Orlando's crew scampered along the *Seahawks* gunwale with their hatchets and cutlasses and filled the air with war cries.

Fighting a man on deck, Jamie cut a main shroud line with his axe and a lantern full of oil crashed onto the wooden planks in front of Catana. A crewman from the slave ship charged Catana on the left and she swung around with her cutlass to defend herself. She hit a brazier of hot coals. The oil blazed up with a roar in front of her and she sprang back. Backing farther, she watched the flames take hold, run up the shroud lines, and catch the rigging. Her first thoughts were of the slaves trapped below in the hold. Racing toward a hatch, she snatched a hatchet imbedded in the bulkhead. She heard cries of help rise from the deck below, smashed the lock, and swung open the door.

"Look out, Catana," a voice cried out. She whirled like a cat. The ax blade flashed as she aimed it at her attacker. She hit him with such force that the blade sank deep into his chest, and he dropped like a sack of rocks.

The flames leaped higher. Catana screamed for help to rescue the slaves. Jamie, Louis, and five crewmen rushed to her aid. Some of the imprisoned were able to climb the ladder, and Tom guided them to the *Seahawk.*

Down in the hold, Catana found women and children cowering against the bulkheads. The bile in her stomach rose at the smell of human waste and stale air. She grabbed a small child and passed it on to Jamie behind her. He in turn handed the child to Louis at the foot of the ladder. They continued to assist people up the ladder who were able to walk and carried those who were too weak to stand. The dead they left behind.

Catana was the last one up. In the few seconds between Jamie's climb to the top of the ladder and her appearance topside, a wall of flame sprung up between her and the others. She was cut off from the safety of the rail. Looking around, she spotted a water barrel and scooped handfuls of water over her until she was dripping wet. With fumbling fingers, she untied the sash around her waist, dipped it into the water, and covered her face and hair. Saying an *Ave* under her breath, she bolted through the wall of flames and did not hesitate as she flew over the rail into the sea below.

Swinging her turquoise sash in the air, she shouted for help. She knew the men aboard the *Seahawk* realized the danger if their ship caught on fire and would immediately separate the two vessels. She watched them swing their axes to sever the taunt ropes that held the ships together.

She sighed with relief when Louis saw her and the *Seahawk* swung around. Louis threw her a line, and in seconds, she was aboard the sloop.

As Catana watched the *Seahawk* sail from the burning inferno, she was amazed that she did not sustain any burns. Exhausted, she slid down the bulkhead to a sitting position on deck and watched the reflection of the flames dance on the water. Jamie hunkered down next to her. "Be ye all right, lass?"

She nodded. "I am a bit winded. That was close."

"Look around ye," Jamie swung his arm to encompass the breath and beam of the deck. "I think we have up to fifty men, women, and children aboard, and we have nothing to feed them."

Catana scanned the rescued slaves who filled the deck. "What are we to do with them all?"

CHAPTER TWENTY-SEVEN

When Catana entered the captain's cabin Orlando was hunched over the table with Jamie, Louis, and Jabulani studying a map in the Waggoner. "This will not do," the captain said pointing to the chart. "There is no fresh water on the island." He turned several more pages until he found what he was looking for. "This one looks perfect. It has food, water, game, and is not far."

"Aye," Jamie agreed. "And it is away from the trade lanes where ships will not bother them."

Jabulani looked up from the map and noticed Catana standing in the doorframe. "Come and join us. We have found an island where we can take our guests ashore."

"Do you plan to maroon them?" Catana asked.

"Of course not," Louis replied. On the island our guests can start a new life, build homes, and live in freedom."

Jamie placed his hand on Catana's shoulder. "Ye know, lass, we canno sail into a port or colony without fear of arrest. Even if we could, slave traders would capture them and put them on the auction block."

Orlando stood tall and looked at his men. "Do you agree we leave them on the island and continue our pursuit of Lancaster?"

"Aye," the men replied in unison."

"Do the slaves have anything to say about their future?" Catana asked.

"I spoke to them earlier," Jabulani replied. "This is what they want."

Orlando closed the Waggoner and looked at Catana. "Is there something you wanted?"

She pulled the map that she had drawn of the La Isla del Espiritu Santo from her waistband along with the attached letter. "I am sorry. I had this all the time and never realized it was what you were looking for."

Orlando unfolded the papers, studied them, and handed them back to Catana. "These are worthless now. When I spoke to Governor Rogers, he told me the Spanish had overtaken the island and the British have no authority over it."

"You spoke to the governor?"

"Yes, the day of our capture. He swore that if anyone asked, he had no contact with me. He could have arrested me for piracy when I was in his office, but he did not believe Lancaster's version of the story. He allowed me to go free."

She pressed the map and letter into Orlando's hand. "Hold on to them. They might come in handy in the future."

* * * *

The wind moved the ship effortlessly over the sparkling water. On the morning of the second day, they were in site of the island where they would disembark their passengers. Catana stood at the rail watching the island draw closer. Tall pine trees topped the grey woods that covered most of the islands surface. White sand fringed the shore. Hills covered with vegetation clambered toward peaks of bare rock.

Louis came up behind her and spoke. "According to the map, we should be able to take her in close to shore before we anchor." The schooner drew closer, and Catana could hear the thunder of the surf as it tossed its foam along the beach. Orlando's order to furl the sails rang out in the tropical morning air. The anchor dropped sending clouds of sand to the surface.

Jamie and Tokala lowered a small boat. "Ye coming with us, lass, or would ye rather stay aboard? Ye come along, too, Louis. We're going to take a look around."

Catana scrambled down the rope ladder with Louis not far behind. The ebbing tide had been out for some time, and when they came ashore, they waded through a belt of swampy sand covered with willows and vegetation. When they came to its edge, there was an open area where low undulating hills covered by trees, bushes, and tropical flowers met a steep hill covered in pines.

The small group strode among the tropical plants until they came to a wide stream where the twisted boughs of live oaks were interlaced. As they climbed higher, the air grew fresher leaving the heavy smell of rotting vegetation behind. Catana charged ahead and climbed to the summit of the highest peak. Turning in a circle, she observed the size of the island. "There are several coves to fish in," she called out to the men following her. "On the opposite side of this hill there is plenty of open land where they can farm."

"I saw several species of birds and small animals they can hunt," Louis added.

Breathing heavily, Jamie sat down on a rock. "We will return to the ship after a wee bit of rest. I'm getting on in years and the walk up this slope has me worn out."

While Jamie sat to catch his breath, Catana found a guava tree and picked some fruit. Returning to the men, she offered them their midday meal. "We will be able to load a large amount of supplies from here," she said and used her sleeve to wipe away a trail of juice running down her chin.

The marsh steamed in the hot afternoon sun as the four explorers returned to their beached boat. The heat was sweltering and Jamie grumbled. "I dona think I can take much more of this. There's not a wisp of breeze from the sea, and the place smells rank in this heat."

"It is the greatest disadvantage of the island that I can see," Tokala said. "Our passengers are from Africa and no strangers to heat."

After they boarded the *Seahawk*, Jamie gave Orlando the report, which met with Jabulani's approval. The black man agreed the heat and marshland would not bother the new inhabitants of the island, especially since they would be settling on the higher land. By sunset, everyone had been ferried ashore. Jabulani took charge of helping the Africans set up a camp. A few crewmen remained aboard the *Seahawk* while the others went ashore to gather supplies.

Orlando joined Tokala, Jamie, Louis, Inez, Percy, and Catana at a large campfire where Inez was cooking fish stew in a large iron pot. "We will gather food and water in the morning," Orlando announced. "Jabulani will remain with his people until our departure. This will give him time to settle them in and explain to them what they must do to live successful off the land."

"I think he is attracted to one of the women," Jamie said.

"If this is so, he may choose to remain on the island," Louis added.

"Jabulani is free to choose his course," Orlando said. "I would miss him like a brother if he did decide to stay. He has been the best helmsman I ever sailed with."

* * * *

After three days of hunting, fishing, picking fruit, and filling water barrels, the crew of the *Seahawk* was ready to set sail. When Jabulani stepped to the helm, Jamie gave him a slap on the back. "Glad to see ye decided to sail with us."

After Jamie went on his way shouting orders to the crew, Catana approached Jabulani. She was curious about his decision to remain with the ship. "Jabulani, we noticed that you had affection for one of the women. Would you rather stay with her than sail with us?"

A broad smile crossed the black man's face. "Some day I will return. But first, we of the *Seahawk* are sworn brethren, and I will stand by my oath until our mission is accomplished."

"Tell me about her. What is her name?

"Jahzara. She is a very beautiful woman. Her luminous eyes are like black onyx. Her skin like polished mahogany and lips soft as rose petals," he said wistfully.

"My, she has enchanted you." Catana stood on tiptoe, stretched, and kissed Jabulani on the cheek. "I wish you and Jahzara a wonderful future."

Crewmen climbed on taunt ropes toward the sky and unfurled the sails. There was a flurry of sheets cracking and the canvas filled. Calm water gave way to foam and the ship lifted to the open sea. Catana savored the delicious taste of freedom, as the *Seahawk* got under way.

Catana sat at the foot of the main mast, engrossed with mending a piece of canvas when Louis approached. "Five of the men we rescued from the slave ship have joined our crew," he said. "They have no families and would like revenge for the way white men have treated them."

Catana rethreaded her needle and sighed. "Why do religions give slavery their blessing? Even our own church allows the practice."

Louis shrugged. "I have no idea. No religious organization is guilt-free. Catholics, Protestants, Jews, and Moslems all take slavery for granted."

Orlando joined them. He had called a meeting to have the crew witness the five men take the oath. Once the men were sworn in, everyone cheered, and Orlando raised his hands for silence. "We will be going up against great odds by pursuing Lancaster. I have forty men under my command, with fourteen cannons, and two swivel guns. We do not have a lot of ammunition. If a fight goes on too long, we will run out. I have learned that Lancaster's ship, the *Retribution* has twelve guns each side and one hundred men. We must use our heads; we cannot take them by strength. What say you, men, do we continue to go after Lancaster?"

The brotherhood of the *Seahawk* took on reality for Catana as crew roared with approval. It was a strange group who called themselves blood brothers and they would stand by Orlando no matter the end.

* * * *

Catana climbed the shroud lines to relieve the lookout. Settling in a comfortable position high on the mast, her eyes traveled along the vast, empty sea. It was a moonless night, and but for the stars, all was black. She took a deep breath savoring the smell of iodine from the sea along with the odor of kelp and salt. It was almost a week since they had left the island to search for the *Retribution* with no sign of her. The rolling motion of the ship made her sleepy. She shook her head to clear it. What was the use of standing watch when there was nothing to see?

Concentrating on staying awake, she scanned the blackness until her eyes rested on a small glimmer of light far in the distance, then it disappeared. Was it imagination? She trained her eyes on the spot and saw it again. This time it was visible for a longer time. Was there land ahead, or was it a ship with her lamps lit? She called down to a crewman at the helm. "Ahoy. Have someone wake the captain. I see a light ahead at one o'clock off the port."

Moments later, Orlando stood at the foot of the mast. "Are you certain, Catana?"

"Aye, Captain. We are drawing closer, and I see it more clearly now."

Orlando stepped to the bow with his spyglass and called up to Catana. "I see the light. I cannot tell what it is, but there is no land charted in this area. It must be a ship. We will shorten our sails and slow the *Seahawk* to remain at this distance. We will not be able to make her out until dawn. Helmsman, warn me if we draw too close or she changes course."

"Aye," both Catana and the helmsman replied.

"Put out any lamps aboard," he called to the watch. "If we can see their lights, they can see ours."

Orlando climbed the ratlines and handed Catana the spyglass. "It is only an hour before dawn. You should be able to see who is out there at that time. When the watch relives you at sunrise, come to my cabin and report your findings." He placed his hand on her shoulder. "And, Catana, pray that it is Lancaster."

With the *Seahawk* sailing in darkness, the helmsman drew her closer to catch the first sign of a change of direction. The anticipation of what the dawn would reveal kept Catana alert. Soon the sky grew light in the east, and Catana steadied the glass on a dark spot along the horizon. As the sky continued to lighten, the dark mass turned into the outline of a ship. She watched it turn to the port and was able to distinguish that the ship had three masts. She scanned the direction the ship had turned and noticed an island.

"Do you see the ship?" she called to the helmsman. "She's heading toward an island ten degrees to our port."

Catana's relief arrived, and she handed the glass to him and pointed out the ship. He looked through the glass. "Aye, she's a man-o-war. It could very well be Lancaster's."

Catana shimmied down the lines and hastened to the captain's cabin to relay her relief's suspicions.

"Jamie," Orlando called through the open cabin door and spoke to the quartermaster as Jamie charged into the cabin. "If that ship anchors off the island, give orders to go around to the opposite side and hide. When we get a positive identification we will ready the *Seahawk* for battle."

CHAPTER TWENTY-EIGHT

The *Seahawk* hid from view of the man-o-war until the warship anchored off the island at dusk. Sliding into an inlet on the leeward side of the island, the crew of the sloop dropped anchor. Orlando sent Jamie and Tokala to row a small boat along the shoreline until they were within sight of the ship. When they saw her colors and name their orders were to return to the *Seahawk* to make their report.

Loud voices woke Catana at dawn. Sitting up in her bunk, she noticed Inez was not in the cabin. She dressed and slipped out the door to see what the ruckus was. Crewmen were running back and forth shouting at one another. Catana spotted Inez standing next to one of the cannon holding a ramrod while Louis attempted to put a black iron ball down the bore of the weapon. Catana sprinted across the deck to join them. "It's the *Retribution*," Inez shouted over the noise. "Jamie confirmed that it is Lancaster's ship and that he is here to take on fresh water and food."

Before Catana could offer her help, Tokala and Percy appeared to help Louis. "If you ladies want to help," Louis said, "clear the deck of debris and prepare it for battle."

Both women went to work freeing the deck of loose barrels, coils of rope, and any object not needed for an attack. At the gunner's command, the men on the cannons rolled them into place with their black mouths gaping at the sea. Other crewmen loaded flintlocks and sharpened knives and swords. Within half an hour there were men stationed in the rigging where they could shoot from good vantage points. A small group was crouched along both sides of the gunwale. Orlando instructed that they would fire their seven port cannons first. The starboard seven would be primed and ready to fire a second round.

The *Seahawk* slid in silence through the early morning fog that covered the sea along the coastline. With their schooner's shallow draft, they were able to stay close to shore and remain out of shooting range of the larger ship until *Seahawk* was turned broadside to the warship, her port cannons ready to fire.

"Stay undercover until the last moment," Orlando ordered.

Catana crouched low next to Jamie at the cannon nearest the stern. "What can I do to help?"

"Would ye like to fire a cannon?"

"I…I never fired one before."

"'Tis quite a thrill. I'll show ye, lass. When the gunner says 'fire,' all the cannons are to go off at the same time. Four of these are loaded with chain shot, the other three with shrapnel."

"Aim for the masts and sails," Orlando ordered.

Jamie pointed the cannon's mouth higher. "Ye see, lass, chain shot is two balls connected by a piece of chain. When fired, the chain flies into the mast. The balls whip around, shatter the wood, and tear through the rigging. The grapeshot is nothing but spikes, nails, and whatever will fit into the barrel of the cannon. When it flies through the air, it tears through canvas and anything in its way."

The thought of it hitting a man and ripping him to pieces made her stomach muscles tightened.

Jamie patted her on the hand. "'Tis chain shot ye have there," he said as though he knew her thoughts. "If it strikes well, it will bring down her mast. Are ye ready?"

"Steady," Orlando ordered.

Catana looked at the slow match in her hand.

"Steady…Fire!"

Catana placed the wick with the red coal onto the touchhole at the end of the barrel. A slight flash followed by earsplitting boom filled the air. Shrouded by fog, *Seahawk*'s line of fire erupted in a solid blast of smoke. Flame and grape shot tore across the British warship. Smoke rolled skyward, blackening the early morning sky. Catana barely saw Lancaster's ship staggering under the blows of the broadside.

She heard echoing sounds of thudding ramrods from across the water as the British forced powder down the barrels of their cannons.

"She's got her guns run out," Orlando shouted.

"Helm a' ler," Jamie called to Jabulani and raced to add his weight to the wheel. The *Seahawk* heeled and tilted as the *Retribution's* full broadside reflected off the fog like a sheet of lightning. Responding to the thrust of the sail and rudder, the *Seahawk* twisted around with the wind, her canvas flapping. Waves crashed over the rail. Because of the sloops erratic turn the warship's cannon shot missed. The wind that had saved them was also blowing away their cover.

High on the fore mast of the *Retribution*, a man cried, "We were short. Reload while we come about."

"Are ye ready with your starboard cannons?" Jamie called to his men.

Tom, who was in the rigging and above the clearing fog, shouted, "We need to draw a bit closer. Yep. I say twenty yards closer."

"Right," Jabulani replied. The jib over the bowsprit flapped and filled on another tack.

"Hurry men, before the *Retribution* comes about," Jamie added.

The *Seahawk* fired her second round. The dense cloud of smoke obscured everything, but Catana could hear the screams and moans of the wounded British seamen.

The *Retribution* fired her second round. The cannon shots were high, but several balls came crashing onto deck. The wood next to Catana splintered, and she felt a sharp pain where a spear of wood pierced the flesh of her thigh. She yanked it out and bound the piece of cloth tight around her leg. The wound was a dull ache, and she was able to walk. Grabbing her flintlock from her bandoleer, she peered over the gunwale and saw through the thinning smoke that the main and mizzenmasts of the British ship were broken. Her sails and rigging lay strewn on her deck.

"Do you call for quarter?" Orlando shouted.

Catana recognized Lancaster's voice. "What are your colors? What port are you from?"

"We are from the sea," Orlando replied. He heaved on the signal halyard and the silken bundle of the pirate flag soared to the masthead of *Seahawk*. There, it burst open, and the skull and crossbones along with an hourglass appeared on a field of red.

Lancaster seemed startled when he recognized Orlando. "What are you doing under the *Jolie Rogue*?"

"You forced it upon me, Lancaster. Strike your colors and surrender."

"I will see you in hell first," came Lancaster's fierce cry.

"Than we will board."

The two ships came together with a grinding crash. The men of the *Seahawk* threw grappling hooks over the warship's rail and bound the ships. Catana joined her brethren and sprang across the narrow strip of water as the two hulls bobbed along side one another. The boarders fired their guns while those in the rigging of the *Seahawk* fired onto the warship's deck.

A British seaman charged toward Catana with a drawn sword. She raised her flintlock, pulled the trigger, and a thick cloud of sulfurous powder flashed in the pan. A pungent cloud filled the air as her arm jerked from the recoil, and the man dropped to the deck.

Her flintlock could serve only as a club now, so she grabbed the downed man's sword. Looking around, she saw bodies everywhere and the deck was slick with blood. The blade of a sword swished by her ear. She swung around to face her opponent, whose size would give him the advantage. The power of his thrusts taxed her skill and she struggled to meet and parry him. The steel of her blade rang out under the blows. A feeling of despair swept through her when she realized she could not hold out against his force.

Her advantage was her speed. Sidestepping a slashing blow, she noticed the hate in his eyes. Fear dulled her responses, and she realized she was about to die. Suddenly her opponent lunged toward her, knocked her to the deck, and landed on top of her. He lay still as a stone. She pulled herself out from under the dead weight and scrambled to her feet. Scanning the area, she saw Tom clinging to the ratlines on the *Seahawk*. A large grin was on his face as he waved his rifle at her. Looking to the deck, she saw a hole in the back of the attacker's head. Exhaustion and the close brush with death overwhelmed her. She sank to her knees and wept.

Dabbing tears from her eyes with the sleeve of her blouse she noticed how quite it had gotten, and in the distance, she heard Jamie's voice. "She's ours, lads."

The *Retribution* canted toward its starboard, drawing the grappling lines taunt as a bowstring. She was sinking. "Return to the *Seahawk*, now!" Jamie ordered. What was left of the sinking ship's crew jumped overboard and swam toward the island. Seven British agreed to surrender and were taken aboard the *Seahawk*.

As the *Retribution* took on water, a grappling line that held the ships together snapped. One end of the line shot through the air and barely missed Catana's head. Louis and Tokala grabbed axes and severed the two remaining lines. The freed sloop's bow swung clear, her sails filled, and with Jabulani at the helm, she bore away as the British warship slid beneath the waves.

The wound in Catana's thigh throbbed. While her mind was on the battle, she had forgotten about the spear of wood that struck her. She searched for Damien to clean and put a new bandage on the injury.

Wounded men either sat or lay on the deck at the stern where Damien worked with his medicines. Tokala, who assisted with cleaning and stitching of wounds, noticed Catana limping toward them and motioned to her. "I see by the bloody bandage on your leg that you need our services."

"Yes, but it is not serious. It looks as if others need your attention more."

Tokala looked at her wound. "I think there is still a sliver of wood lodged in your flesh. Damien will have to remove it with his knife."

Damien, hearing the conversation, put the finishing touches to a bandage and joined Tokala. "He's right, Catana. If we do not remove the splinter, infection will set in. The only thing I have left to clean it is rum. There is a British doctor in the captain's cabin with Orlando. He will do a better job removing the piece of wood.

"British doctor?" Catana asked.

"Aye, he is one of the men who surrendered.

Tokala grasped her by the arm. "Come, I will take you there." When they reached the cabin door, Tokala rapped loudly. A voice called for them to enter. The Indian herded Catana into the room and followed. "This young lady needs your help, doctor."

Catana stared into the sparkling blue eyes of a middle-aged man. There were smudges on his face, his silver hair sprinkled with gunpowder. His friendly smile put her at ease. He gently pushed her onto a chair and went to work on her wound.

"I am Doctor Evans," he said as he probed her flesh. She did not want to watch him dig out the splinter; instead, she scanned the room. She gave a start not because of the pain, but because she saw Orlando lying in his bed still as stone. He had a bandage rapped around his head.

"Is he going to be all right?" she asked in a whisper.

"Ah, I have it," the doctor said and held up a piece of wood covered in blood. "Yes, he will be fine. A few stitches to close a cut on his head. I gave him something so he would rest. When he awakes, he will have a sore head. Other than that, he will be back to normal." Catana sucked in her breath when the doctor poured liquid onto her wound. "This will keep infection from setting in." With sure hands, he placed a bandage around her leg and tied it tight. "Leave this on to keep it clean, but change it each day until the wound has closed."

"Why did you surrender instead of swimming to the island with the others? Were you not afraid that pirates would kill you?"

Doctor Evans chuckled softly. "I am not a good swimmer. As for fearing pirates, I did not think Orlando would harm me. Maurine, Orlando's mother, and I are cousins. Her father and my mother were sister and brother. We are both part Irish and part English. When we were young, I would spend time with her family in Ireland, and she would come to London and stay with us during the theatre season."

"How interesting. Did you know Orlando well?"

I saw little of him as he grew up. The differences between our countries and religions kept Maurine and me apart when we grew older. I did attend Orlando's baptism and asked Maurine why she chose to christen him Orlando."

"Yes, I never realized it was an Irish name."

"It is Teutonic. Maurine loved the theatre, especially Shakespeare. Her favorite play was *As You Like It*, and she named Orlando after one of its characters." The doctor stood and stretched. "Will you do me a favor, Catana? Look after my patient until he awakens. I have wounded men on deck that need my services."

"Of course."

Catana moved her chair close to Orlando's bunk and peered into his pale face. There was much about this man she did not know. He was kind toward her, and yet, she had the feeling he only tolerated having her and Inez on his ship. For some reason, he seemed to have his guard up when around her. Then there were times when he did or said things to make her angry. She thought she heard him moan and leaned closer. When his eyes flew open, she straightened up in surprise. He sat up, moaned loudly, and sank back down onto the bunk.

"Orlando," Catana said in a soft voice, "you have been injured. Doctor Evans took care of your wounds."

"Doctor Evans?"

"Yes, he is one of seven British seamen who chose to join us. What happened? Who did this to you?"

"Lancaster. He came at me with a knife. His blade slashed me across the forehead as I tried to leap aside, and I fell to the deck. The blood running into my eyes blinded me. I wiped the blood away in time to see the sneer on his face as he stood over me with his weapon pointed at my heart. I rolled to one side and kicked his legs out from under him as came at me. He fell forward and hit the deck face down. When I rolled him onto his back, he lay limp. Somehow the blade of his knife had turned toward him. The weapon was sticking in his chest up to the hilt. A thin trickle of blood seeped from his mouth as he lay still in death and his eyes gazed at me with a wide glassy stare." Orlando shuddered.

"I will remember to my last day that empty stare. I thought once I had my revenge it would make me happy, but now I feel hollow inside."

Catana took his hand in hers. "Lancaster did terrible things to people. With his death, the natives of the island where you were enslaved will no longer live in fear. You were defending yourself when he was killed. You did what you had to in order to remain alive."

There was a light knock on the door. It opened, and Doctor Evans stepped in. "I see you are recovering nicely." Pulling up a chair, he joined Catana at Orlando's bedside. "Do you remember me? When you were a young lad, I came to visit your parents in Ireland. Your mother and I are kin."

Orlando thought for a moment than a smile touched his lips. "Yes, I do."

"It is because I know what sort of a boy Maurine raised that I and six British seamen surrendered to your crew. Now, I would like to ask you a favor."

"And what would that be?"

"Take the seven of us to New Providence."

Orlando shook his head. "I cannot. If I go into the harbor there, Governor Rogers will have me arrested and hanged for piracy."

"What if you leave us off at Watkins Point just outside the harbor?"

"Before I give you an answer, I will present the idea to the crew for a vote. When the Governor receives word that Lancaster is dead and his British warship destroyed, Governor Rogers might send men out to hunt us down. It would be like signing our death warrants if we go near his domain."

Doctor Evans moved his chair closer to the bed. "I do not think so, lad. I have an idea that will put you back into the good graces with the governor."

CHAPTER
TWENTY-NINE

Catana had just come awake when she heard Louis rap on the cabin door and call for Inez. Her cousin rolled out of her bunk and padded to the door. The door swung open and Louis greeted Inez with an embrace.

"The captain is calling a meeting at the foot of the mast right away," he informed the two women.

Catana rubbed her eyes and yawned. She knew the reason. What Doctor Evans had proposed to Orlando filled her with doubts and kept her awake half the night.

Inez shooed Louis out of the cabin so she and Catana could dress. Inez preferred a simple cotton frock while Catana struggled into a pair of breeches that barely fit over the bandage on her right thigh. Once she slipped into a loose shirt, her turquoise sash, and sea boots, she was ready to go.

The *Seahawk* was sitting dead in the water on a sea smooth as glass. The sails were furled, and every man aboard gathered around the mast. Without a breath of air, Catana felt the heat of early morning radiate from the wooden deck. She wiped away a trickle of perspiration running down her forehead.

Orlando stepped into view; Doctor Evens followed. When the two men reached the foot of the mast, Orlando held his hands up for silence then spoke. "Doctor Evans and I have gathered you here this morning because the doctor has a proposal that I want you to vote on. I will let him explain."

"Good morning, gentlemen and ladies." He nodded toward Catana and Inez and continued. "For almost a year, the Spanish have been building an attack force in Havana. Its target is New Providence."

A wave of muttering flowed through the crowd. When there was silence, the doctor continued. "Governor Rogers asked help from London to defend the island. London has not responded. The governor is in the process of recruiting those who were once pirates in the Caribbean to come to his defense. He has also emptied jails and armed old men and children. None of this is enough against the Spanish Armada.

"If the *Seahawk* returns me to New Providence, I will speak to Woodes Rogers and ask him to give you men a pardon in exchange for your assistance."

Orlando stepped forward and spoke. "Are there questions before we vote on taking the British men to New Providence?"

"How much sea power does Rogers have?" a crewman called out.

"Three schooners that I know of," the doctor replied.

"And how many does the Spanish have?" another crewman asked.

The doctor cleared his throat. "Five warships, three brigantines, and eleven sloops."

More mutters floated through the crowd.

"I do not think I like those odds," Percy piped up. Heads nodded in agreement.

"That is only part of the plan," Orlando said. "There is a small fleet of pirates who refused to take the governor's offer for a pardon. Men such as Captain Charles Vane, Calico Jack, and our old shipmate Ben feel safe in Trinidad. If we sail there after we drop the British men off in New Providence, we will ask the pirates to join us in our own armada.

"Rogers would likely hang us if he catches us in his territory," Tom shouted. "Why should we bother to help him?"

"When we take the doctor and his companions to New Providence we will stay outside the harbor," Orlando replied. "We will row them ashore at Watkins's Point. If Rogers has only three ships, and is busy setting up a defense against the Spanish, he will not have time to chase after us."

"Is there a guarantee Rogers will pardon us if we help him?" Jamie asked.

"No," The doctor answered. "But what are your chances of peace if the Spanish overthrow New Providence? Rogers has been lenient on pirates by giving them a choice. He has offered them land and a new life if they swear an oath to him. Do you think the Spanish would treat you well? I say we keep Rogers as governor of the Caribbean."

The crew shouted their approval. Only Catana stood silent. These were her people they were talking about.

"What say you, Catana?" Orlando asked. "Do you agree?"

She saw the expectant look in his eyes. This was his chance to prove his loyalty to the governor, and if the Spanish were defeated, Orlando would regain claim to his island. She took a deep breath and answered. "I say we do what it takes to win a pardon and freedom for everyone on this ship."

The crew of the *Seahawk* had made their decision. As a good omen, a breeze picked up. The crew unfurled the sails, and the ship lunged forward with the wind to embrace the sea. They set a heading for New Providence.

* * * *

The voyage to New Providence was uneventful. Catana had the opportunity to get to know several of the British sailors and learned that they had been treated poorly by Lancaster and were not sorry about what happened to their captain.

The *Seahawk* anchored off Watkins point while Jabulani and Tokala rowed the seven British men ashore. After the two men returned to the schooner, Orlando ordered the crew to set sail for Trinidad.

Orlando selected a few of his crew to go with him into the Red Rooster Tavern in Trinidad. Inez remained aboard ship while Catana, dressed as a cabin boy, was able to persuade Orlando to let her tag along. When they entered the tavern, a cluster of pirates were drinking and joking loudly in the back of the room. Most were dressed in fine clothing and draped in gold jewelry.

"I heard that Captain Charles Vane is here," Orlando shouted over the noise. "Find a table, men, and I will invite him over to talk."

There were two empty tables in the large common room and Jamie chose the one in the far corner. Catana, Louis, Tom, and Damien settled into their chairs while Jamie went to fine a bar maid to order a round of rum.

"So, this Captain Vane is a powerful pirate?" Catana asked no one in particular.

"He is not on the best of terms with the governor," Jamie said as he joined them. "When Woodes Rogers offered Vane a King's Pardon, the captain turned him down. Instead, he set fire to several of Rogers's ships and slipped out of New Providence harbor."

Louis nodded. "I have heard of Vane's many deeds throughout the Caribbean along with those who follow him. He has made his crew rich and is said to be a natural leader. If Orlando can win him over, other pirate captain's will follow."

Catana saw Orlando and Vane heading their way and made room at the table for them. Orlando introduced the pirate before the two men took a seat. Vane was dressed in a well-cut burgundy coat trimmed in gold braid. His hair hung in dark ringlets to his shoulders framing the face of a man in his mid-years. The grim look he wore did not look promising to their cause.

"Now that you know why we have come, will you join us?" Orlando asked Vane.

A smile played at the corner of the pirate captain's mouth. "If we leave immediately with our fleet of sloops we should arrive in New Providence about the same time as the Spanish."

"You agree to join us, yet you consider Governor Rogers your enemy?" Louis asked in delighted surprise.

"Aye," Vane said widening his smile. "I would rather defend the British than see New Providence in papist hands."

Catana swallowed her words before she said something that would change Vane's decision. Now was not the time to defend her church.

"Some of the men who did take Rogers's oath are still my friends," Vane continued. "If the Spanish captured the island, they would hang them all, oath or not. Those men may have chosen a different path, but we're still all brethren."

* * * *

After thee days in Trinidad, seven ships had joined the *Seahawk*. The small armada slid out of port with the tide and set sail for New Providence. Captain Vane led the way in his swift three-masted schooner followed by *Seahawk*, two schooners, and three sloops.

The ships made one stop along the way for fresh water. While in port, they learned that the Spanish had passed that way and had a substantial lead. There were nineteen ships in the Spanish armada, and it was under the command of Don Francisco Cornejo.

With this news, the high spirits of the pirates deflated until Vane managed to restore a positive fighting attitude in them. Before they continue their voyage, Vane came aboard the *Seahawk* to relay his plan to Orlando. "Captain Cordova, I want you to sail ahead and observe the situation."

* * * *

The setting sun cast long shadows from the mangroves at Watkins Point as twilight approached. Through the spyglass, Orlando had spotted Spanish ships anchored off the point's eastern tip. After the *Seahawk* sailed back to relay the information, Vane thought for a moment and then spoke to Orlando. "Return as close as you dare, hide, and when you think the time is right send up a signal flag. Our best chance is to have the element of surprise."

The *Seahawk* returned to Watkins Point and remained out of sight in a small cove. The crew furled the sails so moonlight would not reflect from the white canvas. If caught, they were dead.

At dawn, Catana scanned the shoreline with the glass. There was no sign of Rogers, or that he had prepared for an attack. Turning the glass on the Spanish ships, she saw they had launched three long boats and they were heading for shore. She handed the glass to Orlando, who stood next to her at the port bow.

He looked first at the longboats then toward the five heavily armed warships and three massive brigantines. They were moving into position across the harbor to batter the settlement from the sea. Behind them were eleven smaller ships ready for action. The *Seahawk* slipped in closer to get a better look.

As the Spanish longboats drew near the beach, a small cavalry sped over the dunes toward the boats rolling in with the tide. Before the Spaniards could beach their craft, the ex-pirates on horseback attacked and drove them back. Catana grabbed the glass to get a closer look. "Rogers is leading the riders."

Orlando nodded. "That man is either too stupid to be afraid or he is incredibly brave. The landing Spanish have signaled their ships for support."

Thunder echoed across the harbor as Spanish ships open fired and moved forward. Their deep draft kept them from coming in much closer. The cavalry fell back, leaving bodies littered on the beach. Orlando gave the order to run up the flag to signal Vane and his fleet.

The Spanish made a second surge ashore with feeble fire coming from the thickets along the top of the dunes. One hundred fifty attacking soldiers gained a foothold on the beach and fired into the bushes without advancing.

"They are waiting for reinforcements," Orlando observed.

Looking out to sea, Catana saw the six pirate ships approaching. Jabulani swung the *Seahawk* around to join the small fleet. They swept around the point of land, into the harbor, and sliced between the Spanish warships and their men on shore. The pirates open fired on the beach, blowing the Spanish landing party to bits. Rogers' troops stopped firing at first, and then their gunfire joined the barrage from the pirate ships.

The crew of the *Seahawk* knocked away the wedges from under the wheels of the cannons, ran them out and fired. Once the breech lines relaxed, the gun crew reloaded the cannons while the schooner came about. Cannon balls cut Spanish longboats to pieces; debris flew into the air.

Catana put her hands over her ears to block out the screams of the dying Spanish heard over the gunfire.

Vane signaled the pirate fleet to turn their broadsides toward the sea and fired at the Spanish ships. A cannon ball hit the powder magazine on a warship. Flames and smoke sprang high. The enemy launched longboats, but this time, they headed toward an undamaged warship.

The pirate ships buzzed around the warships and brigantines like mosquitoes, hitting one side then the other. Although the Spanish armada had greater power, the maneuverability of the pirate ships in shallows gave them the advantage.

Catana crouched beneath the rail. Keeping her head down, she approached a cannon. After plunging the slow match into the charcoal brazier, she held the lit end to the touchhole. A fizzling puff of smoke blew back, and she tensed in anticipation of the explosion. With a loud boom, everything around her disappeared in a cloud of grey smoke. The black powder was like fine dust and stuck to the perspiration on her skin. Her back ached from crouching for so long under the protection of the gunwales.

A cannon ball from the *Seahawk* hit a Spanish sloop. Her mast came crashing to the deck causing a tangle of rigging to cover the gun crews on her starboard side. *Seahawk* darted around the damaged ship and shot her second mast. It fell clear of the deck and dragged the crippled ship over to one side.

The Spanish stood their ground and flung cannon shot at the pirate ships, and Catana wondered how long *Seahawk*'s luck would hold. Peeking over the rail, she noticed Rogers leading his navy of three sloops into battle from around a small island near the harbor. One opened fired on the remaining warship, bombarding her. The sloop crippled the Spanish ships guns. The two brigantines turned and headed out of the harbor in retreat.

"Wheel about," Orlando ordered. The *Seahawk* tipped to her port so quickly that Catana lost her footing and fell to the deck. As she picked herself up, the Spanish warship sailed past a few feet from them. Behind her, two of Rogers' ships followed. The Spanish ship had her swivel guns ready on her stern and blew lead at two of Rogers's sloops. One sloop came to a jolting halt and sat dead in the water. She was hit and sinking.

The retreating Spanish ships continued to the open sea, and behind them, the pirate ships sailed in pursuit. The *Seahawk* drew near Rogers' flagship. If they remained here, Rogers would arrest them although they helped save his island. As the *Seahawk* passed the flagship, Woodes Rogers stood at attention and gave Orlando a snappy salute.

"Meet me on the island outside the harbor after dark," the governor shouted. Then he turned his ship to go to the aid of his injured craft.

CHAPTER THIRTY

The sun dipped toward the horizon, and the *Seahawk* slid to the far side of the island, a dark silhouette on the water. The moon rose behind them and lit the scene ahead with silver and shadows. Dropping anchor, the ship came to a stop and bobbed on the water. The trade winds blew across the deck, keeping the mosquitoes away.

Jamie paced the deck. "What if it is a trap?" he muttered to no one in particular.

Catana stepped in front of him and fingered the pistol she carried in her bandoleer. "If it is, I am armed and ready to fight. So are Louis and the others."

Orlando stepped up to Jamie and Catana. "I do not think that is necessary. Governor Rogers has little to back him with two of his ships out of commission. He does have the authority to give us a king's pardon. After today, and with Doctor Evans' testimony, I think Rogers will grant us our freedom."

Tom, who was up on the mast as a lookout, shouted, "Sail to the starboard ten degrees."

Orlando picked up the spyglass and trained it on the white speck reflecting moonlight. "It's Rogers' flagship."

"Have the crew ready to fire the cannons if he does us wrong," Jamie said with a growl.

Rogers' sloop slid close to the *Seahawk*, and the governor called across the water. "Captain Cordova, select a shore party and meet me on the beach."

When Rogers launched his longboat, Orlando trained his glass on the vessel. "He is taking four men with him. I will do the same. Jamie, you stay with the *Seahawk*. If there is any sign of trouble, you know what to do."

"Aye, Captain."

"Louis, Tokala, Jabulani, and Damien, come with me."

"I'll get them for ye, Captain," Jamie said and headed toward the stern where the four men stood near the swivel gun.

"May I come ashore with you, Sir?" Catana asked. "My leg is stiff, and a walk on the beach while you negotiate with the governor will stretch the tight muscles."

Orlando thought for a moment. "I guess there will be no harm in that, but do not wander far, in the event that something does go wrong and we must make a fast retreat."

Catana stretched up on her toes and kissed him lightly on the cheek. "Thank you, I will be right back."

Orlando touched his cheek with a surprised look on his face and cleared his throat. "Where are you going?"

"Esmeralda has not had an opportunity for a romp on land lately. I thought I would take her with me."

Orlando heaved a great sigh. "If that cat causes problems or runs off into the night, she will make her home on the island because I will not have the time to look for her."

"Aye, Captain," Catana replied smartly.

Seahawk's longboat came to a grinding halt as its hull scraped the sandy beach. The moonlight reflected off the white sand dunes, giving the island a ghostly glow. Catana was the first to disembark and set Esmeralda down on the wet sand. Rogers' small band of men approached and the two groups merged into one. Catana recognized Doctor Evans as one of the governor's party and smiled at him. The jovial look on his face rested any apprehension she had. She would enjoy her walk.

"Give a whistle when you are ready to leave," she told Louis, "and I will come running."

Esmeralda scampered around Catana's feet, dogging the incoming waves. Catana looked down at her bare feet and watched a wave wash over them. As the water slid out to sea, little flecks of green phosphorous flickered in the sand. She kicked at the next wave, and a spray sprang to life in an eerie green glow. She fell into a brisk walk, hoping to work out the dull ache in her thigh and noticed that Esmeralda was nowhere in sight.

"Here, kitty," she called, looking around. Leaving the tide line, she checked behind the first row of dunes. Sea oats cast moon shadows across the silver sand, but there was no sign of the cat. Maybe she was in the shadow of a dune. Easing toward the blackness, she heard the cat growl. She eased closer and heard a second noise. It was the sound of someone groaning in pain. Staring into the darkness, she was able to make out the form of a man.

She fumbled in her waist pouch to find her tinderbox. Grabbing a stick of driftwood, she wrapped a handful of sea oat grass around it and tied it in a bunch to make a torch. Esmeralda was still growling when she set it alight.

"Whoever that is has you spooked," Catana muttered to the cat. She drew closer to get a better look.

"Help me," she heard a voice moan in Spanish.

It was a man with large areas of his Spanish uniform burned away. His face was burned so badly it was hard to identify him as human. Bile rose in Catana's throat. She quickly planted the torch in the sand and ran to the sea where she got sick. She splashed water on her face, drew herself up, took a deep breath, and turned to head back to the dying man. What could she do to help that poor soul? In the moonlight, she noticed three figures coming toward her on the beach. A beam glinted off the blades of two drawn daggers. Catana had no idea who they might be and her hand stole to her flintlock.

It took her a moment to make a decision, and she called out. "I need your help." The men did not seem to understand so she called out in Spanish, "*Ayudeme, por favor.*"

The men stopped as she proceeded toward them while explaining in Spanish that she had found a man badly burned. They quickly followed her. The men explained that they were survivors of the battle earlier. She would not betray their existence on the island but wondered what would become of them.

"Here," she said, stopping. Bending down, she checked to see if he still lived.

The torch had burned out so she tied more oat grass to the stick. Relighting it, she held it close to the injured man. One of the Spaniards looked closer and gasped. "It is our Captain-General Carvajal."

A second Spaniard, dressed in robes, stepped forward and made the sign of the cross. "Señorita, I am Father Juan Velazquez. We were aboard the *Conception* when we were hit by cannon fire and our gunpowder blew the ship to pieces. A few of us made it to the shores of this island. Carvajal was the captain.

The vengeful feelings she had held toward the captain all these months mixed with pity. The priest placed his hand on her shoulder. "Pray for him, my daughter, for he will soon be in the hands of Our Lord."

Catana shook her head slowly. "I do not think I can, Father. He has wronged me and those I love in too many ways."

The priest turned to his two companions. "Go. Find the others and tell them to come here."

"How many of you are there?" Catana asked the priest.

"In all, a total of eight."

"Remain hidden." Catana warned. "There is a party of five British and five pirates ashore down the beach."

"Are you with them?"

"Sí, but your secret is safe with me."

Father Velazquez pulled a crucifix from his tattered robes and proceeded to give the last rites of the Catholic Church to Captain Carvajal.

"Please forgive me, señorita," Carvajal moaned.

Catana stood speechless. Could she forgive a man who had been so cruel to her and others? She thought of how he had beaten and enslaved her friends Jabulani and Tokala. Could she forget how he arrested her and Inez with the threat of hanging them? And there was her father. Was he responsible for her father's disappearance? She remembered her mother telling her how Christ had forgiven his pursuers. Could she do the same? She thought about what her mother would want her to do.

The priest spoke. "Forgiveness is a choice, my dear. Maybe one of the hardest choices our Savior asks of us. But to forgive the captain will give you peace."

Bending down, Catana spoke in a low, steady tone. "I forgive you, Señor. Go to our Savior in peace."

The captain took a ragged breath then lay still.

"He is gone," the priest said and leaned down to place a cloth over the dead man's face.

The priest was right, Catana thought. For some reason, forgiving Carvajal lifted a burden from her mind. "What will happen to you and your companions?"

Father Velazquez shrugged. "I will pray that Our Lord will deliver us somehow."

Moments later, the other Spanish survivors appeared. When they learned their captain-general was dead, they knelt in the sand to pray for him.

Catana saw movement from the corner of her eye. Esmeralda was stalking a small creature in the moonlight. The torch had gone out, but no one seemed to notice. Standing, she brushed the sand from her breeches. "I must retrieve my cat and return before someone comes looking for me. I wish there…"

An idea slipped into her mind. It might not be good, but worth a try. She explained why the men had come to meet on the island. "Once Rogers leaves the island, I think I and my companions can help you. My Captain and my friend Louis are Catholic. The rest of the crew is not opposed to our faith. I can persuade Orlando to do his Christian duty by helping you. We will take you to an island where you will be safe."

"You destroyed our ship," one of the Spaniards spat. "Why should we trust you?"

"We fought you to win a pardon." Catana replied. "I and my companions have no animosity toward you. Father spoke to me about forgiveness. Maybe it is time we all practice it and help one another." She heard a shrill whistle. "I must go. Think about what I said." Snatching Esmeralda from her hunt, Catana turned toward the priest. "I will tell Orlando and Louis about you in confidence. If they agree to transport you to safety, I will return for you. If they do not, they can be trusted to keep silent, and we will sail away."

Another shrill whistle cut the air. With Esmeralda folded in her arms, Catana sprinted toward the longboat. She trusted the men with her, and after Governor Rogers' departure, she took Orland and Louis aside and relayed her walk on the beach.

Louis gave her a dubious look. "We received our pardons, and we are free to go where we like. Why should we destroy every thing we fought for to help our enemies?"

"No one would ever know," Catana pleaded. "We will transport them to a neutral port. If they remain here and are captured, Woodes Rogers will hang them. We were just in that situation ourselves."

"And we do not want to return to that situation," Louis grumbled.

"One is a Catholic priest," Catana added. A long silence followed.

Finally, Orlando spoke. "I will agree, but they are only to go as far as the nearest island that will provide food and water."

"Thank you," Catana said, handing a reluctant Esmeralda to Orlando. She ran down the beach to collect the new passengers of the *Seahawk*.

* * * *

Once the landing party was back on board, Orlando explained the extra men and ordered Jamie to open a barrel of rum to celebrate their freedom. The Spanish guest, including Father Velazquez, lifted full cups to toast to peace and freedom.

"Where do we sail after we disembark the Spanish?" Catana asked Orlando.

"I asked the governor to assist us in driving the Spanish from our island, but he does not have the manpower. If we want La Isla del Espiritu Santo, The Island of the Holy Spirit, we are in for another fight."

"Do you have any idea who is holding the island and how many we will be up against?"

Orlando took a sip of rum. "None at all. Only the Spanish seem to know what the Spanish are doing."

Catana looked into Orlando's eyes and noticed a gleam. Her gaze traveled to his lips where a smile twitched in the corners of his mouth. She in turn gave him a large grin.

"Are you thinking the same thing I am, Catana?"

Nodding, she called across to Father Velazquez. "Padre, would you come here, please?"

CHAPTER THIRTY-ONE

Catana led Father Velazquez to a sea trunk at the stern of the ship and invited him to sit. Sitting next to him, she began her questions. "Father, do you know who captured La Isla del Espiritu Santo?"

"*Sí*, the captain is a close friend. Why do you want to know? I will not have you harm him."

Catana shifted to a more comfortable position on the trunk. This was not going to be easy. She did not want to lie to a priest, but would he help them if he knew the reason she was questioning him? "We do not want to harm anyone, but the land was deeded to our captain and his crew by the king of England, and they would like to claim their land.

The priest shook his head. "My friend was one of those treated badly by Captain Carvajal. When Antonio announced to the captain-general he wished to retire from the Spanish Navy, Carvajal threatened him with arrest for treason. Spain was at war, and Carvajal said he needed every officer in the service of the king. Antonio confided in me that he would never have the chance to keep his promise to his daughter…."

Catana's mouth went dry, and her heart skipped a beat. *The man who took possession of the island was Spanish Naval officer who made a promise to his daughter?* She brought her mind back to what the priest was saying.

"…disregarded what the captain-general wanted, sailed to La Isla Espiritu Santo, and has been defending it since. Carvajal planned to go after Antonio once we captured New Providence. I prayed he would change his mind, but he was determined. Often in the past the captain-general sent ships to capture Antonio, but each time, the Spanish Navy was defeated. I do not think your captain will fare well if he tries to take the island. Antonio has built a strong fortress that—"

"Excuse me Father," Catana interrupted. "Would you tell me Captain Antonio's full name?"

"But of course, my dear. It is Captain Antonio Molino de Cataluna."

Catana's heart pounded in her ears like a loud drum. Orlando would have to fight her father to gain control of the island. She closed her eyes and took a shuddering breath "He is my father."

"Then you must be Catana," the priest said in a surprised voice. He took her hand and smiled warmly at her. "Everything he did was for you. He wanted to find a place to settle and spend the remainder of his life in peace with his daughter."

"There must be a way to resolve this land dispute without fighting. Excuse me, Father, I must find Captain Cordova."

Catana knocked lightly on the cabin door and entered. Orlando was at his desk studying a map of the island. "We cannot attack the Spanish on La Isla del Espiritu Santo, sir. It is heavily fortified."

"If it is beyond our means to take the island, I think Jamie and I can persuade Ben to join us. He is off the cost of the island now. Since you gave him the map he has made several attempts to go ashore but was unsuccessful." He moved aside to allow her to look at the map. "As you can see it is a large island. If we could go ashore on the west side and come up on the fortress from behind—"

"No. The man who has captured your island is my father. I will not have anyone fight him."

Orlando gave her a puzzled look. "Are you sure?"

"Yes, Father Velazquez informed me." She told Orlando of her conversation with the priest.

Orlando sat back in his chair. "This is most unexpected."

"There must be a way we can get near enough so I can talk to him. Father Velazquez said that he would blow us out of the water if we came too close."

"What if we flew a Spanish flag?"

"No," Catana answered abruptly. "He would attack thinking it was Carvajal. There must be a peaceful way of doing this."

Orlando heaved a deep sigh. "I have no idea what Ben's plans are. If he tries to go ashore from another direction, your father will be on the defense, making it difficult for us to convince him we mean no harm."

Catana studied the map. "As you said, it is a large island, and there is more than enough land for us all. If we can persuade him to agree to share, it would settle the problem."

Orlando carefully folded the map and placed it in the desk drawer. "I have fought too hard and long to give up. Jamie," he called out through the doorway, "gather the crew for a meeting."

Moments later Orlando explained the situation to all those men who were not on duty.

"Captain," Jamie piped up. "I think the first thing we should do is find Ben before he makes another attack and convince him to leave."

"How are we to do that?" Tom asked. "The ijit thinks there is a treasure awaiting him. Words won't stop him."

"There is no treasure," Louis shouted.

"We all know that," Orlando replied. "But as long as he thinks there is, he will do all in his power to get to it."

Inez joined the crowd and spoke. "When you find Ben, Catana and I will talk to him. There may be a way to convince him to take his search somewhere else."

Louis turned to Inez. "And how do you plan to do that?"

She smiled sweetly at him. "Why, with your help of course."

"Is it agreed that we intercept Ben before he makes another attack?" Orlando shouted.

"Aye, everyone agreed."

Catana followed Inez and Louis into the cabin she shared with her cousin. Inez bid them to sit. Louis took a chair, and Catana settled on the sea trunk.

Taking a seat on her bunk, Inez bent forward and spoke in a whispered voice. "The natives who joined our crew told me a story of a creature that lives on the Island of the Holy Spirit. It is half-man, half-bird. It has red eyes; on each hand, three fingers; and on each foot, three toes. They are magic and can cause bad fortune."

Louis laughed. "Do you think a silly story like that will deter Ben?"

Inez gave him an indignant look. "It is not a silly story. The islanders call them *chickcharnies*, and they live in the tops of pine trees. Not only that, there are other stories about the island."

"Louis," Catana said, "you have often told me that pirates are a superstitious lot. It is worth a try."

Louis shook his head. "Even if Ben did believe such a story, it would not be enough to have him give up his search."

"We will explain to him there is no real treasure." Inez insisted.

"We already tried that," Catana replied.

"Yes, but we never tried to convince him."

Louis ran his fingers through his hair. "He actually believes Morgan buried a treasure on that island."

"Where is Morgan now?" Inez asked.

Louis shrugged. "The last I heard was that King Charles II knighted Morgan and made him deputy mayor of Jamaica where he lives as a wealthy and respected planter."

"Why would he leave a treasure buried on an island in the Caribbean?" Inez asked. If by chance he did bury on La Isla del Espiritu he would have returned to reclaim it when it was safe."

"That sounds reasonable," Catana added.

Louis shifted uneasily on the chair. "That may be, but how do we convince Ben to leave the island alone?"

"That is where you come in," Inez said. "You are to convince him there is a richer treasure somewhere else." Louis opened his mouth to speak but Inez held up her hand to silence him and continued. "You once told me that Black Beard buried a treasure on an island off the coast of the colonies. New York, I believe. Now that Black Beard no longer lives, Ben will be able to claim it."

"Yes," Louis agreed, "many pirates have heard this tale, but there is no map, no proof."

"Catana and I will see that there is. Catana, will you please get your letter box?"

Standing, Catana opened the trunk and pulled out the box containing her father's letters, several Letters of Marquee, and documents that would give slaves their freedom. On the bottom were several blank sheets of paper, a bottle of ink, and a quill pen. She handed the writing materials to her cousin and affectionately fingered the letters from her father before replacing them.

Inez in turn handed them to Louis. "To the best of your memory, I want you to draw the coastline of New York, the island and mark an *X* where Black Beard buried a great treasure. Catana will write a letter composed by the pirate."

Louis took the items. "I am not sure Black Beard knew how to write."

Catana grabbed one of the blank papers from him. "Then the letter will have been written by a trusted crewmember."

* * * *

Tom was on lookout watch midmorning of the next day when he spotted Ben's ship. Orlando gave orders to pursue, and the ship responded to the wind as the men worked the sails. By mid-afternoon, they were near enough to hale her.

The *Vengeance* came around, her cannons ready to fire, as the *Seahawk* struck her flag in surrender. Drawing alongside, Orlando shouted to the other ship. "Ahoy, Captain Benjamin Noyes. We request a parley."

Ben returned his flintlock pistol to his bandoleer and summoned Orlando aboard. Orlando called back to him. "It is the two young ladies and the Frenchman that wish to speak to you. May they come aboard?"

The sea was too high to bring the ships close in without smashing against each other. Tokala lowered a longboat to ferry them over. Once they were aboard the *Vengeance,* Ben led Catana, Inez and Louis to his cabin joined them at the table with several crewmen.

"Tell me, what brings you aboard my ship?" Ben asked in a gruff voice.

Catana made herself comfortable, waited until all were seated, pulled out the papers from her packet, and set them on the table. Ben gave them a quizzical look.

"We are here about the treasure," Catana announced.

"Ah," Ben said with a chuckle. "So you do believe there is one? Now don't think ye can talk me into sharing it with you just because ye gave me the map."

"Was one," Catana corrected. "Morgan did bury a treasure on the Island of the Holy Ghost but reclaimed it after Charles II made him governor of Jamaica."

Ben sat back in his chair. "Humph. 'Tis a trick."

"No," Louis said sliding an official looking paper in front of Ben. "Ye know I don't read well," Ben said.

"Aye, but Jonathon here does," one of the crewmen offered. Ben slid the paper over to a middle-aged gentleman dressed in black. Jonathon scanned the paper. "It says Morgan was made governor of Jamaica and is a wealthy land owner."

"Tell me, Ben," Catana said, "if you were Morgan and a governor, would you leave a treasure you buried unclaimed?"

Ben shook his head.

"The island not only has a number of Spanish defending it, it also has supernatural creatures called *chickcharnies.*

One of Ben's men sucked in his breath and turned pale as sea foam.

"What is wrong with you, Jack?" Ben snapped.

"I have heard of them. Are they on the island?"

Catana, Inez, and Louis all nodded in unison.

Ben grunted. "What in the son of a sea cook be a *chickcharnie?* "

"They are strong elf-like creatures with burning red eyes." Catana answered.

"Aye," Louis added leaning over the table and speaking in a whispered voice, "they are half-man and half-bird."

Catana held up three fingers. "They have three fingers on each hand and three toes on each foot."

"And what is worse," Inez inserted, "they cause bad things to happen."

"But if there is no treasure, why are the Spanish so determined to hold on to the island?" Ben asked in a bewildered voice.

"They have been possessed," Catana replied.

"Yes, possessed by the demon creatures," Inez confirmed.

Jack nodded. "If it be true, Captain, that there are *chickcharnies* on the island, I will no go ashore."

Catana leaned to face Ben nose to nose. "That is not all. Did you notice on your map all the small lakes? The island is almost cut in half by water."

Ben nodded.

"In the watery depths of those lakes lurk octopus-like sea creatures called *lusca*."

A loud gasp escaped from Jack's mouth. Ben scowled at him. "I suppose you heard of them too."

"Aye, Captain. They take pleasure in coming up out of the water and dragging men and small boats down to their doom."

"He is right," Catana confirmed. "If you wait long enough, eventually the Spanish will either be devoured by the *lusca* or have gone mad. Then you can move in to look for a treasure that does not exist."

"If what you say is true," Jonathon asked, "how is it Morgan came and went without a problem?"

Louis shrugged. "Who is to say he did not have a problem? He came and went so quickly that—"

"Or who is to say that he never came at all?" Catana interrupted. "If you are looking for the treasure, it will take time, and in that time, who knows…"

Louis cleared this throat. "Of course, if you really want to find a treasure, there is always Black Beard's."

"I have heard he buried one," Ben said with skepticism. "But no one knows the truth."

Louis pushed two more papers in front of Jonathon. "Maybe this will prove it."

Jonathon scanned the map and handed it to Ben. "This shows where Black Beard buried a treasure up north off the coast of the colonies."

Picking up the letter Jonathon read it aloud.

I, Samuel Sutter, along with Captain Teach rowed
to Long Island to bury one hundred bars of gold,
silken cloth jewels, and various coin we took from
the India Queen. *We are being pursued by English*
warships, and as soon as we lose them, we will return.

Catana nodded toward Ben. "As you know, Captain Teach, Black Beard, and his crew were captured off the coast of the Carolinas. Therefore, the treasure still must be there."

Ben took the map and letter in his shaking hand and stared at them. "Why are ye giving this to me and not going after the treasure for yourselves?"

"The men on the *Seahawk* want land," Louis said.

Scratching his head, Ben slumped back in his chair. "But that is ridiculous. Why land?"

Catana slammed her fist on the table so hard that everyone jumped. "Men have fought over land since the beginning of time. The French attacked the settlement where I lived and captured the only home I ever knew. Why? Because they wanted land. The wars between Spain, France, England, and the Netherlands that continue, what is it over? Land!"

Ben nodded. "So it is."

Catana stood. "Will you take the map and look for a real treasure and leave us to continue our quest for land?"

"Aye, lass. Ye have been a good friend to this old pirate. Thank Orlando, too, for me, will ye?"

Catana grasped Ben's hand. "That I will."

Everyone at the table stood and filed out of the cabin behind Catana. A smile played on her lips. She, Inez, and Louis had arrested a potential battle between Ben and her father. Now it was time to contend with the old Spanish captain.

CHAPTER THIRTY-TWO

Catana sat at the captain's table on the *Seahawk*, drumming her fingers on the polished wood, while she waited for Orlando. The map of The Island of the Holy Spirit lay at Orlando's place at the table. She pulled map in front of her and fixed her gaze on the island. It was large enough for both, Spanish, English, and any other race, if everyone agreed to get along. She ran her fingers across the center of the island where a system of inner land waterways cut across from east to west. Maybe Orlando's men would agree to settle one side and the Spanish on the other.

Ben had told her that he was unable to take his ship near the coast on the west side. The water was so shallow that even a sloop was unable to draw close. What puzzled her was how her father knew when and where Ben would attempt to come ashore from the east side. Three times the old pirate made an effort to land his men at three different points. Each time, gunfire was waiting. Did her father have enough men to guard the entire east coast?

The loud voices of men entering the cabin brought her out of her reverie. Orlando, Louis, Jamie, and Damien joined her at the table.

"Will it be a difficult task to deal with your father?" Orlando asked Catana.

"He has always been a just and kind man," she answered in a wistful voice. "But I do not know if his encounters with Carvajal have changed him."

Orlando reached toward her and pulled the map in front of him. "According to this, we will not be able to land on the west side. On the east is a reef, but the *Seahawk* should be able to slip over it easily."

"Aye," Jamie agreed. "But when we grow close Antonio can shoot us with cannon fire and, from what Catana says, he fired at Ben from several locations twenty-five miles apart.

"We must find a way to send a party ashore." Louis said. "One in a small and unthreatening boat he would not fire upon."

"My father would not fire on me," Catana announced.

Jamie stroked his beard lightly. "Aye, lass, but how is he to know it's you in the boat?"

"I could signal him in some way."

The small group threw suggestions back and forth until they were satisfied they had a plan.

* * * *

The next day the *Seahawk* slid silently toward the east coast of The Island of the Holy Spirit, anchored out of shooting range, and furled her sails. Catana climbed into the longboat with Louis.

"Are you certain you want only Louis with you?" Orlando called from the ship's rail.

"Yes, if Father sees there are only two of us he should not feel threatened. When we are close to shore he will be able to see us through a spyglass. He knows Louis and will welcome us ashore."

Orlando trained his spyglass on a small stretch of sand that interrupted a wall of mangroves along the shore. "I see no sign of anyone. Maybe your father is not in this area."

"I hope he is, so we can confront him and settle our business," Louis replied.

Catana crossed her fingers, hoping the same thing. She was anxious to see her father. She tied a white cloth on the end of a pole and jammed it upright between the gunwale and seat. "Flying a white flag will make them think before firing."

She watched it flapping in the wind as they neared the shore. Suddenly a loud boom echoed across the water. A cannon ball arced toward them. Catana ducked as it hit the water next to their boat shooting a plume of water into the air that drenched them.

"I do not think your father wants your company," Louis said in a bemused voice.

Catana gave him an irritated look. "He does not realize who we are." She grabbed the turquoise sash wrapped around her waist. "Father gave this to me for my fifteenth birthday. I hope he remembers." She reached up and tied the scarf to the pole just below the white flag. The longboat sat still in the water for a moment. No shots followed. Taking up the oars, they continued their heading toward the beach.

The small craft slid onto the shore the sound of the hull grounding against the sand. Catana and Louis jumped out and pulled it up beyond the tide line. There was no one in sight. The only sounds they heard was the lapping of waves on the shore and the cry of seagulls wheeling in the startling blue sky. Back from the beach was an inlet choked with trees and underbrush. "What should we do now?" Louis asked in a loud whisper.

Catana opened her mouth to speak, but before she could utter a word, a voice rang out in Spanish. "We have our rifles trained on you. Do not take another step and put your hands in the air."

Catana and Louis did as the man said, and four men, their weapons trained on the intruders, stepped out of the shelter of the trees.

A tall lanky man stepped forward. His salt and pepper hair fell to his shoulders, and he glared at them with dark piercing eyes. He gestured to one of his companions. "Jose, check them for weapons."

A short man who was almost as wide as he was tall stepped toward Catana and gave her an uncertain smile. "Sorry, señorita." When he reached out to run his hand down her body to search for hidden weapons, she stepped back. "Do not touch me. I am the daughter of Captain Antonio Molino. Take us to him."

Jose stood with his hand suspended in midair, then turned to his leader with a questioning look. The man in charge of the group stepped forward. "I am Raul Martinez. If you are our captain's daughter, can you prove it?"

"Sí. This scarf was given to me by my father. Allow me to untie it from the staff and you can take it to your captain. Tell him his daughter Catana Molino and Louis LeClaire would like a parley with him."

Raul nodded. "Hand me the scarf. Jose, you, Hector and Miguel keep an eye on these two until I return with an answer." Receding into the trees, he disappeared.

"May I sit?" Catana asked. "My leg is bothering me."

Jose nodded his approval, and Catana sank to the sand cross-legged. Louis followed suit, and soon the guards made themselves comfortable on a piece of driftwood.

Catana shifted to get more comfortable. "How long has my father been on the island?"

Hector, a balding man with a beak-like nose and close-set eyes cleared his throat. "It has been nine months now."

Pulling a piece of oat grass sticking out of the sand, Catana studied it carefully. "I have not heard from him in over two years and thought he might be dead."

"He almost died at the hands of Captain Carvajal," Jose said.

Miguel nodded. "*Señor Dios* was looking over Antonio when that evil man shot him.

"Sí," Jose agreed. "Captain Molino has sworn vengeance."

Catana smiled sadly. When she saw her father, she would tell him there was no longer need for revenge. "How has my father managed to keep others off such a large island?"

"The natives here are our allies." Jose replied. "Our group defends this area, and Antonio has placed twenty cannons at strategic places along the coast. He taught the natives how to fire them."

"Sí, we do not receive much company, but we have deterred a few the British ships." Miguel said with a wide grin.

"And an insistent pirate ship," Jose added.

Catana looked at Louis and smiled. "Ben," they both said in unison.

Hector spit onto the sand. "Captain Molino has been on the lookout for Captain Carvajal since our arrival on his island. We thought you might be him, at first. We saw no colors flying. When we saw your white flag, we issued a warning shot. If this is a trap…" He let his voice trail away.

Catana fingered the head of the piece of oat grass pensively. "There is no trick I—"

A voice called out and interrupted what she was about to say. "It is true." Raul approached at a jog and stopped in front of them to catch his breath. "I showed our Captain the scarf and saw tears come to his eyes. He wants me to bring you directly to him, Catana. Your friends aboard ship are welcome to come ashore."

Catana stood and brushed the sand from her trousers. "I must return to the ship first. The captain of the *Seahawk* is awaiting an answer. If Louis and I do not return to the ship soon, he may think something has gone wrong and attempt an attack."

"I could return to the ship on my own and tell Orlando—"

"You cannot row the longboat back on your own," Catana cut in. "The tide is coming in and is too strong for one man."

Jose turned to Raul. "I will go with Louis, invite the captain and men ashore, and bring them to Captain Molino."

Catana and her father's men watched while Louis and Raul departed for the *Seahawk*, then they headed inland. Catana was puzzled that her father did not return with Raul to meet her. Was he suspicious that this might be a trap? She did not know how many men were under her father's command, but with a crew from a Spanish warship plus the island natives, they would outnumber the men from the *Seahawk*. Inviting them ashore would be no threat to her father.

The small group made their way through a dense grove of trees with large sprawling roots. The marshy ground was slippery, and Catana had to catch herself from falling several times. Peering through the trees, she saw a clearing ahead and a wooden wall.

After reaching the gate, Raul rapped loudly three times before the door opened. Inside the large compound, buildings were scattered throughout. Raul led her to a small wooden building nearest the gate and directly inside. It was dark except for a few dancing flames in a fireplace in the back corner of the room. As her eyes adjusted to the dimness, she saw her father sitting behind a desk along the back wall. His appearance disturbed her. The gauntness of his face sharpened his features and gave him a hard look. She notice his eyes soften when he looked at her.

"I am sorry I cannot get up to greet you, my dear. Please come closer so I can see you better."

Catana drew near and noticed a scar on his left cheek. She stood motionless for a second then rushed around the desk to hug him. They held each other in silence and tears ran down Catana's cheeks, soaking into her father's coat. Stepping back, she took a deep breath to steady her voice. "I read your last letter many times, but since it has been two years, I feared you were dead."

"Carvajal told me Santa Maria de Galve was captured by the French and that you, Inez, and Jacinta were killed. I did not want to believe him for he has told so many lies. That is when I made my escape from his prison. I wanted to learn the truth. During our battle for freedom, I was injured. After stealing a ship, my men brought me here. It is on this island that we made a stand. Carvajal said he would never rest until I was recaptured, and I am ready and waiting."

Your wait is over, Father. Carvajal is dead."

She told him how she had found him after the battle, her meeting with Father Velazquez, and Carvajal's death. "He wanted forgiveness, Father, and I forgave him. I did not realize the pain he inflicted on you."

Antonio drew a deep breath and let it out slowly. "So, it is over. He died a horrible and painful death. That was his punishment. I wanted to defend myself, my men, and my island more than I wanted revenge." He shook his head sadly. "Father Velazquez is right. It is God who has the authority to judge men such as him." Her father's tone brightened. "Now that I am free of Carvajal and you are alive, we must celebrate."

"Sí," Catana agreed. "Come with me to meet my friends as they come ashore."

Sadness returned to Antonio's face. "I cannot. Carvajal shot me in the leg and the musket ball shattered my knee. I can only walk a short distance and need crutches."

"Oh, Father, I am so sorry."

"Please do not feel sorry. I have been able to cope quite well. And now I am a very happy man. We will start a new life together. This is the dream for which I fought—a place where we can live in peace."

"Would you not prefer to return to Santa Maria once it is under Spanish rule?"

Antonio shook his head. "Even if Santa Maria is once again under the Spanish I do not want to go back. It was a soldier's fort and not a proper place for you or any woman. I want to settle here among the happy, peaceful natives. You may have beautiful memories of your childhood in Santa Maria, but since your mother is no longer there, I want to find a new direction in life."

Catana took her father's hand. "The men who brought me here have the same dream. This land has been deeded to them by the King of England. They are here to claim their land. Would you agree to share La Isla del Espiritu Santo with them?"

Antonio grasped Catana's hand like a vice and fire smoldered in the black depths of his eyes. "Absolutely not."

CHAPTER THIRTY-THREE

Antonio slammed his fist on the table. "No Englishmen are welcome on this island."

"Father, hear me out, please." Catana pleaded. "The men of the *Seahawk* represent a mix of cultures and religions. Captain Orlando is both Spanish and Irish, his first mate Jamie is a Scot. Then there is Tokala, a native from a village outside Santa Maria, and Jabulani, an African slave. Louis is with us. Do you remember Louis? His father and you were once friends. When the French attacked Santa Maria, Louis was the one who helped me escape. Orlando saved my life more than once. These men…"

Antonio held his hand up to silence his daughter. "If they have no affiliation with the England, how is it that countries king awarded them land?"

Catana quickly informed her father of her adventures first on the *Dove* and then the *Seahawk*. Antonio stopped her several times to slow her down and ask questions. She saw a pleased look on his face when she told him of the defeat of the British ship *Retribution*.

"And without the interference by Orlando and the pirates, Carvajal would be off the coast with Spanish ships pounding the island with cannon shot." She stopped to take a deep breath.

A slight grin quivered at the corners of Antonio's mouth. "I must say you make a convincing case. I will discuss the matter with your friends, but I will make no promises. Help me to my feet, dear. I would like to greet them at the gate."

Antonio gripped her arm and pulled himself to a standing position. "Fetch my crutches. They are up against the wall in the back corner."

Taking the crutches from her, he hobbled out from behind the desk. Catana turned away so he would not see the tears that came to her eyes. Her father, once strong and full of life, was now a man who wore the woes of his past on his face and who was barely able to walk. She stayed by his side as he limped across the room and opened the door. They slowly made their way toward the gate in the wall.

Catana heard voices in the distance and two guards opened the gate. Louis and Inez entered first. Inez paused for a moment, looked at Catana, and turned to Antonio. A smile crossed her face as she approached her uncle. Standing on tiptoe, she stretched to give him a kiss on the cheek.

Orlando, Jamie, Tokala, and Jabulani trailed in behind Louis, who greeted Antonio and introduced his companions.

"Raul," Antonio called. "I want you to take Inez and Catana and show them around our settlement while I speak to the gentlemen in my office."

"I want to be at the meeting," Catana said.

"This meeting is for men only," her father informed her in a stern voice.

Catana threw her hands in the air in defeat and turned to join Inez. "Men," she grumbled.

Inez squeezed Catana's affectionately. "You should know your father by now. He has enough pride to fill all the men of the *Seahawk*."

"Sí," Catana agreed. "That is why he wanted to be at the gate to greet his guest. Oh, Inez, it is so disheartening for me to see him this way."

"I know. When I first saw him I barely recognized him, but we must not show our sorrow. It would wound his pride."

"Come, ladies," Raul called. "I will take you to Captain Molino's house and introduce you to Ramona."

The two women gave each other a quizzical look and followed Raul. They passed a number of small buildings and walked through a narrow gate in the back of the wall that surrounded the compound.

"We have a number of small farms." Raul said. "They are protected by swampland on three sides and our fortress on the fourth."

"What do you raise here?" Inez asked.

"Mostly fruits and vegetables," Raul replied. "We were able to collect some pigs, chickens, and a small heard of cattle before we lost our ship. There is an abundance of fish and birds, so we do not worry about going hungry. The natives taught us how to get the most from the land."

Raul led them up a pathway to a pleasant bungalow surrounded by flowers and shaded by a large oak tree. Numerous birds of various colors flitted about.

"This is the Captain's quarters," Raul announced and rapped lightly on the door.

When the door opened, an attractive woman with flashing black eyes stood in the doorframe. Catana guessed her to be in her late thirties. Her long silken hair was tied back by a red scarf. She wore a loose, white blouse and a brightly colored skirt the same color as her scarf. Her warm smile made Catana feel welcome as she invited them inside. When Raul introduced them, Ramona gave Catana a hug and in turn Inez. "So you are Antonio's family. This is wonderful. Sit. I will bring us fruit juice and cakes."

Ramona left the room for the kitchen while Raul escorted them to a pair of chairs near the fireplace. Scanning the room, Catana sensed this was not only a house but also a home where her father lived.

"I think Antonio wanted you to get to know Ramona because they have become quite close," Raul said drawing up a third chair to join them.

"Do you think they will marry?" Inez asked.

Raul shrugged. "It would not surprise me."

Inez giggled and clapped her hands together. "Maybe we can arrange a double wedding. Louis and I; Ramona and your father."

"You need a priest for that," Catana said in a dry voice.

"Ah, but Father Velazquez has agreed to establish a mission on this island when things are settled." Inez rubbed her hands together. "Is that not wonderful, Catana?"

"Sí, wonderful," Catana echoed. Her emotions were churning inside. Her father remarry? The idea was so new to her. Then she realized there were many new changes in life she still must face.

She was certain her father would allow Inez and Louis to remain on the island. If they married, and her father married, she would be the odd man out. What if he turned away the others? Would she want to stay here, or would she join the crew? Would Orlando fight her father or look for another place to settle? Her head begin to hurt thinking about it.

Ramona entered the room with a tray and set it on a low table between the chairs in which Catana and Inez sat. With a flashing smile, their hostess handed a cup of fruit juice to Catana then served Inez and Raul. Taking a cup for herself, Ramona sat on the nearby settee and faced her three guests. "Antonio has spoken of you often, Catana. He did not believe the reports of your death and prayed daily you would be reunited. And now you are here. Your father must be overwhelmed with happiness."

Catana took a sip of juice. "I think he was quite happy to see me until I told him of Orlando and his reason for coming here."

Inez continued to chat about the crew's dream of settling on the island and her forthcoming marriage to Louis. When Raul joined the conversation, the three talked about the future of the island. Catana's mind wandered to the meeting and what was happening. The suspense was making her restless.

"Excuse me," Catana said during a lull in conversation. "I feel the need to get some air. May I go out and admire your flowers?"

"Sí," Ramona replied. "Would you like some company?"

"No, thank you. Waiting always makes me nervous, and a walk will calm me."

Once outside, Catana paced up and down the path several times. "*Madre de Dios*, I will go see for myself," she muttered to herself. With a determined stride, she sailed through the back gate of the fortress and to her father's office. Maybe if she stood near the small open window she would be able to hear what was said.

"And that is your final decision?" she heard Orlando ask.

"Sí," her father replied. "Return to your ship and prepare to sail. I and my men will see you off in the morning."

Dios, her father was sending them away. She must do, or say something to change his mind. She burst through the partially open door and into the room. "If you will not let my friends remain here, I will leave with them."

Silence hung heavy in the air, and everyone stood staring at her.

"Would you leave me for the sake of this mixed group of vagabonds?" her father asked.

She looked around, shuffling back and forth from one foot to another, and tears came to her eyes. "Sí, Father, I think I would. Your narrow-minded attitude toward them is unfair. You are a hypocrite when you say you want to live in harmony with your fellow men."

Her mouth snapped shut when everyone broke out in laughter.

Catana started to speak. "What is—"

Orlando grabbed her arm before she could say more and pulled her out the door. "Your father has agreed to share the island."

"But I heard him tell you to get ready to sail and he will see you off in the morning."

"That is right. We have some unfinished business before we settle here. The natives in our crew are ready to return home, and Jabulani wants to return to Jahzara and his people. Your father is sending a few of his men with us as crew to take the others home and for our return trip.

"After we return to the island, your father has offered to let us log off some of the timber to the north. Jamie and I plan to start our own shipbuilding company. I have ideas for building swifter sloops and schooners. Tokala wants to become a fisherman and—"

Catana grabbed him by the arm. "If you are sailing in the morning, Inez and I have a few things aboard we must get."

"I can take you aboard now and have you back before dark. Let me tell the others where we are going."

Orlando disappeared into her father's office. She waited, for what seemed like forever. He returned with a big smile on his face. "We are all set. Your father has invited us for a fiesta this evening, and I assured him we would be back in time."

As soon as they boarded the *Seahawk*, Catana went to her cabin and pulled her box of letters from the sea trunk. Searching the ship, she found Esmeralda sleeping on the bowsprit in the late afternoon sun. Catana crawled along the spit and reached out toward the cat. When she made a grab for the animal, it jumped out of Catana's way, scampered over her would-be captor, and jumped to the deck. Catana muttered a volley of oaths and backed up to the safety of a solid footing. Orlando was waiting and helped her onto the deck.

"I see Esmeralda is giving you the run around," he said with a smile. "While you chase after your cat, I will have my men load your and Inez's things onto the longboat."

"That will be fine," Catana muttered, looking around for the cat. She tripped over the letterbox, picked it up, and handed it to Orlando. "Please put this in the boat. It contains important papers."

By the time she was able to retrieve Esmeralda, the longboat was loaded and the men were waiting on her. She entered the boat and found a seat while tightly holding onto the cat. Four men were at the oars and Orland took a seat next to her.

"I will send the boat back for the remainder of the crew so they can join the fiesta. Your father told me he has a small house next to his where you and Inez can stay.

"Until my cousin marries," Catana said wistfully.

"Jamie, Louis, Tokala, Tom, Percy, and Damien will be returning with me to settle on the island, and we have all agreed that Antonio should be voted governor of The Island of the Holy Spirit."

Catana nodded with approval. When they came ashore, Catana set the cat down. "She has all the fish and birds she will ever need, here. I will let her run free."

When she and Orlando entered the courtyard preparations had been started for the fiesta. A pig was roasting over a fire, and tables had been brought out from various buildings. Native women piled bowls of fruit and bread at each one. Catana saw her father giving orders to several men and waited until he was finished before approaching him. "Father, come and sit with me at this table a moment."

Antonio eased himself down onto a bench and propped his crutches next to him. She set the letter box onto the table and opened it. "Here are the letters you wrote to Mother while you were away on different voyages. She saved them all and read them over and over." Pulling out a separate letter, she opened it. "This was the last one I received from you. You promised to return home. That is why I wanted to return to Santa Maria once the Spanish had regained it."

Digging to the bottom of the box, she handed her father a sheet of paper. "Since you are governor of this island, I would ask you to sign this letter of marquee for Orlando in the event he runs into an enemy ship. This will give him amnesty."

Handing him, a second paper she added. "If you sign this paper it will give all those people we rescued from the slave ship their freedom. Jabulani already has a paper freeing him from slavery."

Antonio stared at her. "Where did you get these?"

"I took them from Governor Matamoras' desk after the siege of Santa Maria."

Chuckling, Antonio placed the paper in his belt pouch. "Sí, my dear, I will see to it."

Catana noticed Louis and Inez entering the courtyard. "I must speak with my cousin," she said standing. Making her way through the tables, she motioned to Inez. As they approached one another, Inez called out in a stern voice. "Where have you been? Did you hear the good news?"

"I have heard. I went to fetch our things from the ship. Several crewmen have taken our trunks to our new home."

"That is wonderful." Inez turned to Louis, who stood behind her. "Catana and I will leave you for a while to dress properly for the fiesta."

Catana rolled her eyes. "Is that necessary?"

Inez grabbed her by the arm. "Yes, it is."

The house was small but clean. There was a main room with two chairs, settee, and table. The kitchen had an iron stove and was only large enough for one person to cook. The one bedroom had two cots and at the foot of each were their trunks.

Inez insisted on putting on her best gown. Catana dug through her trunk and pulled out a comfortable cotton one.

Inez gave Catana an exasperated look. "Why not wear that ivory lace dress that Orlando loaned you? It looks so lovely on you."

"I refuse to put on that tight gown and have its stays gouge me in the ribs all evening."

"Louis likes this dress on me," Inez said, smoothing her skirts. Her cousin did look attractive in her buttercup yellow gown of soft material. The neckline swooped low but there was lace along the edges gave her a demure look. The skirt was full and swished with each step she took. Catana's red cotton dress was of a similar cut trimmed in white lace. Although the bodice was not as tight, it did fit snug and the skirt flared out from a low waistline.

The two women stepped into the balmy evening breeze and headed for the fiesta where the sound of laughter and guitars floated on the air. Catana found a seat next to her father while Inez joined Louis. As the evening wore on and the men talked of politics, battles, and weapons, Catana grew restless. Inez and Ramona were deep in conversation so she slipped away, strolled to the back wall, and went out the gate. A full moon lit the path, and she thought she saw some movement among the flowers. Drawing closer, she saw it was Esmeralda. "Come here, kitty."

The cat, with her tail straight in the air, padded over to Catana and rubbed against her skirts. Catana bent down, picked up the ugly orange animal, and found a flat boulder to sit on. While looking at the moon, she stroked the cat lightly and her mind wandered. Now that Lancaster was dead, would Orlando ask Ana to be his wife? It was true that Ana betrayed him, but they say love is blind. Would he forgive her? A knot tightened in her stomach. Was she in love with Orlando? Why else would the thought of him returning to Ana hurt so much?

Esmeralda's claws dug into Catana's arm as the cat tensed then bolted from her lap. A shadow fell across her. "What are you doing here, Orlando?"

He joined her on the boulder. "I have been talking to your father. He is a very content man. He has you back with him, is the governor of his island, and no longer has to worry about his old enemy Carvajal. When Father Velazquez arrives, he plans to marry Ramona."

"At first, the idea of his possible marriage bothered me, but then I realized how selfish that was. I know Ramona will make a wonderful wife."

"I think so, too. There is one thing he lacks and wishes for, and only you can give it to him.

"What is that?"

Orlando gave her a sly smile. "Grandchildren. I told him that if you agree, we would work on that after Father Velazquez marries us."

"Marries us?" You say this without consulting me? What—"

Orlando put a fingerer to her lips to silence her. "I love you, Catana Molino, and have for a long time."

Tears blurred Catana's vision. She had been so busy living life that she had not thought about how deep her love for Orlando had grown.

"Think about it, Catana," he said in a hoarse voice. "All of us can live in harmony in this place of beauty. You as my wife and the mother of our children can fulfill your father's remaining wish. You can give me an answer on my return."

Orlando stood and walked toward the gate and fiesta. Catana sat staring after him. Was this the reason for his odd, uncomfortable behavior toward her? Was his noncommittal look when he saw her in Ana's dress to hide his feelings toward her? Other things came to mind. How tenderly he held her hand when she was recovering from being shot. The time he sat next to her on the boat. It all seemed to make sense. Now she understood why she really wanted to go with the others if her father sent them away. She wanted to be with Orlando.

Esmeralda jumped into her lap and brought her out of her trance. Grabbing the cat, she ran after Orlando.

"Yes," she called to him.

He stopped and turned.

"Yes, I will marry you."

He reached out and pulled her toward him. Esmeralda gave a loud yowl. Catana dropped the cat to the ground and threw her arms around Orlando.

THE END